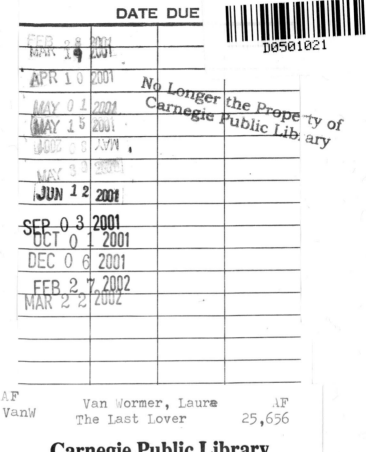

DATE DUE

FEB 2 8 2001		
MAR 1 4 2001		
APR 1 0 2001		
MAY 0 1 2001		
MAY 1 5 2001		
MAY 0 8 2001		
MAY 3 9 2001		
JUN 1 2 2001		
SEP 0 3 2001		
OCT 0 1 2001		
DEC 0 6 2001		
FEB 2 7 2002		
MAR 2 2 2002		

Carnegie Public Library
Big Timber, Montana

RULES

1 Books may be kept two weeks and may be renewed once for the same period, except 7-day books and magazines.

2. A fine of two cents a day will be charged on each book which is not returned according to the above rule. No book will be issued to any person incurring such a fine until it has been paid.

3. All injuries to books, beyond reasonable wear, and all losses shall be made good to the satisfaction of the Librarian.

4. Each borrower is held responsible for all books drawn on his card and for all fines accruing on the same.

GAYLORD F

THE LAST LOVER

LAURA VAN WORMER
THE LAST LOVER

MIRA®

ISBN 1-55166-590-5

THE LAST LOVER

Visit us at www.mirabooks.com

Printed in U.S.A.

25,656

For the whole gang, with love
Benjamin Francis Van Wormer, Marjorie Law Van Wormer,
Robert Law Ault, Jocelyn Discher Ault, Susan Forth Ault,
Peter Michael Authier, Frances Elizabeth Van Wormer
and Christine Anne Robinson.
(boy, do we have long names in this family)

ACKNOWLEDGMENT

With grateful thanks to Kerry McEntee,
for sparking the idea for this story,
and Bea O'Brien, for taking care of business while I wrote it.
And, as always, heartfelt thank yous to the dynamic duo,
my agent, Loretta Barrett,
and my publisher, Dianne Moggy

THE LAST LOVER

PART ONE

CHAPTER ONE

Liam Neeson isn't here after all, which means I've used up three vacation days and twenty-five thousand American AAdvantage miles to stand around watching some actress babe flirt with my beau.

Usually I'm immune to the carefully orchestrated Hollywood publicity party, but when Spencer—aforementioned beau—mentioned last week that the Irish film star was supposed to be here, I said, "Okay, I'm there," and flew into preparations, including the purchase of the short silk dress I'm wearing, which I bought at Syms yesterday on the way to the airport.

Only Liam Neeson isn't here. He's in Europe shooting a movie.

Bummer.

Still, it's a pretty cool party. It's Monday and we're at Del Figlio's, one of the newer "in" restaurants on the Beverly Hills-West Hollywood border. Since I used to work at an "in" Los Angeles magazine in years gone by, I still know the criteria: it's convenient to the powermongers, has vaulted ceilings and a unique decor (lots of heavy beams, red fabric and textured stucco—kind of Dracula's Castle gone Mission Viejo), and boasts delicious and extremely complicated food that will take people years to figure out isn't as healthy as everyone thinks.

I am, by the way, Sally Harrington, a small-city journalist with the Castleford *Herald-American* who has a brand-new side career as a special assignments reporter for WSCT-TV in New Haven. My beau, Spencer Hawes, is an executive editor with the book publishing firm of Bennett, Fitzallen & Coe in New York, and that's how I have come to be in L.A. Spencer is Malcolm Kieloff's editor, the CEO of Monarch Entertainment, in whose honor this party is being given. Kieloff has written, as the publicity kit describes it, "his amazing life story that is sure to be a bestseller."

The real story is, of course, that the CEO of Bennett, Fitzallen & Coe, Andrew Rushman, bought this dog of a book for a million dollars because he wanted to hang out with Kieloff. Kieloff, I should explain, is a superstar executive of the millennium, having taken the helm of an ailing movie and TV studio in the late 1980s and turned it into a massive communications conglomerate by way of buying a cartoon factory, a radio network, a TV network, a chain of theme parks, some magazines, ten newspapers, a children's-book publisher, a children's book club and several Internet companies.

"At least," Spencer confided in me, "Monarch's having every employee of every division, including Monarch Studios, purchase a copy of the book in bookstores."

"And how many employees is that?" I asked.

"Forty-five thousand. The idea was to get them to buy all those copies during the first week and hope the velocity of sales would pop the book on the bestseller list." (This is the kind of thing you learn when involved with an editor, that the bestseller list is not based on how many copies of a book is shipped to stores, but the velocity of its movement from shelf through the register.)

"Did Monarch give their employees the money to buy the book?"

"I didn't ask," Spencer sighed, hating this kind of crap his CEO is in the habit of getting him into. Because when you get down to it, what Spencer was describing between Bennett, Fitzallen & Coe and Malcolm Kieloff is a glorified vanity press deal.

I guess the strategy worked, though, since the book debuts next week in the number-thirteen slot on the *Publishers Weekly* bestseller list, and the Bennett, Fitzallen & Coe CEO is here, although the guest of honor whose company he sought, Malcolm Kieloff, doesn't seem to be paying much attention to him.

Kieloff seems like a nice enough guy. He's rumored to be fighting some kind of health problem, but he seems robust enough tonight. His pretty wife (shockingly, for this town, the only wife he's ever had) and their three children are all here. And it's definitely a happening party. Since Monarch has a finger in so many pies, every agent and publicist in L.A. has made an effort to roll out big names in his honor.

The person I am most interested in at the moment, however, is young Lilliana Martin. She's not a tremendous star (and I suspect she's not all that young, either), but she has moved successfully from a TV show to a movie—which Monarch Studios produced—that is coming out in April. The word of mouth on it is that it's excellent and everyone here is talking Oscar nomination in connection with her performance. When the actress made her entrance, I could plainly see that she does have *it*, whatever *it* is that makes for a movie star. Some people say she's the new Drew Barrymore, others, the new Kathleen Turner, still others say a remodeled version of Kate Winslet. (Only in Hollywood do they talk about actresses as if they were cars.)

Lilliana Martin is supposed to be twenty-six, but I suspect she is closer to thirty from the way she handles herself; hers is an almost flawless performance of calculated move and gesture. She has that intelligent blond thing going, too (although her skin is too olive for me to believe that her hair color is real), and she's wearing a clinging red silk dress that is ridiculous but nonetheless a knockout. She also timed her entrance to occur right after the major female movie stars—Sharon Stone, Sandra Bullock and Anjelica Huston—had left.

To be honest, though, the reason why I am so interested in Lilliana Martin is because since she met Spencer forty minutes ago, she has latched on to him in such a way that every time she laughs, she dips forward slightly and presses her left breast into his forearm.

Hmm.

My relationship with Spencer Hawes is at an interesting point. Five months ago, when we threw ourselves into this relationship (literally threw ourselves at each other), we had no doubts but that we had met our soul mates. Now, after a couple of months of having sex beyond my wildest dreams (yes, it has been that good, that free, something quite new to me), we are having difficulty in that area. Suddenly we are self-conscious. The passion is absent and we have to kind of jump-start sex now by going through the motions until our bodies start responding in ways our minds no longer seem able to.

I suppose it is me. (To be honest, I wonder if Spencer or any guy ever *really* cares if the mental part ever catches up with the physical part of sex, so long as the physical part happens?) Spencer says not to worry, we'll grow out of it, but I do worry. I worry that I'm finding myself in the same state of half dread, half longing I used to have with my last boyfriend, whom I abruptly left to be with Spencer.

Doug. I can't even let myself think about him.

I knew there would have to be consequences to my behavior, but somehow I thought I might be able to just skip over them for once and live happily ever after. I truly thought Spencer was the answer to the loneliness I have always felt, loneliness I find hard to articulate, even to myself.

Sometimes I think I just should have married the first guy I saw right after college and made a go of it. I seem to do better with relationships that are simply forced on me than with the ones I choose out of complete freedom.

Did I say *relationship?* What I mean is, when I meet a man and feel overwhelmed by sexual attraction, when the very air seems to go *bzzzzzzt* with sexual connection, my whole self can drop into free-fall desire and I am determined to make it work. It is absolutely ridiculous, I know, but that is how all three of my significant love affairs started.

I certainly did not expect the passion between Spencer and myself to go on without interruption, but I did expect, I think, a little more content to have developed in our relationship by now. The problem is (I prefer to think), we're both so damn busy and so involved with our careers—the processes of editing, writing and reporting literally suck the emotional energy out of you—that there is very little left at the end of the day. And then on top of that Spencer and I are in a long-distance relationship, together on weekends either in Castleford, in central Connecticut where I live, or on the Upper East Side of Manhattan, ninety miles away, where Spencer lives.

It is the first week of February, when the dark days of slush and ice back East have settled blues over the land, and I feel those blues now as I watch Spencer.

The gorgeous and fatally glamorous Lilliana Martin has just done it again, pressing that large left breast of hers into Spencer's arm, so hard this time her breast has flattened and threatens to altogether spill out of her red halter top.

No, no doubt about it, Lilliana Martin likes my beau. And

here I am, across the room, nervously sipping white wine, trying to get rid of this annoying short guy wearing horrid little black metal glasses who insists on talking to me. He tells me he has just been made the new production head of Monarch Studios.

"Congratulations," I tell him, not believing it for a second. This guy couldn't get membership in a seventh-grade audiovisual club.

"Thanks," he says, lofting forward a little on the balls of his feet. "Maybe you'd like to help me celebrate and have dinner with me."

"Thanks," I say, "but I'm afraid I have plans with my boyfriend," although I am beginning to have my doubts. We're supposed to stay and have a celebratory dinner with Kieloff and his family and some of the Monarch stars. Presumably this will include Lilliana Martin, and I really don't feel like sitting around watching her with Spencer.

To be fair to Spencer, though, I know firsthand how tricky it can be when a VIP guest starts misbehaving at the party you're supposed to be hosting on behalf of your company. I'm not sure, exactly, what I expect Spencer to do in this situation, other than what I've seen him do three times already: physically detach himself from the actress and step away.

The studio executive rises up on the balls of his feet once again to get taller than me. "And who is your boyfriend?" he says in a tone of voice that also says, *He can't be more important than I am.*

"He's Malcolm Kieloff's editor," I explain. "We flew in from the East Coast."

"Huh, a book editor." He's not impressed. "And what do you do?"

"I'm a newspaper reporter," I say. "And I'm also doing some TV reporting for the DBS affiliate in New Haven, Connecticut."

"Ah." He's trying to maintain the slight height advantage, which is making his stance a little precarious. "Did you go to Yale?"

"No. Here, actually, to UCLA."

He grimaces slightly. He does not approve. "I went to school in Cambridge."

This means Harvard.

"Harvard," he adds, in case I missed it.

"Yeah, I've heard of it," I can't help but say.

He laughs.

Why doesn't he move on? Surely he knows this room is packed with great-looking women who would do almost anything to get work from him at the studio. So why waste time on me?

Because I don't like him, I answer myself, *and he knows it.* (Remember, I used to live in this town and know the certain weirdness that pervades the rules of sexual attraction.)

Suddenly I see that Spencer and his new friend, Lilliana Martin, have turned around and are looking at me. And the actress is smiling broadly, laughing, dipping that breast into his arm again and then, shockingly, is offering me a friendly little wave. In the next moment Spencer is bringing her over.

"I made a deal with Ovitz this week," my short companion says with some urgency.

"That's great," I say, eyes on Spencer.

"This is Sally," Spencer announces proudly when they arrive, in a way that makes me want to forgive him for anything and everything. "Sally Harrington, this is Lilliana Martin."

I smile politely and extend my hand. "Congratulations on your upcoming film. I've only heard wonderful things about your performance."

"Thank you," she says. Her voice is soft, smooth, but I

can tell by the exaggerated care in her enunciation that she has been drinking.

In Los Angeles, being high in public this early in one's acting career is not a terribly good sign. In New York, it doesn't seem to faze people one way or the other. But here, where the body is worshiped over almost everything, drinking or drugging nowadays is perceived as a slap against the studio about to release the actor's movie. (If Lilliana Martin isn't careful, before she lands her next movie she might *have* to go to New York to prove she can show up for work on time. This is called "doing something marvelous in the *thee-ayah-tuh.*")

Still, I find it somewhat comforting to know that Lilliana Martin has been drinking, not performing this breast-into-Spencer's-arm routine stone cold sober.

"Spencer's been talking my ear off about you," she says in a low, friendly voice. "He's been telling me I should give you an interview for DBS."

I can't help but smile. Spencer's trying to help me. Push me out of the local-schmocal *der hinderlander* pieces I'm supposed to be doing for WSCT in New Haven and put me at the door of *DBS News Magazine* with a national piece. And if Lilliana Martin's movie is as big a hit as people think...

I try to introduce my new friend, but I don't know his name. He supplies it—Jonathan Small (I could have guessed this)—but apparently these two already know each other.

"Jonathan," the actress says, leaning down to brush his cheek with a kiss. "This is Spencer Hawes from New York, Malcolm's editor."

This momentarily stops him. Then he swallows and turns to inform Spencer that Malcolm Kieloff's book has all kinds of mistakes in it and needs to be edited. The usual response of an editor to this kind of criticism is "If you think it's bad now, you should have seen it before!" But Spencer lets out a slightly breathless, incredulous *"Really?"* instead.

Behind his dreadful little black glasses Jonathan squints at him and, sounding almost hopeful, asks, "Did I offend you?"

"No, not at all," Spencer tells him. "You only surprise me. I had no idea someone like you could read."

Lilliana Martin bursts out laughing and even Jonathan snickers a little, rolling forward onto the balls of his feet again and clasping his hands behind his back. He turns to me, as if we are alone. *"This* is the boyfriend?"

"This is the boyfriend," Spencer confirms, and something akin to cold fury is building behind his smile and I don't think it has to do with me. Spencer knows that Jonathan knows this whole Kieloff book deal is a put-up job, but what is getting him mad is Jonathan thinks Spencer *wanted* Kieloff to "write" this drivel, that Jonathan thinks Spencer's just like him, just trying to hustle a buck, only Jonathan's tipping off Spencer he should hide his crass motives better.

I know, it's complicated, but I told you, I used to live here. It's one of the countless little face-offs the guys do in L.A.

"As I said," I murmur to Jonathan, "we have plans."

"Ditch him and call me," Jonathan whispers. He presses a card in my hand, kisses me softly on the ear and walks away.

I am at a momentary loss for words.

"Who the hell *is* that guy?" Spencer asks, stepping forward to pluck the card out of my hand. He frowns at it and shoves it in front of Lilliana. "This can't be right."

"It is," Lilliana says softly. "Jonathan's head of production now."

Spencer and the actress's eyes meet and I feel a small chill. His anger has vanished in the presence of the obvious electricity between them. Thankfully, Spencer backs

away and moves to slide his arm around my shoulders. "I
need to check on Malcolm," he explains, "make sure he's
talking to the book buyers. Maybe you guys can talk about
doing an interview."

"I don't want to pressure Lilliana," I say.

"You're supposed to," Lilliana says good-naturedly.

"Okay," Spencer says, moving off, "I'll be back."

I look at the actress. "Truly, I don't want to put you on
the spot. I'm sure the studio's lined up everything they
want you to do."

"God," the actress says, ignoring me, "I need a drink."
She looks around, adding sarcastically under her breath,
"I've only fallen off these heels twice tonight...."

I look down. They are very high spiked heels. She's
probably only about five five in her stocking feet. "I'll get
you something," I offer.

"No way, you can't leave me," she says. "Here comes my
agent."

"Lilliana, darling," the guy says, taking both of her hands
and kissing her on one side of the face and then the other.
"You look fabulous. When I walked in all I could see was
you."

Lilliana rolls her eyes and introduces me. "Sally, my
agent, Richie Benzler. Richie, Sally Harrington. She's a reporter from DBS News in New York. We may be doing an
interview."

Trying to live up to the promotion she has just bestowed
upon me, I smile and shake the agent's hand. He turns back
to Lilliana. "Where's Cliff?"

"In hell, I hope," Lilliana says out of the side of her
mouth.

"Oh," her agent says, hesitating. "Does that mean...?"

"It means it's over."

"But—"

"No buts, Richie! He's a glorified thug and I'll thank you

very much not to introduce me to another one." She is sounding pretty sober now.

"He's not a thug," the agent begins, murmuring, trying to hold on to her hand. "He's very influential with the studio."

"Save it," Lilliana says, shaking her hand loose. "Listen, Sally and I were just going to powder our noses." She looks to me for confirmation.

"Yes, we were just on our way," I say.

But instead of walking toward the front of the restaurant, where the bathroom is, Lilliana leads me to the back of the banquet room, to an alcove in the corner. She peers around the partition and the manager of the restaurant magically appears. Lilliana whispers something and he smiles, bowing slightly, gesturing for us to walk back through the alcove, which we do. He opens a door for us and points up a carpeted stairway. "To the top and to the right."

"Thank you," Lilliana says, leading the way. "Nine times out of ten," she says over her shoulder to me as she climbs the stairs—I slow down because I'm nearly getting clipped in the nose by the wide swing of her silk-covered derriere, "they'll let you duck the mob for a bit."

At the top of the stairs, to the right, is a basic bathroom à la Mobil station, clearly meant for the help. (Downstairs, for the patrons, they have marble bathrooms, complete with hovering servants.) There is no sign of the Dracula-gone-Mission decor up here, either. It's all-American restaurant office: indoor-outdoor carpeting, fake wood paneling with attractive advertising pieces from food and alcohol distributors tacked up, furniture from Staples, or maybe it's Office Max.

Lilliana moves past the bathroom to lead me through an open office door on the left. There are receipts and paperwork everywhere and not one, but two adding machines sitting on either side of a computer terminal on a massive and very messy desk. She drops down in one of the two chairs in front of the desk and gestures for me to sit in the other. "Ah, that's better," she says as she kicks her shoes off and reaches to pick up the phone. She punches the red button on the bottom. "Hi, this is Lilliana Martin calling from the manager's office. I wonder if you could bring up two glasses of Moët and some of those cheese pastry things? Great. Oh—and do you have a pack of cigarettes around?" Pause. "Marlboro Lights, if you have them."

I have to smile. This is a woman who knows how to use her celebrity.

Lilliana hangs up, crosses her legs in my direction and settles in, arms resting along the arms of the chair. Her muscle definition is something and I suspect she is showing it off.

"So," she says, "are you really going to try to hang on to Spencer or what?"

CHAPTER TWO

"Excuse me?" I say to Lilliana Martin.

"I have to ask. It saves time. You never know what's really going on in a relationship unless you do."

"I see," I say. She asked the question in a very deliberately constructed way. Am I really going to *try* to hang on to Spencer? I don't know whether to praise the actress for her insight or slap her across the face for her insolence. "I take it you're interested."

She shrugs. "I'm alone right now."

Only in L.A. could this conversation be taking place.

"And have you asked Spencer if he's take-away-able?"

"Actually," the actress says matter-of-factly, "he said he was thinking about getting married."

I smile slightly.

"That may not come as news to you," she continues, her eyes moving behind me to the doorway, "but it sure did to me. Come in. You can put it on the desk."

A waiter enters carrying a circular silver tray. On it are two flutes of champagne, two cocktail napkins, a small round plate of cheese hors d'oeuvres, a glass ashtray and a pack of Marlboro Lights—open, with cigarettes carefully tapped out—and matches. After placing the tray carefully on the desk, he bows slightly and says, "With the compliments of the house, Ms. Martin."

"Thank you," she says demurely. The waiter nods slightly to me and leaves the room. Lilliana hands me a glass of champagne and I take it, scarcely waiting for her to pick up hers before I take a long sip.

It is cold and crisp and tastes wonderful. The actress holds out the hors d'oeuvres and I shake my head. She puts the plate back, takes a swallow of her champagne, puts the glass down, and then sits back in her chair with the cigarette and matches in hand. "If I were you," she says, "I'd think long and hard before marrying a man like Spencer. You'll get pregnant and feel like killing yourself when you see the way he looks at other women."

"You would know, I assume," I say icily.

"I never needed to be pregnant," she continues in that matter-of-fact voice, putting the cigarette between her lips. "Just watching my lover look around makes me feel like killing myself." I sit there in semistunned silence while Lilliana lights up and tosses the matches on the desk. She takes a deep drag, lowering her lashes, and then she lets her head fall back to exhale a slow stream of smoke toward the ceiling. Her neck is long and her hair falls softly off her shoulders; there is red lipstick left on the cigarette filter. She smiles to herself and then brings her head down to look at me. Her eyes are a deep brown. "I am being absolutely awful and I don't even know why. Because I think I even rather like you."

I sip my champagne. No way is this babe twenty-six. She's done *far* too much living—far too much, I suspect, for me to handle.

"And I think I might be envious," she continues. "I'm just throwing my boyfriend out now. I think I hate him," she says. When I don't say anything, she adds, "He's like a preppie gangster, you know?"

I don't know if she's talking about her boyfriend or Spencer, which, either way, is not a very good sign.

"What kind of work does your ex do?"

Her head kicks back slightly with a laugh. "He's a union executive, which means—" She shrugs, reaching for her glass. "I don't want to know. You don't want to know, nobody should want to know." She takes a deep swallow and looks at me. "At least Spencer's got talent, you know? He can do something. But he's trouble, you must know that. A guy his age not married? Nice-looking? Not a serial killer?"

"Now, there's a personality trait," I mutter into my glass, "*not* a serial killer."

"You must know what I mean," she insists.

I lower my glass. "No. Why don't you explain it to me?"

"A guy like Spencer will fuck you royally—"

I cringe at the vulgarity.

"Because that's what he *does,* that's his thing, fucking," she continues. "And hooray for that! We need men like that. We *all* need a man like that at least once. But then," she adds, frowning, pulling heavily on the cigarette, "they fuck us *over.* Big time. Sooner or later, they're on to the next conquest." She exhales, looking at me. "Boo, hiss. Audience doesn't like it."

I can't believe I'm still sitting here. The better part of me told me not to go upstairs with this woman to begin with, but now I find myself morbidly interested in what she has to say.

Twenty-six, my foot.

She puts out her cigarette, pops an hors d'oeuvres into her mouth, drains her glass and then lights another cigarette. She glances over at me. "Don't marry him," she says gravely.

I laugh and sip my champagne. Hell if I'm responding to that.

"You shouldn't laugh," she tells me.

"It's better than crying," I tell her.

"Mmm," she murmurs in agreement, pulling on her cigarette. She smiles then, exhaling, and looks at me admiringly. "Do you know," she says with a sense of wonder, "that this is the first conversation I've had in I don't know how long where I don't feel like I'm taking a screen test with somebody?" She sighs, briefly touching her forehead but being careful not to mess up her makeup. She pulls on the cigarette again. "It's weird. Take the dog groomer—he knows my dog and cares about my dog, and he pets him— and I don't know, he might even love him. But me, after all this time, he still talks to me like we're doing a screen test. Everything's exaggerated, you know? Like the only reason why we're talking is to see how good he looks for a nonexistent camera he's always posing for."

"It takes time to make a home, to feel a sense of community," I say. "You haven't been in any one place very long, have you?"

I'm trying my best to recall the details of Lilliana Martin's life. She's from the Midwest, I think, modeled some, got a part on a soap in New York for a couple of years. Then she landed a role on a prime-time TV show, *Roommates,* and moved to L.A. That wasn't very long ago.

"A year," she argues, eyes widening. "I've been here a year. I miss New York."

"It takes time to settle in out here, find your people," I say, lowering my eyes to sip my champagne. I wonder how much of this nonsense I can put up with in order to get an interview for DBS. The most disturbing aspect, though, is I find myself liking her. This insulting, vaguely alcoholic, home-wrecking actress. Worse yet, on some level I seem to identify with her.

She looks at me again, smiling now. "Someone told me that success as an actor means being able to make friends with people you like." She is silent a moment, eyes drifting to the floor before coming back up to me. "Someday I'd like to have friends like you guys. People who can actually do something." She laughs to herself, head kicking back slightly. "Like read and write."

I smile. "Thank you. But you'll find there are a lot of wonderful people here in L.A. Who read a lot of books, as a matter of fact."

She appears to be studying me. "Spencer says you're wicked bright."

"Oh, only slightly wicked, maybe," I say.

She laughs, taking one last drag of her cigarette before leaning forward to stamp it out. "We better go," she says, now all business. "Dinner must be soon."

While she puts on her shoes, I drain my champagne glass.

"You're looking forward to this dinner as much as I am," she observes while rising, one hand on the desk to keep her balance. Those are some heels she has on. "Don't worry, Malcolm will want the dinner over as soon as possible. He's a real family guy." She carefully smooths the silk of her dress while I get up.

"That's quite a dress," I can't help but say.

"Hideous, isn't it?" she laughs. "But anything to steal the stage. That's my job, steal the stage, steal the attention."

I follow Lilliana back downstairs and we slip into the party the way we left and find that people have started to leave. Spencer spots us and hurries over. "I thought you guys had escaped without me. We've got to go over to the Garden Room for dinner. Lilliana, Malcolm wants you to sit next to him, if that's all right."

"Sure," she says.

"Darling," he says to me, "I'm so sorry, but that asshole Jonathan Small has talked his way into this dinner and he's supposed to sit next to you."

"Oh, I can handle him," I assure Spencer.

Spencer leans closer, taking my elbow. "Where did you guys go?"

"Upstairs. To some office. We had some champagne, and she wanted to have a cigarette."

We have to walk to the Garden Room, which means the guests must thread their way through the main dining room. People are staring as we walk, trying to figure out if we're "anybody," but it's only when Lilliana is spotted that a murmur moves through the crowd. In the next moment, the diners all put down their silverware and start to applaud.

Her new movie must really be Oscar material.

"It was only a minor role," Lilliana mutters over her shoulder to me.

I can't believe it. I think she's embarrassed.

The setting for dinner is exotic. A lush indoor garden surrounds us and I smell orchids. There is a long table set for twenty-two, with Malcolm Kieloff on one end, and the CEO of Bennett, Fitzallen & Coe, Andrew Rushman, whom nobody is paying any attention to, on the other. "Surprise," I hear a voice whisper in my ear.

It's Jonathan slipping into the chair next to me. Beaming. I look down the table to Spencer, but he is talking to Mrs. Kieloff. I look at Lilliana, who is sitting there, slightly glassy-eyed at this point, politely listening to Malcolm. My eyes move to Spencer's boss, Kate Weston, publisher of B, F & C, and she winks at me. There are two other actors at the table, a comedy actress who is the lead voice in a hit animated feature released by Monarch and a supporting actor on one of Monarch's popular teen dramas.

The food and wine are excellent and the dinner conversation actually isn't half bad when I remember how many doors Jonathan can open for me at Monarch. One that I'm particularly interested in is the possibility of interviewing the actor James Van Der Beek, who grew up in Cheshire, near Castleford. A piece would be a big hit back home, both for the paper and the New Haven DBS affiliate.

I am having a difficult time fully taking in the scene the way I want to. I'm supposed to be a journalist and I know many people would die to have my seat at this table, to meet and talk with movie executives and famous actors in a posh Beverly Hills restaurant. So I take careful note, mentally, of the food and decor, of the conversations taking place, what people are wearing, but I feel detached and unaffected.

Actually, I'm bored.

In the five months I've hung out with Spencer, I'm afraid the powers of celebrity no longer work well on me. Barely a week has gone by that Spencer hasn't asked me if I have any interest in meeting this famous person or another. Half his job, it seems, is going to fashionable parties, openings and screenings. As his companion, it quickly struck me that these occasions in New York are just like the ones I witnessed out here in L.A., including this very dinner: they are *work,* everyone is *working,* no one's here because they want to be, even the guest of honor.

A couple of months ago, I shrieked when I found myself described on page six of the *New York Post* as "The beautiful Connecticut reporter on the arm of one of New York's most eligible bachelors." True, I did inherit some nice looks from my mother (the light brown hair and big blue eyes people seem to like), but this was a bit much. But then when I appeared in a photograph with Spencer in *Avenue,* taken at a book party at a swanky Fifth Avenue apartment, and then again in the *New York Times* Style section when we went to an opening at the Metropolitan Museum (Spencer had edited the companion book to the exhibit), I was only grateful for the *professional* exposure. Name recognition is everything these days.

By the time coffee and dessert are being served, I realize I have had too much to drink, because instead of being outraged that Jonathan has slid his hand over my thigh, I think it's funny. I take his hand, give it a squeeze and return it to him. "Another time, but not now," I promise. He need not know there will never be another time, that I will move to Alaska before I ever talk to this man again, studio or no studio. He seems satisfied with my answer and we manage to get through the remaining half hour without much ado.

"We're giving Lilliana a ride home, okay?" Spencer tells me on the way out.

"We're going to a new club," Jonathan tells Spencer.

"No, I'm going to Lilliana's," I correct him. "I promised." I lower my voice. "I'll call you later." At this, Spencer's head turns so fast it nearly snaps off his neck.

"Where are you staying?" Jonathan murmurs back.

"The Four Seasons," I tell him, and then I see Spencer smile (because we are staying at Shutters in Santa Monica). "I'll call you later."

"You do that," he says, grabbing my arm and kissing my cheek.

"God, Sally!" Spencer says, nearly yanking me out the front door.

"Well I had to get rid of him. You want a scene?" I am laughing. This is all so unreal, the lights, the paparazzi outside. I feel as though I am in a movie.

We get into the limousine, Lilliana and me on the back seat and Spencer facing us on the jump seat. We recount the party and laugh and Lilliana gives us gossip about the people we just dined with as we wind up the Santa Monica Mountains to Cold Water Canyon.

We reach Lilliana's house, a split-level set back off the road and nestled into the side of a mountain. I say, "Lilliana, it was great," and hold out my hand to her, but she says, "Please come in for a quick cup of coffee or something."

She says it with the intensity of a person who does not want to go in alone.

I look at Spencer, who is waiting for my decision. "Okay, sure," I say.

The driver holds the door as all three of us pile out and walk the brick path to the front door. The house is built of gray limestone and white wood and is lovely. "Oh, hell," Lilliana says as she opens the door, "he didn't pick up his stuff." She sighs heavily. I don't blame her. The foyer is full of boxes.

"What does this guy do?" Spencer asks, touching a ten-thousand-dollar Bose stereo system, stacked neatly between a tennis cannon and a box that says it contains a complete digital photo lab.

"A business executive." She sighs, waving us on, leading us into a great room with a vaulted ceiling and a nice view of the canyon. "A funny-business executive," she adds. She whirls around. "So what can I get you, Sally?"

"Oh, nothing, I don't think."

"A cognac?" Spencer suggests.

"Ah, good idea," Lilliana says.

I look at him. "I thought we were having coffee."

Lilliana fixes a tray and comes over to sit on the couch with a bottle and three snifters. She has Spencer do the honors. I take mine and sip. At this rate, I'll be on the floor in no time. Lilliana slips off her shoes and slides to the floor, resting her back against the couch, looking up at me. "Spencer said you used to live out here."

"I went to UCLA. Then I worked at *Boulevard* for a couple of years."

Spencer has sat down at the piano and is picking out "Around the World in Eighty Days" with one hand. It is, I know, the only song he knows, which his mother taught him when he was eight. He always does this whenever there's a piano around and he's had too much to drink.

"I lived in Connecticut once, did you know that?" Lilliana asks me.

"No."

"Greenwich." Lilliana smiles down into her cognac. "For two weeks. Short romance." She takes a sip.

"Well," I say, "Castleford, where I'm from, is very different from Greenwich."

"Mmm," she says absently.

I don't think she's very interested in Castleford.

Suddenly she looks up. "Maybe I will have coffee after all. Or tea. Would you like some tea, Sally?"

"As a matter of fact..." I begin, putting the snifter back on the coffee table.

"Spencer?" Lilliana asks, rising from the floor with amazing grace. She touches my shoulder. "Come with me."

Spencer stops plucking notes to look up.

"Would you like coffee or tea?"

"I'm fine," he assures her, and resumes his recital.

I follow Lilliana into the kitchen and marvel at how beautiful it is. This is Martha Stewart land, with every charming feature one can think of: a butcher block island, shiny copper pots and pans hanging on iron hooks, a large stainless steel range with hood, magnificent wood cabinets with glass windows—showing perfect china and glasses, all in their place—large glass canisters with all kinds of dried grains and herbs, a recessed bookcase that holds a collection of cookbooks....

"Like all people not allowed to eat," Lilliana explains, "I'm completely obsessed with food."

I laugh politely, putting my hand on the counter to steady myself. I hear Lilliana putting water in the kettle and then the oddest thing happens. I feel her hands on my shoulders and then her breasts gently, but firmly, press into my back. And then she murmurs in my ear, "I'm not sure how to approach this."

I take a breath and pull away to the side, resting back against the counter to face her. "Then don't," I say a little more sharply than I mean to.

She purses her lips slightly, nodding, and then lowers her head, as if ashamed.

"Hey," I say, touching her arm. "It's okay, don't worry about it. It never happened."

She looks at me. "I didn't think you'd want to, but Spencer—"

"Spencer?" I say, my whole body stiffening.

"It's my fault," Spencer says from the doorway. "I said I didn't know, but she could ask you."

I cannot believe it. And evidently my expression shows this because Spencer looks alarmed when I demand, "You didn't know *what?*"

"If you'd want to—well, you know."

Lilliana groans and turns away. "Just shut up, Spencer."

"No, tell me," I say, angry. "You didn't know if I wanted to...*what?* Be with Lilliana?" I narrow my eyes. "Or a threesome, Spencer?" I don't have to wait for an answer. I close my eyes for a moment, trying to stop the rage I feel flooding through my body.

When I open my eyes, I find that Lilliana is wisely leaving the room.

"How dare you," I whisper, seething.

"Oh, for God's sake, Sally," he says, moving toward me. "She only asked. All you had to do was do what you did, say no thank you."

I make a sound of disgust and push past him to the living room, where Lilliana's sitting on the couch, her face buried in her lap.

"You knew him for less than an hour and pegged him perfectly," I say loudly to Lilliana. "He's exactly what you said."

"What did she say?" Spencer asks, following me.

"Would you please just keep your mouth shut," I mutter over my shoulder.

"Oh, God," Lilliana moans in her lap.

"Come on, Lilliana, don't," I plead, kneeling next to her but being careful not to touch her. "You're going to ruin your pretty dress." I pause, thinking how much I sound like Mother. "Spencer and I are both idiots. We should have just dropped you off and left. We know how vulnerable you are right now, with your boyfriend and everything."

Slowly she raises her head and looks tearfully at me. She sniffs, rubs her eye with the back of her hand and tries to smile. "You're a nice person, Sally Harrington."

"But I'm really tired," I murmur, "and I've had too much to drink."

"You can stay over if you want," she says automatically. "In the guest room."

"That's all right, we've got the driver to take us to the hotel." I stand up. "I just want to make sure you're all right."

Somewhere in the house, the telephone starts to ring. Lilliana's head turns and then she seems to make a decision. "I'll see you to the door," she announces, standing up, sounding suddenly pretty close to normal.

Awkwardly we move to the front foyer, where Lilliana opens the door for us. "Good night," I say, holding my hand out.

She ignores it to lean forward and kiss me lightly on the cheek. "Thank you."

"Good night," Spencer says gruffly.

She kisses him on the cheek, too, without saying anything. Spencer and I walk out into the driveway and the front door closes behind us.

"How mad are you?" he asks, taking my hand.

"I'm not talking about it here," I say, shaking his hand off.

The driver has spotted us and jumps out of the car to open the door.

"Come on," Spencer whines, "don't be like this."

I get into the car and slide across the seat. I turn on the FM radio.

Well, it's over, I am thinking. *The relationship that was going to last a lifetime is over.*

Spencer gets in and closes the door. Then he fumbles for, finds and pushes the button that raises the divider between us and the driver. "What is the big deal?"

I look at him in amazement. "You're not really asking me that, are you?"

"Yes," he says, looking for the volume control to turn down the radio, "I am really asking you that."

"You are unbelievable," I mutter, looking away. Then I look back at him. "You set it up, you son of a bitch!"

"I did *not* set it up!"

"Then explain to me how this happened."

"She asked me."

"She asked you *what?*"

"If we'd ever done a three-way."

"Oh, God!" I cry, turning to my window.

"I said no," Spencer says, defending himself. "Look, the whole thing started when I said my girlfriend was here. She was coming on to me and I was trying to tell her no, while not getting her all upset—"

"Poor, Spencer," I tell the window.

"I told her I was thinking about getting married!" he cries.

"Right," I say, whipping around. "So how did you get from 'I'm thinking about getting married' to 'Why don't you make a pass at my girlfriend and see how it goes'?"

"I never told her that."

"Well you told her something!"

"No, she told *me.* She asked me to introduce her to you and let her find out for herself."

"Find out what, Spencer? If I wanted to celebrate our engagement by having a ménage à trois? Or were you planning on just standing around and watching?" I look at my window again. "You're a freak."

"We weren't even talking about bed," he insists, pulling on my arm to make me turn around. "We just wanted to—"

"What?"

"Maybe just fool around a little. Kiss." He lowers his voice. "We weren't going to go to bed or anything. She just wanted to make out a little." When I don't answer but only stare at him, he adds, "Look, Sally, obviously it was a bad idea. We had too much to drink and—" He sighs, looking into my eyes. "I just thought we needed a little... Something. Something to wake us up."

"You've done this before, haven't you?" I ask him. I look away. "Where the hell have I been? Of *course* you've done this before."

"Sally," he whispers, "I love you."

"Right."

"I do. But you've gone dead on me, Sally, cold fish— what the hell am I supposed to do?"

"You could try talking to me about it before dragging another woman home."

"I didn't bring her home, we're not home, that's just the point," he says with maddening calmness. "She's a nice girl, she's very attractive, she's discreet and she was interested. So shoot me. We're three thousand miles away from home."

I look out the window at the greenery rushing by. The weirdest thing is, instead of feeling like killing Spencer, I feel like slitting *my* wrists. I always do when I know a relationship is finished, or screwed up beyond repair. I feel as though I want to die.

"Don't make this a big deal," Spencer says.

"It is a big deal," I say.

"I just want us to have a decent sex life."

That's it. *Decent sex life.* I slam the partition button. "Stop the car!"

"Sally!"

The driver is pulling over into someone's driveway. "Get out!" I scream. "Get the hell out of here!"

"I'm not getting out," he tells me.

"Get out of this car!" I scream.

He glares at me a moment, and then jerks the door handle and pushes the door open and gets out. "You want to know why I didn't talk to you about our sex life?" he yells. "Because I can't! Every time I try to, you go crazy!"

I lunge to pull the car door closed and lock it. "Shutters!" I tell the driver.

He's looking at me in the rearview mirror. "But, lady, he, um, leased the car."

"My father will squash you like a bug if you don't get this car moving!" No need for him to know my father's been dead for twenty-one years.

The driver hesitates, no doubt thinking over the complicated family dynasties in this town, and arrives at a decision. He'll drive me to Shutters and leave Spencer at the side of the road.

CHAPTER THREE

The telephone is ringing. I surface from beneath the pillows to see that it's almost 8:30 a.m. "Hello?" I say softly.

"Hi, Sally. May I speak to Spencer?" It's Kate Weston, Spencer's boss.

"Um, he's not here right now," I say carefully.

"Well maybe you can help me. Lilliana Martin's agent just called, wanting to know if I know where she might be. She left with you guys after dinner, right?"

"We gave her a ride home," I say, reaching toward the glass of water I left next to the bed last night. I put the two Alka-Seltzer tablets I also left there into the glass and wait for them to dissolve. "Up in Cold Water Canyon."

"And she was all right?"

"As far as I know. We went in for a cup of coffee and left."

Kate sighs. "Well, would you mind talking to her agent? He's freaking out. She was supposed to be picked up this morning for some kind of publicity shoot and they got there and found the front door unlocked and no Lilliana."

Huh. "Sure, tell him to call me."

"Thanks. And have Spencer call me when he gets back."

I sip my Alka-Seltzer and try not to think, only lie back

against the soft pillows and try to register the morning sunshine that is slipping through the tall wood shutters. That's
why they call the hotel Shutters. Right on the beach, the
hotel is reminiscent of Havana in the 1920s. Each room has
shutters over its large windows and they're also in a window that peeks from the bedroom into a Jacuzzi. It's a
knockout of a place to stay. Until last night, it was also a
romantic place to stay.

The telephone is ringing again. It's the agent, Richie
Benzler. "So you took Lilliana home last night?"

"Yes. We had some coffee and left. Around eleven, I
think."

"Was she plastered or something?"

"She was a little tipsy," I admit.

"I wonder..." His voice trails off. "Was she alone? Was
Cliff there?"

"No, but his stuff was in the front hall."

A pause. "You took her home with that Spencer guy,
right? The editor?"

"Yes."

"Did he sleep with her? Stay over or anything?"

I've been wondering the same thing. "He left with me,"
I say.

"Okay, thanks. I'll keep looking." And he hangs up.

The Alka-Seltzer is settling my stomach, but I am one
step away from breaking into tears.

I wonder if Spencer went back to Lilliana's. I wonder if
he went back to get her and take her to a hotel so I couldn't
find him. Or maybe *she* took him to a hotel so I wouldn't
find *them*.

I've got to do something and so I opt to put on gym
shorts over a one-piece swimsuit and go blading on the concrete walk along the beach. I dress quickly, trying not to
think. I leave the room, cross the pool area and take the

stairs down to the lobby to find out where I can get roller blades.

Now that I am half resigned to the idea I'll never see Spencer again, I'm startled to find him sitting downstairs in the lobby. He looks dreadful, dressed in the same clothes as the night before, only his jacket is nowhere to be seen, his shirtsleeves are rolled up and his socks, I notice, are missing. Next to him on an end table is half a glass of chocolate milk and a *New York Times*.

"Did you go back to Lilliana's?" I ask quietly, sliding into the seat next to him.

He looks at me with bloodshot eyes and an unshaven face.

"Because she's missing this morning," I continue in a low voice. "Her agent called Kate and then me to find out when we last saw her. I told him we took her home, had a cup of coffee and left together around eleven. So if you know where she is, you should call him. Or tell her to call him." I hand him the room key and stand up. "His number's next to the phone." I start to walk over to the concierge's desk.

I feel his hand firmly grasp my arm. "We need to talk."

I sigh, avoiding his eyes. "I'm not sure I want to."

"I don't care if you scream your head off," he continues, "we *have* to talk." He steers me toward the elevator.

Part of me is tremendously relieved to see him, another part, however, now that I know he's safe and sound, wants to slap him bald-headed for wrecking everything. We return to the room in silence. He unlocks the door and steps back for me to go in first. "I'm ordering room service," I say. "Do you want anything?"

"A Bloody Mary," he says.

I look at him.

"A Bloody Mary," he repeats, going into the bathroom.

I call room service and order some eggs and bacon and orange juice and Perrier and a Bloody Mary while I hear him in the shower. Room service tells me it's too early for alcoholic beverages so I say make it a Virgin Mary.

The food arrives as Spencer emerges from the bathroom, towel around his waist, hair dripping water. He has shaved and brushed his teeth, too. He walks over to the table and picks up the Virgin Mary and tastes it—looks at me but says nothing, knowing there is no vodka in it—and drinks it down, anyway. Looking down at the table, uncovering the napkin around the toast, he says, "I walked back up to Lilliana's house and called a cab. I came here and slept outside in a lounge chair by the pool."

I am relieved, but will die before letting on. "Maybe you should call her agent," I say. "And tell him that you saw her."

He bites the toast and raises his eyes. He swallows. "But I didn't. She wasn't there. The front door was wide open."

"Where could she have gone?"

"Anywhere," he says, sitting on the edge of the bed. "But she must have left right after we did." Suddenly he tosses the remains of the toast on the table and buries his face in his hands, rubbing his eyes. "What the hell are we going to do, Sally?" He drops his hands and looks at me, miserable. "I don't know how to fix this. I wasn't thinking. I don't know, I just thought—" He sighs. "There's no excuse. But you've got to understand I didn't mean it in a disrespectful way."

I know better than to try to respond to this because I will start screaming. How he rationalizes having Lilliana hit on me as being respectful, I have not a clue. We've been together for five months. God only knows what he'll have in mind after a year.

"What I want to know is," he says softly, "if you would be willing to go into counseling with me. When we get back. Before things go any further. Before I do any more damage."

If there is one thing he could have said that might save us, this is it. The idea that Spencer is willing to tell a third party what he did last night reassures me. Some.

"I think that would be a very good idea," I say, pulling the cover off my eggs. He is watching me, waiting, I suspect, for me to signal that we're friends again. Feeling light-headed and vaguely ill, I put the cover back down. "It's all falling apart, isn't it?" And the second I say it I know it's true. I lower my head and the tears start to roll. In a moment he's next to me, holding me.

"We have to work through this," he murmurs, kissing the top of my head.

How can I tell him that it's not just this, not just us, but how I've lived my whole life, this all-or-nothing drive and crash I can't take anymore. I start crying for real, feeling grief for this dying attachment, feeling grief about the past. For in the end, all sorrow feels the same to me; the despair feels the same, the sentence of loneliness inescapable. Stupid me for thinking otherwise, for thinking Spencer and I would somehow be different.

After a while I stop crying, exhausted, and Spencer gets me some Kleenex. I use it.

Then I look at him. He feels it, too. The sense of stunned disbelief that has settled over us both. Yesterday we were thinking about getting married, now we are doubting if there was anything real here at all.

If only the tingling between my legs would stop now instead of increasing, as if my body is determined to blast my sadness out of existence. I make the mistake of looking down. Spencer takes my hand and places it gently between his legs.

I take a deep breath and look at him. His eyes are narrowing, his breath picking up. He has grown hard, but I haven't moved a muscle. He swallows, closing his eyes.

I know what I want to do. I want to remove the towel and

I want to sit on him and wrap my legs around him and bury my breasts in his face and feel nothing but the deepest physical part of me sated.

Spencer's eyes are still closed; one hand has pulled down the strap of my swimsuit and raised my breast toward his mouth.

The sensation has my heart pounding, my whole lower body longing. But my heart is unmovable. I kiss the top of Spencer's head, whisper, "I'm sorry. I can't."

He raises his head, leaving my breast cold and wet in the open air. I am crying again. "I can't do it anymore, Spencer. It's not meant to be. It's not who I am."

He swallows and rests his forehead against my cheek for a moment. Then he gets up and walks into the bathroom, closing and locking the door behind him.

CHAPTER FOUR

"Somebody called this afternoon looking for you," Mother says as I come in the back door of her kitchen. She is sitting at the table, half glasses on the end of her nose, working on her school curriculum notebook. She has a sea of notes around her, drawn from the boxes and boxes of them she has written and kept over the past twenty years.

"Who was that?" I say, stomping the snow off my shoes and then squatting to say hi to the dogs. The big collie-shepherd-retriever, Scotty, is mine; the small golden retriever, Abigail, is Mother's. The dogs furiously squirm and vie for position to lick my face hello. They're inside tonight because we are having a snow squall that began shortly after I landed at Bradley International, the airport outside of Hartford.

"He wouldn't give his name," Mother says, taking off her glasses to look at me. "I told him he could reach you at the paper."

This is not the first time Mother has been bothered by people trying to track me down. I am unlisted for a reason.

"Did Scotty behave?" I ask, giving my boy a kiss on the nose.

"He was a love," she tells me. "It was Abigail who was bad. She ate my piecrust on the counter."

My eyes grow large and my mouth opens wide at the culprit, whose reddish-gold silky face I'm holding in my hands. "Abigail!" I whisper. She smiles and pushes her nose under my chin to get closer, which prompts Scotty to try to sit on me to demonstrate possession, and I fall backward on the floor, laughing.

"You spoil them," Mother tells me.

"I don't give them piecrust!" I object, lying on my back, both dogs on me now. We play around a little and finally I get up. Mother, though she thinks me a disgrace ("In your pretty skirt!"), is smiling because she's nuts about these dogs, too.

"So how was L.A.?" she asks, accepting a kiss on the cheek.

"Liam Neeson wasn't at the party after all."

"Oh, that's disappointing," she says, looking at my face. "But something else has happened, hasn't it?"

"No," I insist, turning away, "I'm just tired." Mother's the last person I want to talk to about what I'm feeling.

My mother, Isabel "Belle" Ann Goodwin Harrington, grew up with every advantage as a fair-haired beauty in Newport, Rhode Island. (People often mistook her for the actress Lee Remick, and even now, at fifty-eight, she still gets an occasional startled look from strangers.) When Mother married Daddy, it seemed she had everything to look forward to as well. My father, Wilbur "Dodge" Kennett Harrington, was a promising architect out of Yale. They married, built a house in Castleford, had two children, and my father left the big architectural firm he worked for to strike out on his own. Not long after he was killed in an "accident," and to keep body and soul together, Mother started teaching school again, and with my maternal grandparents' help, managed to hang on to the house.

Mother is one of those unsung heroes you hear about. She raised two children essentially alone, downplayed her loneliness and maintained her integrity, and to this day leaves just about everyone who crosses her path a little better off for having known her. As a role model for me, you can imagine, she is a tough act to follow. Gentle, kind, true, beautiful... Well, I'm not *that* bad, but everyone says I'm much more like my father, a bit of a dreamer, definitely competitive and emotionally—well, kind of up and down.

Four years ago Mother was diagnosed with cancer. That's when I came home from Los Angeles and ended up staying in town. Mother has now survived cancer, too, and although she looks her age, her beauty has quietly transformed into something almost ethereal. Mother says she had to find a spiritual life to make her journey in this world, and she often tells me (hint, hint) that whatever it is she has found that gives her this glow, she hopes I'll find it one day, too.

Meanwhile (and in contrast), I am Mother's thirty-year-old "oldest, unmarried," who has light brown hair—instead of Mother's honey blond—and a fainter version of her large blue eyes. Unfortunately, any spiritual glow I have is probably a combination of a temper tantrum followed by the fear of God striking me down in my tracks. At any rate, Mother is not the person I automatically think of who would understand the messes I get myself into.

"Darling, come into the living room," she says. "I want to talk to you for a minute."

Uh-oh, something's up. The living room is reserved for formal talks.

My father's design for this house was based on a late-eighteenth-century home. There are Oriental rugs and wonderful furniture in this room, almost all of it left over from the old Harrington estate (which is now a convent next door) or from Mother's family, the Goodwins. All of the wood planking, moldings and even the staircase in this room is from trees felled, planed and cured right here in Castleford. At the end of the living room there is a tremendous stone fireplace my father built with a friend.

I see flakes of snow settling in the fireplace and automatically walk over to remove the fire screen and close the flue.

Mother has settled in a wing chair. "Did you see Morning?" she asks, referring to my roommate from UCLA, the dreadfully spoiled but charming daughter of a big-time TV producer. Yes, that's her given name, Morning.

"No," I say, replacing the fire screen, "she's parasailing on the Amazon."

"Isn't that funny," Mother muses, "I just noticed the other night on my insurance policy that if I take up parasailing, my premiums will substantially increase."

I smile, but say, "I wish you wouldn't waste your money on life insurance."

"I'd like to leave you children something."

Daddy was underinsured when he died and I am very well aware of the financial bind it left my mother in. Understandably, she's had a thing about life insurance ever since, but the need to provide for me and Rob has long gone by.

"You have insurance from school," I point out.

"Very little."

"It's plenty to bury you, Mother, and invite the whole county over for a party," I say, kidding. Truth is, I can scarcely comprehend a world without Mother in it.

"After the cancer I can't get another policy," she says. "I need to keep this one up."

"But, Mother, *why?*"

"I don't wish to discuss it," she says, cutting me off. "And that's not what I wanted to talk to you about." She pauses a moment, meeting my eye. "It's about Doug."

Doug Wrentham is my old boyfriend. I mean my really

old boyfriend, as in the guy whom I lost (gave, donated to the cause) my virginity to in my senior year of high school. We later broke up, saw each other again ten years later, after he had come back to Connecticut to work as a prosecutor in New Haven. We had been seeing each other for two years until I met Spencer.

Interestingly, I have spent more days and nights with Spencer in the last five months than I ever have with Doug. Still, I feel a sense of creeping dread at the mention of Doug's name.

I feel a tremendous amount of guilt. Yes, he broke up with me once to fool around with some woman, but at least he had ended our relationship *before* he slept with her. (I had not been as kind.)

Are Spencer and Doug at all alike? Only in the matter of brains, maybe. They both are very, very bright. With Spencer, what you see is what you get: a highly emotional, talented man who is never going to sail on a smooth lake. He has a decided bent for drama, gossip and excitement. Doug, on the other hand, is extremely calm, but his tendency to be quiet can mean anything from he's worried about a case to he's planning to quit his job the next day, and he's not likely to discuss either. His preference is solitude and his passion, sports. And in a different way, justice.

"His mother's in town for Mary Felton's wedding. I saw her at the hairdresser's."

"How is she?" I ask with a brightness I do not feel.

"She looks well. She said her husband is thinking about retiring next year."

Yeah, yeah, yeah, I think, *let's move this along.* "That's nice."

"She took me aside and said she was worried about Doug. That she knew you two had broken up. And she thinks this was not a good thing for him."

"Oh, so she thinks he should marry another woman who

will cheat on him?" I don't even look at Mother before covering my face with my hands.

There is, however, a lot of truth to what I said. Doug's first wife was another "good match" who ran away with their stockbroker.

"She wanted to know if I thought there was any hope for you two."

"Separately or together?" I can't help but crack.

Mother ignores it. "She asked me if you were still going out with this other man, and I said yes, I think so, and she asked me if it was serious, and I said I really didn't know." Mother pauses.

I look at her.

"She asked me for your phone number."

I rub my eyes. "Why?" I drop my hands. "I don't even know her anymore!"

"Well, it doesn't matter because I didn't give it to her," Mother announces, standing up. "But she knows she can reach you at the paper."

This seems to be a trend. First the nameless man who called earlier today, now my ex's mother. At this rate I'll never go back to work again just to avoid all the people who will be calling me there.

Mother goes into the kitchen where she reprimands the dogs, for they are wrestling on the floor, sounding like Cujo, which they always do when they sense tension in the air.

I rent a stone one-bedroom cottage on the Brackleton Farm not far from Mother's house. It is in the middle of nowhere, surrounded by woods and, farther out, acres of fields. As the snow flies, I navigate the Jeep up and over and around all the ruts of the long dirt drive.

The high beams pick out the cottage and I can't help but smile. I love this little place; I love the privacy; I love coming home.

Spencer. I feel sick. How many times did we make love here, how many hours—

Scotty barks, snapping me out of it.

"We're home, boy, we're home," I tell him as I park.

I open the back hatch and Scotty jumps out and tears off to the back of the house. He will go around and around and around the house, searching for the scent of monsters. I drag my bag up the front stairs—the porch light comes on with the motion detector—and I find a large vase of fresh-cut flowers wrapped in cellophane by the door. I turn off the alarm system, stamp the snow off my shoes and let myself in, toss my bag down and turn on some lights, then go back to get the flowers to bring them into the kitchen. On the way I hit the messages button on the answering machine.

A neighbor telling me that coyotes killed one of their cats over the weekend, I better keep an eye on Scotty at night.

Some lady reminding me that I'm to give blood this week at St. Luke's.

I call into my voice mail at the office of the *Herald-American,* nothing important, just Crazy Pete Sabatino giving me an update on the Masons replacing George Bush with George W. as the ruler of the world. And then, switching on my computer, I check my e-mail. Nothing important since this morning. Just a few e-mail memos from the office manager at WSCT-TV in New Haven, the DBS affiliate, where I am supposed to be on the air once in a while, but never seem to be.

Employees must remember to wash out their coffee cups.

Employees must remember to get all changes to the in-house directory by Friday.

Employees must remember to put the Employee Sports Day on their calendars.

I feel like sending an e-mail back to the station that reads, "New employee requires new management to get on the air," but that is another headache I don't feel like thinking about.

I let Scotty in the back door and while he is shaking snow all over the kitchen, I tear open the cellophane on the flowers and open the small enclosure envelope.

> You are unforgettable.
> Jonathan Small

Oh, no.

The studio creep from the party. I rub my eyes, sighing. How the heck did he find me?

I sift through my mail. Bills. A credit card offer (I walk over to the fridge to register it; I'm doing a piece for the paper on credit card solicitations and I'm keeping score. Eleven since the New Year); a long-distance telephone service offer; a credit card protection offer; a life insurance offer from my bank; a sample financial newsletter addressed to "Slay Harring"; a postcard from a friend traveling in Vietnam; and a real, live letter from a friend in Washington. I open the letter and a clipping falls out. And there, front and center, is a picture of Doug Wrentham, my old boyfriend, dark eyes shining, thick brown hair rumpled, great smile flashing.

"Thought you'd like to see the enclosed," my friend writes. "Are you guys ever getting married?"

Clearly this is a friend out of touch. Well, to be fair, I didn't send Christmas cards this year. I didn't know how to even broach the subject of news. What would I write? "Doug finally wanted to marry me, so I had a one-night stand with a philandering book editor and tried to make a relationship out of it."

I scan the piece. It's a short take of what Doug said while participating in a criminal justice seminar in D.C. Someone in the audience asked him, "Why, if the salaries are so much lower, would a good lawyer want to work for the government?"

"Let me put it this way," Assistant District Attorney Doug Wrentham of New Haven, Connecticut, replied, "I worked in private practice to pay off my student loans. Once that was done, I felt free to pursue a career in law."

I laugh out loud. This is exactly why he doesn't do these seminars unless forced to. He gets ticked off at certain questions and makes comments like this.

Before thinking it through, I pick up the phone and punch in the number of his apartment in New Haven. When I hear his voice, I am tempted to hang up. What am I doing?

"Doug? Hi, it's Sally. I just got in from L.A. and my friend Margo sent me a copy of the *Law Bulletin*—"

"Oh, no," he groans. (Who knows whether he is groaning about the article or about me calling?) "My old boss saw it and called me a sack of—expletive deleted." (Before moving back to Connecticut, Doug worked as a tax attorney at a large firm in Boston.)

"You mean to say he actually called you?"

"He finally called me," he says, laughing. "Never called me when I worked there, not once, but this time he called me."

"He's just envious. He hates his work."

"Hates, loathes and despises it," Doug confirms, "they all do."

"All the way to the bank," I add.

There is a pause and he says, "So how are you?"

"All right." I don't know what to say, because everything is horrible. "Busy, you know."

"Haven't seen you around the courthouse."

"Haven't had any criminal stuff."

"Haven't seen you on TV, either."

Until about four months ago, I worked at the *Herald-*

American full-time. When the job offer came from WSCT-TV to do special reporting for them, the paper agreed to let me take half-time pay without benefits in return for a flexible schedule. Both institutions thought they would benefit from my work at the other. Unfortunately, things don't seem to be working out very well at either place.

"I've been doing some off-camera work," I explain. "Writing, producing, stuff like that. I'd feel guilty not doing something to earn that money." WSCT may be a small station, but the pay is miles and miles beyond the paper.

"Huh," Doug says. "Off-camera. How does that make you feel?"

"Fine," I assure him. "It's putting the stories together that's the fun part. At least for me." I sigh. "Well, to be honest, we had kind of a falling-out over my hair. They say I look like an escapee from Miss Porter's—" this is an exclusive boarding school for girls in nearby Farmington "—and our executive producer maintains our audience is working-class illiterates."

"Uh-oh," Doug says. "Come on, out with it, Sally. What did you say?"

"I told him he knows *jack* about who lives in central Connecticut and to stop confusing his own dubious heritage with the demographics of our audience."

"Uh-oh," he says again.

"I know. And I am sort of in trouble," I admit. "The big Kahuna's called me into New York next week for some kind of review."

"Alexandra?"

Alexandra Waring, who offered me this job, is the anchorwoman and star of the DBS News network. She also holds the title of managing editor over the division, which essentially gives her the power to hire and fire.

"I'm afraid so," I say.

"But they're still paying you and everything, right?"

"They have to. I have a contract. Besides, I'm still pro-ducing stories. And I might have landed a big interview in L.A. for the magazine show."

"Really," he says, "with who?"

"Can't talk about it yet," I say. "Don't want to jinx it." *And what might you have to do to get that interview, big mouth?* I whisper, "Lilliana Martin."

"Hey, she's cool," he acknowledges, which means Doug is attracted to her. There is a pause. "So," Doug says then, "how's the book editor?"

"He's okay."

"I saw him in *Vanity Fair,*" Doug says. "At some party. One of the secretaries was looking through the magazine at work and I happened to see it."

"They have a lot of parties," I say. "Publishing seems like nine-tenths promotion and one-tenth content."

He hesitates. "I was going to say something but I won't."

Spencer seems like nine-tenths promotion and one-tenth content, I can imagine him saying.

"I want to see you, Doug," I blurt out.

"I'm kind of busy," he says. "Running around in circles is more like it. I'm working on a child rape case, one of those scumbag 'funny uncles.' Except the niece is a nephew, only nine and has gonorrhea of the anus."

"Oh, God," I say, closing my eyes.

"Tell me about it," he says, sighing.

"Maybe we could have coffee?"

Another pause. "Sally, frankly, I'm not sure I'm up to seeing you. This case is taking pretty much all I've got."

I can't believe it. Doug said no, I can't see him. "Oh, okay," I say, trying to make my voice sound lighthearted, "maybe when the case breaks your way."

"Yeah," he says without enthusiasm, and that is when I know I have really done it, that I am going to get exactly what I deserve.

My throat constricts and my eyes well up. "I'm so sorry, Doug," I whisper.

"Me, too, Sally," he says, and hangs up.

I sit there a minute and then spring into action. I get a couple of large shopping bags and start rampaging through the house. Spencer's blazer. Spencer's dress slacks, shirts. Sports shirts, shorts, jeans, jockey shorts, socks, jock strap.

Picture of Spencer; picture of me and Spencer; picture of Spencer and Scotty and Samantha, his cat, who came out on weekends, too. Spencer's books and magazines; Spencer's yellow pads and pencils and pads of stick 'ems. Samantha's cat food, kitty litter, litter box—I take everything out to the shed and leave a neatly stacked pile by the lawn mower.

Back in the kitchen I get all the food I kept especially for him: the Dr. Pepper, the spicy V8, the health cereal, the rice crackers, all that stuff, and put that in the shed, too.

Then I put on a jacket and boots and gloves and take Scotty out to shovel the front walk. I finally simmer down.

It is very quiet out here, lovely. The snow is drifting down out of the black sky, silently falling on the trees, the lawn. The Jeep is already covered. I throw a snowball for Scotty and he catches it, his teeth making it explode into a hundred pieces. He coughs, dancing, waiting for another. I comply.

God, what a mess of my life I've made. One tear trickles down as I scoop up more snow and softly pack it. Then I swing my arm to toss it high in the air and Scotty rears back on his back legs, mouth open, zeroing in on it, drops to the ground only to spring high in the air to snatch it, exploding it into smithereens.

The telephone is ringing. I'm not going to answer it, but then I think it might be Doug calling back. I run into the house and snatch it up just as the answering machine picks up. "Hold on," I say, clicking the receiver to make the machine shut off. "Hello?"

A male voice says, "I'm looking for Sally Harrington."

"This is she," I say, just as I think maybe I should say that Sally Harrington is out.

"Ms. Harrington, this is Detective Mendoza calling from the Los Angeles Police Department."

I swallow. "Yes?"

"I'm just following up on a missing-person's report that was filed this evening, for Lilliana Martin, and your name was given to us as one of the last two people who saw her."

"Uh, you mean last night," I say. "We—my friend Spencer Hawes and myself—gave her a ride home from a party at Del Figlio's. We dropped her off about eleven o'clock."

"And Spencer Hawes was with you," he says.

"Yes."

There is a pause and I envision him making notes. "Um, Ms. Harrington, do you know where in Honolulu we can reach Mr. Hawes?"

I blink. "Excuse me?"

"Do you have a number where we can reach Mr. Hawes?"

"No. I'm sorry, I don't." *Honolulu?* He's got to be kidding.

"Do you know when he's expected to return?"

"No. But you can check with his boss," and I give him Kate Weston's name and the number of Bennett, Fitzallen & Coe in New York.

"When you were with them last night, did Ms. Martin say anything about going away? Perhaps accompanying Mr. Hawes?"

"No."

"And when was the last time you saw Mr. Hawes?"

"This morning, in Santa Monica, at Shutters, the hotel. It was about nine, nine-thirty. Then I had to leave. I had a noon flight to catch back to Connecticut."

Pause. "Okay, Ms. Harrington, thank you very much. If you hear from either Mr. Hawes or Ms. Martin, please ask them to give me a call." And he leaves his name and number.

I hang up the phone and stand there a minute. *Honolulu?*

CHAPTER FIVE

I didn't sleep much last night, and as I drag myself into the *Herald-American* this Wednesday morning I find everybody wanting to know what Liam Neeson is like, how was my sudden trip to LaLa land?

Where do I begin.

"He didn't come," I say, going to my cubicle. Still, some gather around my desk to find out who I saw, who I met. (We're kind of celebrity-hungry out here in central Connecticut, where the only resident stars are guys like Chris Berman who works at ESPN in Bristol.)

Last night I left three messages on Spencer's machine in New York, two on his voice mail at the office, and I have already spoken to Kate Weston, who seemed at once puzzled and nervous.

"Yeah, that's what the police told me, too," she said. "That Spencer left LAX yesterday afternoon on a flight to Honolulu."

"Kate—" I struggle not to sound like the pathetic ex-lover. "I don't get it."

"I don't, either," she says carefully. "Unless—"

"Unless he's done a flyer with Lilliana Martin for a few days," I finish. "It's all right, Kate, it's crossed my mind."

"I'm sorry, Sally." Pause. "It's the only thing that makes sense."

"Has he called the office?"

"No. Which is odd."

"And why wouldn't Lilliana Martin let her agent know she was going away?"

"Maybe he wouldn't have let her."

"So she just took off." I try to think. "But they would know if she flew out, wouldn't they?"

"She may fly under an alias."

"The airline would have her real name under the alias on the passenger list," I explain, having tapped those lists many times in the old days to see who was coming and going on what airlines. (Haven't you ever wondered about all those photos of celebrities arriving at airports?)

Kate promises to let me know as soon as she's heard from Spencer, and I do the same. "He'll call one of us very soon," she says, "I'm sure."

I'm not.

In my cubicle I find I have inherited the second part of a featured series on the miserable state of our train station in Castleford. The guy who wrote the first part evidently quit yesterday. I try to make sense out of his notes.

My boss, Alfred Royce Jr., heir to the newspaper, comes into my cubicle. "Sally," he says nicely, which means only one thing—he's got something awful to assign to me. "Something's come up I think only you can do."

As Dorothy Parker would say, *What fresh hell is this?*

"I thought you wanted me to finish the train station piece for Sunday," I say.

"You can still do that."

"It's Wednesday," I point out. "And it's supposed to be in-depth."

"I'll get Hal to cover, this is more important," he says, leaning forward over my desk. Royce's breath smells of pickles, which I don't get since it's nine-thirty in the morning. "As you know, I am the chairman of the Castleford History Week."

"Yes." I draw the word out in a low, expectant tone of voice.

"And this year the board's elected to do Native American history."

"Yes," I say.

"So I want you to go up and see this guy at Tokahna Casino and see if you can't get some money out of him for it."

My eyebrows rise as I look at the card he has handed me. "Why me?"

He leans closer. Yep. Pickles. What is he eating in that office of his? "I can't go myself," he whispers, "because of, er, well, you know, a historic conflict of sorts."

"Historic conflict?" I whisper back.

"My family almost wiped out their tribe," he tells me confidentially. "Royce is not a great name to use around them. They might remember."

"Oh," I say, getting it. Yesterday's scorned and massacred people are today's coveted casino billionaires.

"I'll need Daucy Marinetti to come with me," I tell him.

"Daucy?"

She's our circulation manager and has nothing to do with anything except I like her and know she'll owe me big time if I spring her for a paid afternoon of gambling. "She has an inside track with the Tokahnas," I explain.

Inside track is right; Daucy and her husband are one step away from professional gamblers. Logically speaking, the Marinettis by now should have a mansion and at least one flashy car, but they have opted for a more modest home and cars so they can lose thousands of dollars each year at casinos around the world. To their credit, they do keep receipts on everything and deduct losses from their income taxes.

* * *

"All right, let me see," Daucy says gleefully, sorting through the accordion file we pick up at her house before taking 91 north. "Tokahna... I think I've got about three hundred points on account there and they owe me a suite for a weekend."

"What are the points for?"

"One point equals one dollar in the restaurant or the casino stores," she explains, thumbing through.

"Are you getting this?" I call to the back seat.

Alan, a cameraman from WSCT, nods, camera looking over the shoulder of Daucy. He's a stringer, a freelancer, but the point is, my executive producer at WSCT has allowed me to take Alan to shoot some footage of the casino while I'm there.

In this deal I have with WSCT and the *Herald-American,* I am allowed to use versions of the same story with both, so long as the one who assigned the story gets first run. Al has only assigned me to hit the Tokahnas up for some money, but I've wanted to do a feature on our Connecticut casinos and the effects of gambling on the state for some time, so I figured I'd do a little professional groundwork while I was there.

Offering to promote the casino on TV, I suspected, might give me a little leverage with the Tokahnas. I was right. They were very pleased when I called to ask if I could bring the WSCT camera along for a story.

I'm not sure what, exactly, the story will be. The merit of the casinos in Connecticut is difficult to ascertain. Twenty-five percent of every coin that goes into a slot machine is directed into the Connecticut General Fund. This is good, right? Well, yes and no. State residents were promised revenues would go to education and public libraries, and of course most of it doesn't. (I'm not even touching on the subject of Lotto, it gets me so angry.) But hey, we didn't have an income tax back then, either, and when we got saddled with one we voted in a governor who swore he'd get rid of it, and we still have it, of course, and we still have the highest state taxes on gasoline, so what kind of fools are we? At any rate, on one hand we have whole groups of formerly impoverished people that are now prosperous or, at the very least, are employed in extremely well-paying jobs, and what was merely the in-land "drive through" part of the state has become a tourist destination. On the other hand, we've got the utter ruin and destruction of families who have had one or more loved ones ravaged by the compulsion of gambling, to say nothing of the horrendous highway accidents from all those drivers enjoying all those free drinks.

"So on a good weekend..." I prompt Daucy for the sake of the rolling tape.

"On a good weekend," she says, "I'll break even on the slots and me and Cody will have stayed in a suite, had three free meals each day, had free drinks, gone to a great show for free and had a limousine pick us up and take us home. Once we were flown to Vegas for free. Another time we got a free helicopter ride to Trump Casino in Atlantic City from New York. That was cool. Another time we got a ringside table at a Wayne Newton show. In Vegas, another time, there was a tank of sharks over the front desk of the hotel."

By the time we are making our approach to the Tokahna Reservation, Daucy is explaining the ins and outs of the IRS and gambling.

"So you mean if I win $1,199," I begin, "I do not have to report it to the IRS."

"Nothing under $1,200," Daucy confirms.

"But if I make a five-dollar capital gain on the sale of a stock," I say over my shoulder to the camera, "and fail to report it, I can go to jail."

"Well, I don't know about that," Daucy says. "I don't buy stocks. They're too risky."

Each of the three casinos in Connecticut—Foxwoods, Mohegun Sun or Tokahna—has had a special highway built to lead gamblers to their destinations. You sail through the isolated countryside, and then, quite suddenly, a turn is taken and a vision appears in the distance, rising from the wilderness. Foxwoods is like Emerald City, a huge gleaming complex, a city unto itself soaring up in the middle of nowhere; Mohegun Sun, like a huge hunting lodge in the hills; and finally, Tokahna, the least impressive (for it is the newest), has a cavelike feeling alongside a mountain.

I check into the PR office to clear the cameraman and get our list of rules. (We can't, for example, have anybody identifiable in the shots. That wouldn't be cool, would it, when somebody who's supposed to be at work is seen on the news at the casino?) But Daucy is a great bridge to understanding the lure of the place, and we film how even if you're playing the quarter slots, a waiter or waitress comes around to get you a drink—alcohol or coffee or soda. Daucy explains what are appropriate tips, and gives us a tour of the restaurants and the gift shop where you can spend your accrued points on everything from cigarettes to clothing. You can also, she adds, buy gasoline with the points at the reservation gas station. She takes me to a member's club line where in seconds, after handing them my driver's license, I, too, have a card. Daucy shows me how to slip it into the slot machine, which, in turn, registers points in accordance to how much money I put in the machine.

Alan goes off with Daucy, aka professional gamester, as she hops and skips around to all kinds of slot machines and settles with Wheel of Fortune in the corner, while I take in the amazing number of signs with the telephone number of Gambler's Anonymous. I visit poker, blackjack and roulette tables, and, if you can believe it, an area where people are playing the child's game of War and betting on each card. (Daucy has explained to me that her husband's favorite game, three-card poker, has disappeared from all the casinos because—you guessed it—the patrons won too much.)

My beeper goes off and I look at the number. It's a DBS number in New York. I go to a pay phone to make the call and am put through to Alexandra Waring's office. Against the din of slot machine bells, music, people talking and shouting, I have to strain to hear. "You were the last person to see Lilliana Martin and you're sitting in a casino on an Indian reservation in upstate Connecticut?"

"Um," I say, "it's more complicated than you think."

"Good, then you can explain it to us," the anchorwoman of the *DBS Evening News* says. "Pack a bag for the week and be in the newsroom by seven tonight." She is gone.

I have been summoned. I look at my watch. I've got six hours. Feeling oddly detached about it, I meander over to the fifty-cent slots to put a Kennedy half-dollar into the machine and pull. *Wild cherry, blank, double diamond.* Two half-dollars fall out.

"You keep forgetting your card," Daucy admonishes me as she moves in to sit at the machine next to me, Alan following.

"I'm not going to be able to stay much longer," I tell her.

"Put your card in," she instructs.

I turn around to address the camera. "There are no clocks in here, no windows, either, you'll notice," I say. "It is very easy to lose a sense of time and perspective. Money quickly becomes unreal. I don't know if it's day or night. All I know is to keep putting money in and hope to win back everything I've lost."

I look around. Most of the people here are seniors. Many are in wheelchairs. I realize, with a slight pang, how gambling might easily be these people's last hurrah, that last adrenaline rush for those finding their bodies in, well, decline.

Before it is time for my appointment with him, Mr. River, the casino PR man, comes down to the slot machines to visit. I start to get up to go to his office, but he assures me it's fine to talk here. (Of course it is, as long as I keep putting money in the machine.) No, he would prefer not to go on camera. While depositing more half-dollars and pulling the lever, over and over and over, now with alarming familiarity, I tell him about the Native American theme festival in Castleford. While Al has instructed me to just hit the tribe up for some money—promising to heavily promote their sponsorship and support of the glorious cause of Connecticut's history—I have a slightly different idea.

"I was asked to seek a donation from you," I tell him—*blank, blank, bar*— "but to be perfectly honest, I don't have enormous confidence the board will know how to spend it appropriately. I wondered, instead, if you thought the tribe could send some kind of show or presentation or lecture series to Castleford where people can learn about the tribe's history and heritage?"

"Do you have any suggestions?" he asks.

"As a matter of fact—" *bar, double bar, wild cherry,* five half-dollars plunk into the bin "—I do."

"Okay, Al," I tell my publisher on the cell phone from the car, "you've got a twenty-five thousand dollar donation from the Tokahnas for History Week."

"Great!"

"We have to run a sponsor credit on all promotional and advertising pieces—"

"No problem!" he nearly yells.

"And the only stipulation," I continue, "is that we present a slide show and lecture series at the library for three nights, and print the text of the lectures in the paper the final weekend of the festival."

"Okay, sounds great!"

"One thing, though—the last lecture is about the near extinction of the tribe at the hands of Royce's Raiders."

"Oh, no," he groans.

"I know!" I exclaim in what I hope sounds like an innocent voice. "I just didn't know what to say!"

I left Daucy at the casino, where her husband was joining her. Last I saw, she had taken a hundred dollars into the high-stakes slot machines and hit, with her second five-dollar chip, for sixty coins, which translated into three hundred dollars.

As for me, I lost ninety dollars and have a stomachache and my eyes are burning from the smoke and I feel sick. I did, however, buy a box of chocolates with my casino card in the shop.

I drop Alan at his car, promising to set up a shoot date to fill in the piece. (I note in my diary exactly what I'm wearing so I can duplicate it later, giving the impression the whole piece was executed the same day.)

The snow of the night before has left the road to my house a slippery mess so I put the Jeep into four-wheel drive. I swing around the bend and find a black Lincoln parked in front of my house, engine running.

I park the Jeep and climb out, hearing Scotty going nuts inside the house. The driver of the Lincoln lowers his window.

"Hi," I say, "can I help you?"

"My passenger is looking for Sally Harrington."

I look past him to the empty back seat. "Your passen—?"

"Hello!" I hear from the side of the house. Coming toward me is a man slipping and sliding over the snow in loafers, khakis and a blue blazer. I have not the slightest idea who he is. He's in his late thirties or so, maybe five ten, balding, a bit on the heavyset side. He's not unattractive. "Sally Harrington?" he asks hopefully.

"Yes," I say. As he approaches, holding out his hand to

me, he slips and I end up grabbing his arm before he wipes out completely.

"Thanks," the man says, righting himself. Clouds of frost are coming out of his mouth. "Jeez, it's freezing out here," he declares, slapping his arms around himself. He kicks his head in the direction of the Lincoln. "You want to sit in the car?"

This is a cue to invite him into the house, but forget it. "I'm sorry, did we have an appointment?"

"With me? No. I'm sorry, I haven't introduced myself." He holds out his hand. "I'm Cliff Yarlen."

The name means nothing to me.

He crosses his arms again against the cold. "I'm looking for my girlfriend and I wondered if she was here," he says. "Lilliana Martin?"

CHAPTER SIX

This is getting interesting.

"Why on earth would you think Lilliana was here?" I ask the boyfriend from L.A.

"I was told you were the last person to see her," he explains.

"I see." He is shivering, and, let's face it, it suddenly occurs to me that delivering the missing actress's boyfriend to the newsroom at DBS might do something toward redeeming me with Alexandra. The trick is how to get him there. "Why don't you come in? Your driver, too, if you'd like."

"No, he's fine where he is."

I hear a trace of what I suspect is New York. (Not Manhattan. People from Manhattan, it has been my experience, talk like wealthy characters on sitcoms. Black, white, Hispanic, it doesn't matter. The only exception is East Harlem, where they're still axing questions like they do in the other boroughs.)

I turn off my alarm system (shielding the panel so the boyfriend can't see the numbers) and instruct Scotty not to tear my guest apart. After sniffing him over, Scotty runs outside to take a quick whiz and then trots over to the Lincoln to bark at the driver. I close the front door, confident

Scotty won't jump up on the car and scratch the paint, but will keep the driver in his place.

You can never be too careful.

I offer my guest a cup of coffee and he asks for herbal tea. While I make a cup of instant coffee for me and Sleepy Time for him, he sits at my kitchen table. Happily, the less I say the more he seems to feel compelled to talk, so I stop saying anything at all.

"I'm worried about Lilliana," he says solemnly, and launches into an explanation that her agent called him yesterday looking for her, and then the police called him last night. Richie Benzler told him I was the last person to see Lilliana. He tried to call me yesterday through my mother and decided since he had to go to New York, anyway, he would jump a plane to Hartford and drive down to see if Lilliana might be here.

Since I am unlisted, how he found out where I live has me puzzled. I don't like it that he's found me so easily.

"I only met Lilliana night before last," I say slowly.

His smile is a knowing one. "That's often the way she is."

"She often disappears?" I say, deliberately overlooking his implication.

"Yeah, actually."

"I wasn't the only one to see her," I say.

"Spencer Hawes, yeah, I know," he tells me. "But he's not with her."

"How do you know that?"

"Oh," he says, looking a little startled, "I see what you mean." When I bring him his cup of tea, he shakes his head with conviction. "No, she's not with him."

I resist asking him again how he knows this.

Cliff looks up. "Could I trouble you for some soy milk?"

"Sorry, I'm all out," I tell him, managing to keep a straight face. I love people from Southern California. "I do have one-percent milk, though."

"No, thanks, I don't do dairy."

"Oh, right," I say, nodding, as if I can imagine anybody who would voluntarily bypass milk, cheese or ice cream even for a day. I sit down.

"You see," he says, "Lilliana and I have been having some problems."

I nod. "She mentioned that."

"We were separating for a while. Truth is—" he drops his eyes "—I wanted to see someone else. You know how it is."

Unfortunately I do. "It's hard to believe you could find someone more attractive," I say.

"It's what you're used to, I guess."

I supposed this is to mean he's used to sleeping with beautiful actresses, easy come, easy go.

"So Lilliana wanted all or nothing," he continues. "I don't blame her. But you know, it wasn't like it was a serious thing, this other woman, and it's not as if Lilliana's an angel—" He cuts himself off, looking at me, that knowing smile coming back. "But you, obviously, must know all that."

I do?

He gets a pleading look. "Look, it's not the way she told you. I just want to see her. Talk to her." He pushes his tea to the side. "I'm worried about her."

"I'll tell you what. I've got to go into New York. Now. Tonight."

"I'll drive you," he says without hesitation.

"Okay," I agree, getting up and moving to pick up the wireless telephone.

"Do you think that's where she is?" he asks. "New York?"

"She might be in New York," I say cagily.

And in Timbuktu for all I know.

I excuse myself to ask Mother if she can pick up Scotty; call the paper and leave a message for my boss, Al Royce, telling him that I'm sorry, but I've got to go into New York, DBS business; and then I call Alexandra Waring's assistant to tell her that I'm bringing Cliff Yarlen, the estranged boyfriend of Lilliana Martin, into the studio with me tonight and I'd appreciate if someone could run a background check on him.

"Okay, ready," I announce to Cliff on my return to the kitchen, dropping my bag and hanging up the phone. "Would you like to use the bathroom before we go?"

He gets up, smiling a bit sheepishly. He is kind of cute. "You've got nice manners, no wonder Lilliana likes you."

"How, exactly, do you know that she likes me?" I ask.

"There's no way she would have brought you home, unless..." He shrugs, smiling suggestively.

I show him where the bathroom is.

I call Scotty back into the house and, when Cliff's ready, activate the alarm system and we're on our way.

It's ninety miles to Manhattan from Castleford and I am grateful when Cliff asks me if I'm hungry, do we want to stop somewhere. Since he doesn't "do" dairy, I scarcely know where to suggest out here in red-meat-and-potatoes land, but then he says, "I like the fish sandwich at McDonald's," and so I direct the driver to cross over from the Merritt to 95 at Milford so we can drive through a McDonald's at a rest area in Fairfield.

Now I am content. Cheeseburger, chocolate shake, small fries. Same meal I've chosen since I was seven.

Cliff is impressed by how easily I am waved into the DBS complex. There is no need for him to know that the "nice girl" (as he calls her), Wendy Mitchell, who escorts us up to Alexandra's office in Darenbrook III is actually the head of security. It's 6:22, two hours thirty-eight minutes to national air, and so it is no surprise that we find Alexandra's executive producer and right-hand man, Will

Rafferty, waiting for us because the anchorwoman is down in the newsroom.

"Nice to meet you, Cliff," Will says in his man's-man voice. (Will is a funny guy; one minute he can be tough as nails, in the next, kind of a wuss. He's married to an equally chameleon-type personality, Jessica Wright, the DBS talk-show host. Every day their marriage must feel like new people show up to be in it.)

"Is Lilliana here?" Cliff asks him right off.

Will glances at me as much as to say, *What the hell is he talking about?* but covers, saying, "She might be doing Jessica's show."

"That's what I thought," I say. "I guess we better check."

"Okay," Will says. "Why don't you have a seat, Cliff, and we'll go check it out."

Outside the office Will tells the assistant to get Mr. Yarlen whatever he might like to eat or drink. "And turn the TV on for him."

We go across the hall to Will's office. He closes the door firmly behind us. "Do you know who that guy is?"

"Lilliana Martin's ex. I found him at my house and so I brought him with me. He's some sort of union guy."

"I'll say," Will declares. "And did he happen to mention he's under investigation by the Justice Department, the Department of Labor and the FBI?"

"No," I say, "he left that part out. He did say he works for the American Federation of Technology Workers."

The AFTW is a newer, booming union seeking to organize all computer technicians in the entertainment business, including, ultimately, TV and radio news. This does not please the existing unions, to say the least.

"He's the union *president,* Sally!"

"Oh. So what are they investigating him for?"

"Same old union scams—phantom workers, redirection of employee benefits. He's the point man for Southern California."

"The mob?"

"Looks like it. His father died in prison while serving a sentence for racketeering."

"Huh," I say.

The door opens behind us and Alexandra Waring slips in. She is wearing a navy blue dress and single strand of pearls for this evening's newscast, one of what the news director calls her "killer outfits," where everyone remains transfixed by how the color highlights her incredible blue-gray eyes.

She has a very interesting past. Born and raised on a farm near Lawrence, Kansas, Alexandra was the youngest of five, the daughter of a longtime U.S. congressman. She excelled at Stanford University, started her career as a reporter in San Francisco, later moving to Kansas City where she was a reporter and weekend anchor. She moved to New York to anchor the news for WWKK and by twenty-eight was a ratings sensation. She jumped to network news as a correspondent on Capitol Hill, where she was nearly killed on air by a crazed admirer, and was then brought back to New York, handpicked by media tycoon Jackson Darenbrook to head the news division of his new TV network, DBS.

With Alexandra had come Will Rafferty, who had been her field producer in Washington, D.C., and before that, some sort of production assistant at WWKK.

The idea behind DBS (the Darenbrook Broadcasting System) was simple: to affiliate independent broadcast stations around the country into a part-time network. What was not so simple, I know, was (and is) trying to get the local newsrooms of these stations to pull themselves together as news professionals. WSCT in New Haven is supposed to be one of the best in the lot, but I have yet to see the network newscast use an entire story generated from the Connecticut affiliate.

Alexandra had been engaged twice, but never married. The second time was a widely publicized engagement to television producer Gordon Strenn, but she broke it off. He married someone else and Alexandra eventually took up with a woman, an actress, in fact. The network never acknowledges her private life one way or the other, and nor does the anchorwoman, and since her ratings are terrific I can only assume no one cares what she does.

While we remain standing, Alexandra walks over to sit on the front edge of Will's desk. "So you've brought Cliff Yarlen in."

"I came home from the casino and he was standing outside my house. He's looking for Lilliana Martin and for some reason seems to think I know where she is."

"And do you?"

"I haven't the slightest idea."

"I find that hard to believe," Alexandra says, looking at me directly.

I throw up my hands. "I don't. I just had a cup of coffee with the woman. I don't know her from Adam!"

Alexandra glances at Will before looking back at me. "There is only one reason why Cliff Yarlen would think Lilliana Martin ran away with you to Connecticut, Sally, and I promise you," she smiles slightly, amused, "it's not because he thinks she's having coffee with you."

I feel my face getting red. "She's not at my house," I say, and I'm about to add, *And nor will she ever be!* but I think better of it. For all I know, Alexandra knows the woman, they're gal pals or something.

"Well, then," the anchorwoman says, crossing her arms over her chest, "maybe you should tell us exactly what happened in Los Angeles Monday night."

"I met her at Malcolm Kieloff's publicity party," I begin, "and Spencer and I gave her a ride home."

Alexandra is looking a little exasperated with me. "Sally—"

"Okay," I say, raising a hand. I drop it. "Look, I didn't want to have to go through all this because it's got nothing to do with anything." I take a breath. "Spencer and Lilliana got this idea that we should have a threesome."

Will's eyes fly wide open and even Alexandra looks a little surprised.

"And they set me up at Lilliana's house after the party," I continue, ignoring their expressions. "And so I had a fight with Spencer in the limo on the way home and I threw him out and I went back to the hotel—"

"Wa-wa-wait," Alexandra says, giving me the policeman's signal to slow down. "First things first. You met Lilliana Martin at the Kieloff book party."

"Yes."

"Where was this?"

"Del Figlio's."

"And?"

"And so she and I were talking—there was a chance she'd give us an interview with *DBS News Magazine* when her movie comes out. I met her agent and everything."

Alexandra nods in approval.

"And then she wanted to have a cigarette and so we went upstairs to the manager's office for a while. You know, talked and had a drink, and actually, um, she basically told me she wanted to have sex with Spencer. There was nothing about me in the conversation, not like *that*." I glance at the anchorwoman. "Would you stop smiling? It's not funny."

"I'm sorry," she says, nodding. "Go on."

"Anyway, I actually kind of liked her," I admit. "She was just being honest and checking what the situation was between me and Spencer, and—" I clear the air with my hand. "You don't need to hear all this stuff."

"Humor us," Alexandra insists.

"So we all had to go to that dinner for Kieloff. In the Garden Room. And then after we had a car and we offered her a ride home. So we went to Cold Water Canyon and went in for coffee, and in the kitchen we were talking and then she sort of made a pass at me, which I thought I had gracefully declined, but then when I realized Spencer had set it up I lost my temper. She was very apologetic and was actually crying and stuff, but then I got her calmed down and we left. But then Spencer and I had a fight in the car and I threw him out."

Now Will is smiling.

"Did he go back to her house?" Alexandra asks me, serious now.

"I saw him the next morning, yesterday morning, at the hotel, and he said he did walk back to the house, but Lilliana wasn't there and the front door of the house was wide open. So he went in and used the phone to call a cab, came back to Shutters and slept in a lounge chair by the pool."

"So where's Spencer now?"

I hesitate. "Well, it seems he's in Honolulu. I thought he was on his way back to New York, but the Los Angeles police told me he flew to Honolulu yesterday."

There is an uncomfortable silence.

"So you think Lilliana may be with him," Alexandra concluded.

I lower my eyes. "Maybe. To have a couple-day thing." I raise my eyes. "When I saw him yesterday morning, it wasn't great. I sort of broke up with him. He was upset, so I figure he might have gone off with her."

There is a knocking on the door and we turn around to see Alexandra's assistant.

"I thought you'd like to know that that man, Mr. Yarlen,

just bolted out of your office, Alexandra. He was making calls on your phone—"

Cell phones do not work in the West End Broadcasting Center and guests are offered in-house lines to use. The reason cell phones don't work is because they supposedly interfere with the electronic equipment in the center, but I suspect it's because the news group is paranoid.

"—then he got up and left," the assistant finishes. "I went after him to ask if I could help him with something and he said no, he just had to go."

Alexandra flicks up the phone, presses a number and hangs up. A second later the phone rings and Alexandra picks up. "Cliff Yarlen is coming through. Can you follow him? See where he goes?"

"Maybe I should talk to him," I offer, moving toward the door.

"No," she says, hanging up the phone and glancing at her watch, "you need to go to wardrobe and then to makeup."

My mouth goes dry. There's only one reason why I would need to go there.

"No big deal," she says, taking my arm and steering me toward the door. "You're just going to read one story and throw to tape. We want to see how you look on the news set."

CHAPTER SEVEN

The next thing I know, I am outfitted in a soft beige Armani skirt and jacket, size ten, and a Donna Karan silk blouse, both of which I know cost a fortune, and am being escorted to makeup by a burly news intern named Calvin who has been instructed not to let me out of his sight.

No big deal. Just making my debut on the national news tonight.

"Hello, Sally," Cleo greets me, the master makeup magician who has been with DBS since its conception. I met Cleo five months ago when I was part of the *DBS News Magazine* show investigating the circumstances of my father's death. Cleo is one of those women my mother describes as "interesting-looking." Tonight her hair is on top of her head, she's wearing Lena Wertmuller glasses and imitation leopard-skin pants and a silk blouse.

"'Secure her hair,'" Cleo reads from a small piece of paper in her hand that has the initials A.B.W. on the top of it. She smiles at me. "I hear your hair has created a controversy way out there in Connecticut."

"I don't know why," I say, defending myself.

"If you ask me," Cleo says, looking me over, "the anchors on that affiliate look like something from *The Dating*

Game." The burly intern giggles. She ignores him to ask, "So do you agree? That your hair needs to be 'secured'?"

The front pieces of my hair, which I almost always pull to the back of my head and hold with a barrette, are slipping out every which way. "I got it cut recently and the pieces aren't quite long enough," I explain. "So, yes, I agree. *They* want me to cut it short," I add, referring to the WSCT management.

"Hmm," she says, eyes narrowing slightly behind her butterfly glasses. She takes out my barrettes and plays with my hair. "Did you go to Chapin?" she asks nonchalantly, referring to the private school for girls in Manhattan.

"No, I grew up in Connecticut."

"Miss Porter's?" she asks then.

"No," I say, laughing, "just plain old Castleford High."

"We get a lot of alumni from those schools who wear their hair the way you do." Her eyes shift to meet mine. "It says 'old money.'"

"No money," I assure her. "Just a widowed mother who supported us on a schoolteacher's salary."

"So is this the way you want it?" Cleo is holding my hair back in place the way it is supposed to look and probably hasn't since about ninth grade, the last time I allowed my mother to fuss with it.

I meet her eyes in the mirror. "Yes, please."

"I'm going to have to use a little mousse."

"I hate mousse," I tell her.

"You can hit the shower right after the broadcast and wash it out," Cleo says. "Alexandra often does."

Will comes in to hand me the copy I'm supposed to read tonight. It's an update on a murder trial being held in St. Louis.

"Yarlen went to JFK," he reports. "He's probably heading back to California." He looks at something on his clipboard. "You're in the union, right?"

"Yeah."

"Got a number?"

I recite my number. After he finishes writing it down, I gesture with the script. "Will, can you tell me what's going on with this?"

"She wants to see how you look behind the desk," he answers, writing something on his clipboard. Then he tells the intern to go back to the newsroom. When Calvin leaves, Will says, "Since you're doing nothing at WSCT, she wants to see if we're missing anything before she fires you."

This hits me like a pan of cold water and my eyes show it. I try to cover. "Did it ever occur to you the reason I'm doing nothing in New Haven is because Mr. Jack Crap himself is producing the news? Mr. Redneck, draw-pictures-because-nobody-who-watches-us-speaks-English, Mr. Jack Crap?"

Cleo snorts.

"He's not the best," Will concedes, "but Alexandra doesn't think you've focused on your work at all." When I don't say anything, he adds, "She actually said, and I quote, 'Why do I get the feeling that if Sally dumped that Spencer guy we would have someone who could do something with that affiliate out there?'"

I am stung. And then I feel the anger rise, a sure sign I've been scared and there is some truth to what has been said. Since the day I met Spencer, I've been operating on three cylinders. Running, but not smoothly. To be a good journalist you need excellent concentration, not the scattered energy generated by an addictive kind of affair.

Is he really with Lilliana in Honolulu?

"So she's putting you in tonight to see what the camera thinks," he says, and I try to come back.

Will relents a little and puts a hand on my shoulder. "Just read it and don't worry. It will all work out."

* * *

I'm doing a segment called "Crime and Punishment." I'm supposed to recap a horrendous double murder in St. Louis and then introduce the Midwestern reporter who is covering the trial. I am tempted to rewrite some of the copy, but I think better of it. Best to do exactly as I am told and Will said not to mess with it.

I am sitting on a small set in Studio A, one I've never seen before. It is tiny with a desk and a textured wall in the back that has the scales of justice on it. Clichéd, but to the point, I guess.

Alexandra comes in and takes her place on the main news set. The trend these days is for anchors to stand up while delivering the news, but Alexandra thinks that unless she's planning to run for president it looks pompous and stupid, so nobody but the weather guy and reporters in the field stand up during the broadcast.

The anchorwoman is going over something with one of the writers and is scribbling stuff on her script. The studio floor manager comes out to say something. She nods. Then she evidently hears something in her earphone from the control room, says something into her microphone and makes a note on her script. The burly intern comes trotting across the studio with another sheet of copy for her.

After Alexandra gets her papers settled, she looks around the studio. Her eyes fall on me. I wonder what she thinks of my hair.

She gives me the thumbs-up sign.

I smile; I'll be damned if I let on that I am absolutely terrified and that before coming into the studio I had been hanging over the john in the ladies' room, unsure if my stomach can take this or not. I did some stretches, took some deep breaths, had a little water and seem to be settling down. Every time my hands begin to shake, I dig one of my heels into my ankle until the pain stops the shaking.

The studio lights go off. It is silent except for the voices we can hear through the headsets of the crew.

Around ten minutes into the broadcast, I wonder what I'm doing here. Five months ago I wrote for the Castleford *Herald-American* full-time and now I'm going on the national DBS news. And then I'll probably get fired.

Quite a day.

Meeting Spencer was like starting on a five-month bender. Until I met him, I worked constantly, to a fault. I was driven. And even right now, on the set, I feel myself struggling to focus, to understand how important it is that I do well. It kind of feels like I'm back in college, when someone got sick in a TV class and people called around frantically trying to find anybody who would go into the studio in their place. I did. All the time.

I look at my run-down sheet and see that my segment is coming up after the next commercial. My stomach lurches and I dig my heel into my ankle again. *Ow.*

"And from our 'Crime and Punishment' desk," Alexandra is saying, as if this is a regular feature, "is Sally Harrington with an update on the major trial unfolding in Missouri. Sally?"

The red light goes on and I smile into the camera. "Thank you, Alexandra." And then I pull in my face to get serious and read off the TelePrompter, "Today the accused killer of Steven Balchek and Jennifer Holiday took the stand...."

Suddenly I feel exhilarated, a tide of energy flooding through me. I command myself to focus on the words I am reading, to speak them slowly, to make people listen to me. I fight the urge to gesture and use my facial muscles for accentuation.

I gotta keep it slow, clear, because this trial is complicated stuff and I've got to make it sound simple. I finish my part and introduce the correspondent standing outside the courthouse in St. Louis. And then, suddenly, the red light is off and so am I.

I feel oddly abandoned, like I want to try and get that camera back on me.

"Get the worst of that makeup off," Alexandra tells me on her way by when the broadcast is over, "and meet me in the garage."

CHAPTER EIGHT

Alexandra's limo is waiting outside in the West End drive. The temperature has risen and a freezing drizzle is blowing. The driver takes my suitcase, puts it in the trunk, and then opens the door for me. Alexandra's already inside, reading something under the light over her shoulder.

"Where are we going?"

She looks up. "Just to the Admiral's Club at JFK, where Cliff Yarlen's waiting for a flight to get out. I want you to talk to him and then I'll bring you back to your hotel. Okay? It won't take long."

I'm about to drop dead of exhaustion, but I say fine.

"I'm riding out with you," she says, pouring a Perrier from the car refrigerator for herself, "because we need to talk. Help yourself to something to drink."

In the tiny refrigerator is Perrier and Diet Pepsi and orange juice. But do I see something else lurking in the back? Ah, yes, an Amstel Lite, just what the doctor ordered. But I guess I better be on my best behavior and take a Perrier. She hands me an opener to use and I settle back in the seat, pouring some water into a glass. "I assume you want me to find out why Cliff left so fast."

"Yes," she says, digging into her briefcase and coming

up with a pen and legal pad that has writing all over it, "but we've got other things to discuss." She clears her throat, scanning the pad in her lap.

"You've found out Lilliana and Spencer are in Honolulu together?" I guess.

"Let's forget about everybody else for the moment." She sighs, eyes still on the pad. "I want to focus on you." She makes a note in the margin on the top sheet, joining the several that are already there. She looks up. "It's interesting— the camera likes you. I wasn't sure. We've got this ongoing problem in the studio with flat light."

"Maybe it's the lighting director who's flat," I suggest.

"Tell me about it," she mutters. "We're on our fourth. This one used to be a cinematographer, if you can believe."

I resist commenting that she is at last receiving true star treatment. I also can't help but wonder if her actress girlfriend had anything to do with the choice of a cinematographer for a news set.

"And how's my hair?" I ask enthusiastically. *Don't be a smart-ass,* I tell myself. *This is your career.*

"Your hair is good," she announces, "although I suspect you'll have to work with Cleo to get it to look the same way twice." She sips her drink and then angles herself against her door, crossing her legs toward me and resting the pad on her knee. "I think Will told you we're trying to figure out what to do with you."

"I often have the same problem," I murmur, sipping the cold mineral water. It feels good to my throat.

"Personally speaking," the anchorwoman continues, "I can't figure out if you're lazy or just screwed up."

I feel the hot edge of my temper rising. "I am not a lazy person."

"Your work for us has been erratic at best, Sally, and we've been one step away from firing you."

"But I'm not *working* at WSCT in New Haven," I protest.

"They won't *let* me work! Everything I do or say is wrong." I realize I sound like a whining child and need to remedy that, fast. "Let me rephrase that. I was hired as an on-air special investigations reporter. Rather than be shut out completely, I've opted to produce stories for WSCT and let other people take the credit."

"Assuming that is true," Alexandra says, "why is there such a problem? I just don't understand how you can be blacklisted in such a short time period."

"Where do I begin?" I'm struggling to keep my voice level. "This is a Connecticut affiliate in New Haven whose news producer can't be bothered to learn anything about New Haven County, or *any* county in Connecticut. I asked him why anyone in Connecticut would bother watching us if we don't do any Connecticut stories. So he tells me, when he was in Houston he didn't know anything about Houston, either. What he knows about is pure news. I asked him what, in his mind, is pure news. He says, with a straight face, I swear to God, 'Winning Lotto numbers. That's news.' I said no wonder he's climbing from a major market like Houston to Nowhere, Connecticut, so fast."

Alexandra tries not to smile. "But sometimes Lotto is news."

"Look," I say, "I know a shell game when I see one. That news department is no more about news than a corporate shareholders' report is about the state of the nation. Let me tell you the stories I had lined up—Governor Rowland walking us, WSCT News, through the Adrian's Landing project. Nobody else, just us—it's the governor, for Pete's sake, that's a big deal where I come from. Well, it was nixed before I even got it off the ground—too much free PR I'm told. Fine, I could see that, until I found out the station owner's son is a lobbyist for the Democrats in the state senate."

Alexandra's face is expressionless.

"I wanted to cover the protest at the Capitol over the state giving sixty million to private developers to build a shopping mall in New Haven. Nixed, not interesting, I'm told. We have a ten-car crash near Castleford on 91 and I get a local guy to shoot the film and I do the report. They use the tape, but cut me out and the anchor does a voice-over, completely screwing up the facts in the process. We've got ten cars smashed up, right there on tape in front of people's eyes, and this jackass is calling it a major two-car pileup." I cock my head. "What the hell is a major two-car pileup?"

Alexandra can't help but laugh.

"So then I pitch him a complete puff piece on the Tokahna Casino. My boss thinks, 'What a great idea!'" I lean closer to her. "Dovetails the Lotto-as-news concept beautifully, *n'est-ce pas?* If it turns out to be a piece on gambling as an addiction and where to get help, we all know where that story's going to end up."

"Sally—" she begins.

"And you know what *really* burns me? The Rowland interview was only one facet of an entire series I was working on about Adrian's Landing. I was going to use it throughout, comparing and contrasting what the governor said verbatim with the businessmen, politicos and locals, for and against. It included an overview about the Black and Hispanic populations of downtown Hartford and the pluses and minuses of the project for them. The six biggest businesses that directly benefit from Adrian's Landing and their connection to both sides of the aisle in the Capitol. I also wanted to show the bidding process, and which unions benefit and who is cut out. Well, I was *forbidden* to interview the governor and the entire series was shelved." I glare at her. "It was too controversial for our market, he said. *Too controversial!*" I shout, making the driver glance back through the glass. "It's too controversial to present the facts to the people whose taxes are financing the whole damn project?"

"I hear you," Alexandra says quietly.

But I'm on a roll and I'm ready to tattle everything I know about the station, and I rattle off who's screwing who (the anchorman and the intern from Trinity College), who's stealing from petty cash (the news producer), and who smokes pot before every broadcast (the director), and that's why—

She raises a hand to stop me. "That still doesn't excuse—"

"My lack of productivity," I conclude. I lean forward to rap on the glass partition. It goes down. "Stop the car, there's something I need in the trunk."

"This isn't necessary," Alexandra says. "We're in the middle of an intersection at Ninety-sixth Street and Second Avenue."

But I am not to be deterred. I make the driver pull over and open the trunk. I open my suitcase, extract an enormous three-ring notebook. The tome has to be four hundred loose-leaf pages thick, neatly separated by dividers. I jump back in the car and clunk the book into Alexandra's lap. "There are the nine stories, soup to nuts, I worked on for WSCT, and every single one—except the gambling one— has been thrown out."

Alexandra turns the pages, skimming. Evidently she knows shorthand. "You did an awful lot of work on this Adrian's Landing story," she murmurs. "What did you do with your research?"

"Gave it to a friend at the *Hartford Courant*." The *Herald-American* is not the appropriate place for an in-depth investigation series on Hartford. The friend, not coincidentally, is related to a star player for the UConn Huskies women's basketball team, and I 'traded' it for an inside TV interview and player profile for WSCT when the team recently made the final four.

She reads some more. "And this one, about the social worker who employed her teenage gang clients as hit men?"

"I gave it to Clarence for *DBS News Magazine,*" I say, referring to a producer on the show.

She looks at me. "That story came from you?"

I nod. "You can ask him."

"I shall," she says quietly, reading on, pursing her lips. It looks as though she may be changing gears. After we've crossed the Triboro Bridge, she looks over at me. "Why hasn't any of this been told to me?"

"By who?"

"By anyone. But let's start with you. Why didn't you tell me?"

"I don't work for you. I work for Lotto-is-News Man."

"Why didn't you talk to me about the *DBS News Magazine* piece yourself?"

"Because I didn't think I was ready. I thought Clarence would know who was best to handle it."

Alexandra shakes her head, gesturing to my notebook. "This is what I mean, Sally. Obviously you're not lazy."

"Thank you."

"But to do all this work and not talk to the person who hired you, well—that's crazy."

"But it's not your problem," I say. "I don't work for you directly."

"It *is* my problem," she says, "because I can't fix something if I don't know it's broken." She sighs. "For heaven's sake, Sally, I could have fired you. We're cutting WSCT loose as an affiliate, which means your contract with them ends. And, in turn, with us."

"You're dumping WSCT?" I ask gleefully.

"We were hoping to buy the station, but it's not going to happen, so we're ditching the whole Connecticut operation. It really doesn't matter, since most of the state is wired for cable and carries WST." WST is a New York independent that became the first superstation carried on cable across the country.

She shifts in her seat slightly. "Okay, so I understand the situation in New Haven. But I've noticed you haven't been writing much, either."

"You subscribe to the *Herald-American?*" I laugh.

"Since one of our reporters writes for it, yes." She smiles. "It's not as if I don't know anything about the town."

True.

Alexandra personally spearheaded an investigation into the circumstances surrounding my father's death and devoted an entire special of *DBS News Magazine* to it. She knows more about Castleford's history than most of the people who live there. She has also personally interviewed the man, Phillip O'Hearn, who was responsible for Daddy's death in a convenient "accident" during the great Castleford flood. As DBS News and my cop friend Buddy D'Amico discovered, the so-called accident was caused by the detonation of demolition charges while my father was inspecting the high school gym wall.

"That's true. I haven't been writing much at the paper," I acknowledge softly. Suddenly I feel so tired I could cry.

"Does it have something to do with your, well, personal life?" she asks gently. "With Spencer Hawes?"

"It's a lot more than just Spencer," I concede, sighing. "A whole lot more."

She waits patiently for me to continue.

"Relationships take emotional energy," I say, "the very same energy you need to write."

She nods. "Yes."

I find myself sinking into the emotional abyss I've been trying to back away from for months. "It's my whole hometown, Castleford." I swallow. "I'm not sure I feel much like writing about it anymore. I'm not even sure if I want to go on living there, not in the same town with the man who murdered my father." I avert my eyes. "Castleford's split right down the middle over this." I give a bitter laugh. "O'Hearn may have had my father killed, but his construction empire is still one of the largest employers in the area. It's like a psychic version of the Hatfields and the McCoys, one side supporting the Harringtons, the other side resenting us."

I hold my forehead in my hands a minute before dropping them to look at Alexandra. "I had no idea the effect that story would have on our lives. On my family. Sometimes I think my mother is twice as sad as she was before."

She nods. "That's because there hasn't been any resolution for your family."

"Yes," I say, nodding, "that's exactly it. You feel like you're walking around waiting for the other shoe to drop and it never does, never will. I'm so sick of the whole thing. My father's still dead, and O'Hearn's up there on the top of the hill in the biggest mansion in town, and his wife is running around bad-mouthing my mother, telling people she's angling for money." I make a sound of utter disgust. "My mother after money! God in heaven—it's amazing I haven't killed them both myself!"

"There may be other ways to deal with them, Sally," Alexandra says quietly. When I look at her, she adds, "Let me think about it."

I offer an appreciative smile. "Thank you. It helps, you know, to imagine there may be something left I can do." I sigh, looking out the window. "Even if there's not."

I keep close tabs on the man who is responsible for my father's death. In fact, I keep a running file on his life. I keep abreast of his business affairs and his mistresses (currently a thirty-nine-year-old formerly abused wife who works in the city tax collector's office). I don't know what I'm waiting for, but I'll know when it happens.

Mother says to leave it, that Mr. O'Hearn has his own

conscience to live with. I wonder. For God's sake, my father *gave* O'Hearn the ways and means to start his business! He was his friend! And just because O'Hearn skanked out on the caliber of his building materials, why did my father have to die?

In certain restaurants around Castleford these days, I can walk in and the usuals at the bar will literally turn their backs on me. *Oh, that Sally Harrington,* they think, *why is she making trouble when things are finally good again in Castleford?*

"I think Spencer was a way for me to postpone acknowledging how angry I am about my father's death," I say. "And it's not just anger about O'Hearn. Sometimes I think it's about the way of the whole world." I look out my window again. "Maybe this is what growing up is about, realizing that you've been brought up with ethics and morals and have been sent into a world that doesn't give a flying 'f' about anything but feathering one's own nest."

"No, Sally." The way the anchorwoman says this makes me turn. "The world *is* about feathering one's own nest, but only so you can then help others to do the same—and convince people there are enough feathers to go around. That's what I've learned, that people are almost always scared there isn't enough in this world for them. Not enough love, not enough money, not enough security. So they feel they've *got* to go out there and grab as much as they can. And I guess they think the Phillip O'Hearns of this world are the men who will help them."

"My father *gave* O'Hearn a living," I say, as though Alexandra didn't already know the whole story. "He taught him how to start his business, loaned him his reputation, gave him work—"

"And clearly there is something very wrong with O'Hearn."

"But he's not suffering!" I finally cry. I hold my forehead

in my hand. "I can't believe I'm giving the time of day to this guy. Still."

"Sally," Alexandra says gently.

"I'm sick of him, sick of it all," I declare.

"Sally, you have no way of knowing what kind of hole O'Hearn has inside that would push him to do the things he did. I mean, what kind of fear must it take to go to these lengths? And surely he must have to live with what he did—"

"I should just arrange for him to die," I say, finally saying out loud what I've thought to myself in bleaker moments like this. "Another tragic accident. Wouldn't that be so sad. Such a family man, such a philanthropist, such a pillar of the community."

"Sally."

I look at her.

"You can't live this way. You can't let O'Hearn win. You've got to process this anger somehow and get rid of it."

I look down to my lap. "I think I was hoping Spencer might do that."

Silence.

"This must be difficult for you. His disappearance. When you've been spending so much time with him."

I look at her. "To be honest? No, not really. I just want to make sure he's all right."

Alexandra hesitates. "Even if he's run off with Lilliana Martin?"

"I'm almost hoping now that that is the case," I say. "When does her disappearance become public?"

"If she doesn't contact somebody in the next twelve hours," Alexandra says, "she officially becomes missing and it goes out over all the wires."

"How did you know she was missing?"

She smiles. "I've got my sources."

"Come on," I say.

"Her agent called a friend of mine, looking for Lilliana. The friend simply mentioned it, and mentioned, in passing, that she was last seen with you."

"I see." I look out my window. "But what if she isn't with Spencer?" I feel a slightly sick sensation in my stomach, but I'm so exhausted I'm getting used to it.

"Do you think that's a possibility?"

I'm not going to say that I think Lilliana probably liked me a lot more than she did Spencer by the end of Monday night, but that's what I think. In fact, the more I think about it, the more I doubt she would have run off with him. Of course, what do I know? She was bombed the night I met her. Who's to say how she felt the next morning?

"Yes," I finally answer. "I think it's a possibility they went separate ways."

"Why do you think that?"

I shrug. "Just a feeling." Reluctantly I meet her eyes. "If he was trying to hurt me, he'd make sure I knew he was with her." I shake my head. "But I don't think he is. I think—and I'm hoping—he's just angry at me and hurt, and wants me to worry a little." I sigh. "God, I hope so. I hope he's all right."

"I'm sure they're both fine," Alexandra says. "That's why I want you to talk to Yarlen. I think he's heard from Lilliana Martin—or someone who has. I think that's why he's going back."

"How do you know he's going back to California?"

"Wendy," she replies. "She's great on this kind of thing."

"Some security head. She looks like the missing link in the Daisy Chain," I say, making a reference to seven-sister good looks.

"That's just the point. She doesn't *look* like security. So listen, back to this." Alexandra shifts slightly in her seat and taps her forefinger on my notebook cover. "I like this. Big time. How would you like to work for me?" She points to herself. "Report directly to me?"

"Come on, Alexandra, you're supposed to be firing me," I remind her.

"From WSCT, but now I'm making you an offer to come to DBS."

"As what?"

"We'll have to figure that out," she concedes. "You're smart, with it, and you write very, very well. And you have a kind of blind loyalty. I like that. As long as it belongs to me, of course," she adds with a smile. "And, the fact is, I trust you."

My guess is she's thinking about the magazine hatchet job I was hired to do on the DBS network president, Cassy Cochran, but didn't. Or she's thinking about the damage I could have done to *her.* But didn't. The WSCT job was an unexpected payoff for that. I knew that at the time, but what she's talking about now is something else.

"Every once in a while," Alexandra is saying, "you find someone in this business who you know will be pretty good at whatever career track they choose in life. That's my take on you, Sally. You can probably do well at whatever you try your hand at. But right now it seems you're slightly disenfranchised. You're free to go anywhere, do almost anything, but you can't seem to go. Can't leave Castleford, get on with your life. Because if you do, you know, you'll soar."

I shrug. "Maybe I've lost my ambition."

She throws her head back and laughs.

"What?" I demand.

She lowers her head. "Never confuse unfinished business with a lack of ambition, my friend."

Unfinished business.

"Come on, Sally, work for me. I think it'll be great for you."

"And join Alexandra's Merry Little Band?" I counter.

Her eyebrows go up in question.

"One of the interviews I did for the *Expectations* piece," I tell her. *Expectations* is a high-end tabloid magazine. "One of your less-than-ardent fans said something like, 'Here's the drill. You live and die for truth, justice, and above all, protecting Alexandra Waring, and then you get to join Alexandra's merry little band and live happily ever after.' It's not such a bad deal if you're into—" I stop, embarrassed, remembering the rest of her sentence.

"If you're into what?" she prompts me.

I shrug. I know Alexandra's gay; she knows I know she's gay—a lot of people know she's gay, but I still find this embarrassing. I've run through my small ability of dealing with sexuality the last couple of days.

"Sally."

If she really does want me to work for her, I've got to be able to be honest with her. "Well, the inference was about everything being all right as long as everybody is in love with you."

Her head kicks back slightly. "Really." Blink. "And what did you think about that?"

"To be honest, at the time I thought it was an odd thing to say, because it seemed to me that you make a point of surrounding yourself with people who are immune to— well, you know. Immune to you."

She smiles a sad little smile, but she's clearly uncomfortable. "With the hours and the pressure on us all, yes, severe attraction can be a problem." She glances out her window. We're exiting 681 for Kennedy. "So this will not be a problem?"

It takes a second before I realize that she has asked me a question.

"No," I say quickly.

"Good," she says. And then she smiles, relaxing. "But

you're still a woman who likes to live on the edge. I think we're going to have to keep an eye on you."

What's that supposed to mean, I'm not sure I want to know.

We've pulled up in front of the American Airlines terminal. The blowing rain has started to freeze on the pavement and the driver gets out to see that I get safely inside the building.

Cliff doesn't even seem mildly surprised when I slip into the easy chair across from him in the Admiral's Club. "Hey," he says with a smile.

"Hey," I return. "You ran off. Where are you going?"

"Business." He grimaces. "I've got to get back to L.A."

"But what about Lilliana?"

"Oh, she's okay," he says. "She left a message with my office. Said she just needed some time alone, not to worry."

"That's good. So where is she? Home?"

He shakes his head. "Palm Springs, she said."

The desert, not Hawaii. So she's not with Spencer.

"What's in Palm Springs?"

He shrugs. "Hell if I know. She always says," he raises his hands to gesture, as if mimicking her, "'I hate the fucking desert, Cliff, I don't want to go to the desert,' so I guess if she's in the desert, it's safe to assume she's with somebody." He smiles, shrugging. "And it's not you, and it's not me, so that just leaves the rest of the world to consider."

"So where does that leave you?"

"Hell if I know," he says again. "I guess where I've always been. Since the day we met, I haven't known which side is up. She's so—how do you say it? Mercurial? But that's also what makes her so much fun." He winks, as if I am an insider to this woman I do not know.

An attendant comes over to ask me if I want something to drink. I decline.

"It occurs to me that Lilliana could be with my friend Spencer Hawes," I say.

"Yeah, I met that guy."

"When?"

"Yesterday. He was at Lilliana's yesterday, looking for her. I was looking for her, too, obviously. He was sitting outside."

"What time was this?"

"In the morning. Around ten."

Ten. The police said he left on a ten-forty flight to Honolulu.

"Are you sure?"

"Sure I'm sure. He's Malcolm Kieloff's editor, we talked about it. He said Lilliana was with you guys at the party the night before. And then I moved on and left him there." He frowns. "What's the matter?"

"Spencer Hawes is missing, too."

"Oh." His face falls a little. "So maybe he is the one with Lilliana in Palm Springs."

"Maybe," I say softly.

Cliff leans forward, but then lets his head loll back slightly to look at me through half-closed eyes, like he's a cat or something. "That leaves you and me, Sally Harrington, and a nice long flight to get to know each other."

"I'm afraid I'm staying," I say, rising from my seat.

"You're not going to L.A.?" he asks, disappointed.

"No. I just came to check and see if you were all right, you left so suddenly."

He stands up. "Well, I'm very sorry to hear that." He scratches his head, looking around. "Could be a long night. For a second I thought it might be a blessing." He smiles at me fondly and holds out his hand. I shake it and he won't let it go.

He does have a certain magnetism. He is decidedly not what I imagined a union boss to be like.

"I'm not sure anything's going to fly out of here tonight,"

I tell him. "Why don't you let me drop you off at a hotel? I've a car outside."

"Tempting, but no thanks." He releases my hand. "I better wait until something opens up. I really need to get back." The next thing I know, Cliff has slid his hands around my waist and is kissing me. "Bye," he murmurs, stepping back. "Thanks for the nice day. It didn't start out that way."

"You're welcome," I manage to say, backing away.

CHAPTER NINE

The ride back into Manhattan with Alexandra is mercifully uneventful. I briefly update her, telling her that Cliff said he left DBS because he heard from Lilliana, that she was in Palm Springs; that Spencer had been at Lilliana's house around ten yesterday morning, and that Cliff now assumed Spencer was with Lilliana. Alexandra spends the rest of the ride on the telephone with someone named Keefer in Tibet, talking about popular reaction to a Chinese economic summit.

After dropping Alexandra off at her building at Seventy-ninth and Central Park West, the driver drops me off at the Riga Royale. As I enter my room, courtesy of DBS, I feel a surge of gratitude for such a nice hotel room, soft linens and thick towels. Throw in room service and this is my idea of heaven. And tomorrow I get to sleep in.

It's nearly two in the morning and I am starving. (One of the drawbacks of hanging out with Alexandra is that she never seems to eat, or, at best, offers to share a snack like raw baby carrots and unbuttered, unsalted popcorn.)

I call home and find a message from my mother saying I was sensational on the news and that my brother, Rob, saw it with a bunch of his friends in a bar in Aspen.

Golly. I had completely forgotten that. Tonight I had made my debut on a national newscast. In the scheme of things, it seems as real to me as the jackpot of fifty dollars I won this morning at the casino, which I then promptly threw away in another machine.

The next voice on my answering machine at home is also very familiar. It's Doug. "Gosh, Sal," he says, "I turn on the news and who do I see? You were great, honey—" That last was a slip, an old endearment that popped out with his enthusiasm. "I had no idea you were going to be on. Are you going to do more of this or what? You didn't say anything about it last night. Anyway, you were great. And it was great to see you. On national TV and everything." Hurriedly he hangs up, as if he suddenly remembers who he is talking to.

Doug will be sound asleep, but I don't care. I'm just so glad he called. I feel like I haven't talked to him in years.

"Wrentham," he mumbles, assuming it's work calling. As an assistant D.A., the police sometimes call him in the middle of the night to come to a particularly heinous crime scene or when there are already legal problems over an arrest. It's not as bad as in New York, but New Haven has its share of excitement. A shoot-out in the middle of a wedding reception, for example, when the suspects ran up from the nightclub located in the basement of the hotel. That was about a week ago.

"It's Sally, Doug, I'm sorry to call so late."

"You're not sorry in the least," he says good-naturedly, waking up. "Which is sort of flattering, I guess."

I smile. He's glad to hear from me.

We talk a bit about the broadcast, how unexpected my debut was. And, out of habit, I share a little of what Alexandra and I talked about in terms of my career.

"That's so weird," he says, "to go from getting fired to getting hired."

"I know."

"So what are you going to do?"

"I'm not sure."

"What about the paper?"

"I think I hate it," I decide.

A pause. "So you'll be moving into the city?"

"I don't know," I repeat. "I don't know if it's full-time or what. I'm kind of hoping it's not." I sigh. "Let's face it, all I know is what I don't want anymore."

He doesn't say anything.

"Listen, Doug, you know that I was in California."

"That's what you said."

"What I didn't tell you is that I broke it off with Spencer."

He clears his throat. "Well that's interesting."

"I don't know, I guess it was just something I needed to do, to explore that relationship."

"I didn't mean interesting that way," Doug says. "I mean it's interesting that you dumped him and now he's missing."

I'm taken back. "How do you know he's missing?"

"We got a call that Lilliana Martin was missing, and that she may be with him. It came through New Haven because he's been spending a lot of time in Castleford."

"Well, Lilliana Martin's not missing. She's in Palm Springs."

"And he's with her?"

I take a breath. "I don't know and I don't care."

"I find that hard to believe," he says in a low voice approaching a growl. "For you to take a flier on such an incredible womanizer, I can only assume you believed you were the one woman who could reform him."

Score one for Doug. I am just one of a long line of foolish women who thought there was a future with Spencer. I consider trying to explain, but then think, to heck with it. Nothing I say can soften or remedy what I've done. Any pain or embarrassment I feel will not fix how I behaved. "I was going to call you in a few weeks."

"You called me last night," he points out.

"I mean, I was going to call you to tell you. Last night was different."

"Why were you going to call, Sally?" He's trying not to let anger creep into his voice.

"Because I think I made a mistake."

"You think. I see, come back to good old Doug. Got nothing else to do."

"Hardly!" I nearly yell. "And may I remind you who dumped me two seconds before screwing some chickee-poo in the office? Into whose arms you ran straight back into the second you thought we had broken up?"

"I never so much as kissed anyone else while we were going out, Sally."

"You're such a liar!" I sputter. "How about that girl in the bar I caught you with?"

"That doesn't count, I was loaded, it was just a kiss—"

"And then in the parking lot that time," I continue. "You were in a clinch with Debbie Ann Bolton. God only knows what that was about!"

"Oh, come on, that doesn't count."

"Right, right," I say. "Look, I acted in an entirely stupid and irresponsible way, I admit it. And to pretend I'm not suffering—and will continue to suffer—I'm not even going to try. I'm miserable, Doug. I'm scared. I can't believe how I've messed up my life." I take a breath. "So I'm going to focus on my work and in a couple months, if you want to talk, great, if you don't, fine, I understand. I'm not sure what I would do if I were you."

"You can't come crawling back to me," he says. "It's not in your nature."

"I'm not crawling back—I'm returning your goddamn phone call!"

"You're crawling back after acting like a bimbo."

"Fine, you win! Whatever. But Bimbo's calling it a night. Some day, if you feel like talking, call me—"

"Sally—"

"No, I understand. Truly, I do. I deserve it. I'm not fit to have a relationship with anybody."

"No. Listen to me, Sally."

I sigh. "What?"

"You were bored."

That shuts me up.

"In our relationship," he says. "You were bored. So was I. When he came on the scene, my adrenaline finally started running, and it made our relationship seem a lot better than it was. I understood why you would rather start your new career—remember, you were writing that magazine piece—with a slick guy who knew the New York scene. Not some crabby assistant D.A. in New Haven whose only use for New York is Yankee Stadium and Madison Square Garden. That's why I was so crazy, you were leaving me behind. And you *should* have left me behind!"

"Stop it," I say, thinking how like us this is, that first we blame each other and then ourselves, like we're reading a script to a play that has no real plot and never any ending. "Only the part about the New York scene may have been partly right, that the excitement, the newness had me punch-drunk or something."

"Every time we see each other regularly, Sally, we settle in like Ma and Pa Kettle, rocking on the front porch, bored to tears." He imitates an old man. "'Cha see the dog bark, Ma?'"

I can't help but laugh. "That's not true."

"It *is* true, Sally. I don't know what's the matter with us. We do nothing together except eat, drink and sleep."

"And what were we supposed to do?"

"Anything. How about when we were kids? We'd go night skiing over at Mount Southington, remember? We'd play golf. We'd play doubles on the weekend. We were going to take flying lessons...."

"Doug, that was before we had careers—"

"Well, all I know is, if we ever even see each other as friends again, we gotta do stuff together. Because the other clearly never works for long."

I think about this, getting suspicious. "How did you suddenly get so insightful?"

A pause. "I'm seeing someone."

My heart sinks.

"You know, like a therapist."

My heart soars. "Really."

He sighs again. "I've got a lot of crap with the ex I've never dealt with." The ex is the wife who ostensibly ran away with the stockbroker over the same issue, boredom.

Suddenly I realize that a lot of Spencer's appeal lay in the fact that what was part of his work felt like the first social life I'd had in years, accompanying him to all the hot clubs and restaurants, hobnobbing with celebrities, getting our pictures snapped. Doug's work, on the other hand, usually meant eight hours a day poring over law statutes, trial transcripts, police reports, another four hours sandwiched in between running around the courthouse trying to get the wheels of justice moving, and a couple major trials a year, where he literally worked sixteen hours a day, only to come home, crash, wake up in the middle of the night to research and make notes for the trial the next day, all while scrambling to keep on top of the mounting cases in his in-box. Crime never stops. Trials drag on forever.

I can't remember the last time I sat in the gallery to watch one of his trials.

I can't remember the last time Doug and I had time to do anything together except play with the dog.

"You've given me a lot to think about," I murmur.

"Maybe you might see someone, too," he suggests.

Like all people in need of help, I am convinced that I am so crazy that only I can sort myself out. (Read: *There's nothing wrong with me!* I like to pretend. *It's the world that's done me wrong!*) But this five-month episode with Spencer raises a lot of issues.

And, to be honest, so has the aftermath of the investigation into my father's death. There's a lot there, and like Doug and his ex-wife, my way of coping until now has been jamming all those thoughts and feelings into a box inside me and simply adding more chains and padlocks every year in a struggle to keep it from opening and disrupting my life. Of course, the very presence of that box and those chains has been affecting my behavior for years.

"Yes," I say. "I'm going to. Soon. I promise."

Silence.

"It's pathetic, I know," Doug sighs, "but I love you."

I smile. "I don't think our love will ever go away. I know I'll always feel about you differently."

Silence.

"I don't know, Sal. I just don't know."

"Maybe that's the best way to be," I say. "In the meantime, at least you know that I know I have a lot to work on. And the way I feel about you, have always felt about you, comes from the healthiest part of me. I honestly believe that."

"But how *do* you feel about me, Sally?" He says this in a whisper.

Good question. I know I love him, but do I love him romantically? Will that come back?

"I know I love you," I say. "I just don't know—" I hesitate.

"If it can last," he finishes. "I know. So listen, let's give it a couple weeks and let the dust settle. And then—well, let's see if you want to have dinner or something."

By the time we hang up, I am pretty certain he is dating someone.

I get off the bed and go to the bathroom to draw a hot bath. I take off my clothes and look at my body in the mirror, not terribly pleased with what I see. Well, what woman ever is.

It's so weird, sex. What it is, how much of it is physical attraction and how much is intellectual magnetism. Or emotional need to feel as though one belongs in the universe.

Hell if I know why anyone would want to sleep with me.

PART
TWO

CHAPTER TEN

I stay on in Manhattan for Thursday and Friday, getting to know the DBS operation. I told Al Royce back at the paper that I'm getting a promotion and he laughed, saying, "Well you better get something because I'm getting rid of you if this keeps up," to which I replied, "Somebody's got to deal with those Tokahna Indians for History Week," and he hung up on me.

What Alexandra has in mind for me is still unknown to us all, but part of my time has been devoted to double-checking that I have all my union affiliations in order as a newswriter and on-air talent. WSCT in Connecticut had been a nonunion shop. Alexandra has been assigning me stories to write for her to read on the air. I've been giving them my absolute best shot (it's very different from writing for the paper) and have been pleased thus far that she has only made a few changes. (She is notorious, evidently, for disappearing into her office for hours to rewrite everything she is to read.) Will has also put me in contact with the various news desks of affiliates across the country, handing over a few producer chores involving reports from the field.

"You sure you haven't done this before?" he asked at one point, checking the notes I had dashed off for him.

"It's kind of like going to press," I said.

"Whatever," he said. "You're good. It would be good if this works."

I was going to ask him, If what works? Do you have any idea what my job will be? but decided to cool it. They are clearly feeling me out, having me do a little of everything. People in the newsroom are polite but wary; they know I have some kind of standing because of my association with Alexandra, but no one is sure what it might be. (Join the club.)

At one point I was sent to a small office in the back of editing where a very elderly man named Mr. Graham had me watch old newsreel footage of tanks and asked me to pick the shots I thought were best.

"I don't know much about tanks," I confessed.

"It is the quality of the shots, not the tanks I am after, young lady."

Mr. Graham, I was to learn, is like me—an employee of Alexandra's whose job is unclear to everyone except Alexandra. "He worked with Edward R. Murrow in London during World War II," a production gaffer told me in the lunch line in the cafeteria.

"That was sixty years ago," I pointed out. "Any more recent credits?"

He shrugged, shaking his head. "He does something for Alexandra. I'm not sure. So what are you doing?"

"Something for Alexandra," I answered. "Gosh, you don't suppose Mr. Graham has no idea what he's doing, either, do you?"

"If he doesn't, he's been doing it an awful long time," he laughed.

Suddenly one of the cooks turned to wave her spatula at

us. "He iss da prodoocer of estorical documentaree! Of the vor!"

I checked, and sure enough, Mr. Graham was listed as the producer on every video in the extensive *DBS News History of World War II* series.

At any rate, yesterday morning, Thursday, the newsroom received confirmation from two different sources that Lilliana Martin had been seen in Palm Desert, near Palm Springs, but no one knew where she was staying or how to reach her. Kate Weston called yesterday, too, to say she still had not heard a word from Spencer and was worried. So I called Richie Benzler, Lilliana's agent, and asked when he expected to speak to Lilliana again.

"I don't know when I will," he pleaded. "She's in one of her moods."

"What kind of mood is that?"

"When I don't know what the hell is going on!"

"Well if she does call in," I continued, "it's very important you tell her that Spencer Hawes needs to call his boss at work."

"Spencer Hawes! You mean he's with her? I thought you said he wasn't!"

"Well, he's disappeared, too, so we're just putting two and two together," I explained.

"But isn't he your boyfriend?"

"Obviously not anymore," I replied.

So I'm sitting here Friday evening writing some stuff for tonight's newscast in an empty office when Richie Benzler calls me back from L.A. "Lilliana got mad when I relayed your message," he begins.

"Why, what did she say?"

"She said if his boss wants to know where Spencer Hawes is, his boss should call you. So I said, Sally Harrington's the one who called me and asked that I give you that message. So she started yelling at me, 'What kind of person does she think I am?' I told her I didn't know, but I was sure you thought she was very nice—"

My mind is racing now. If he really isn't with Lilliana, that means Spencer has been missing since Tuesday morning. Three days, no call in to work, and Kate said he had a very important meeting this morning in New York. And yet, no word.

Could he really have taken off to Hawaii? To do what? Sulk? Make me worry?

But not to call in to work. That was out of character. It's also vaguely frightening.

"So do you know how to reach her or not?" I ask.

"No," he says, discouraged, "she won't tell me. She keeps saying she needs to stay quiet a little while."

When I get off, I call Spencer's apartment for the hundredth time. The answering machine comes on, but the message tape is full. I have a key to his place and am signed in with the front desk, so I could stop by tonight after the newscast, just to check.

Then I call Kate Weston at home and tell her what Lilliana's agent told me, that the actress denies Spencer's with her.

"Gosh, I don't know what to think," she says. "It's been three days. I guess I should call his parents." She says this last part with such reluctance I know it is a hint.

"I'll call them," I say, "and I'll call you back."

While Mr. and Mrs. Hawes are fleetingly concerned about their son's three-day disappearance, they are not overly concerned because, as Spencer's father explains, "We're used to Spencer calling every other Sunday and there's nine days to go. So I guess you could say we don't worry about him unless that call doesn't come."

"Right," I say.

"We talked to him last Sunday. He was in California. And he said you were flying out, too."

"Yes, I did."

"Did you two have a fight or something?"

The question catches me by surprise.

"Because if you did, he might be trying to teach you a lesson. He used to do it as a kid. If we yelled at him, he'd stage the scene of his drowning at the marina. Leave his sneakers on the dock with a note." He laughs a little and imitates a little boy. "I didn't mean to eat the cookies!"

"That crossed my mind, Mr. Hawes, but now that it's been three days... And the fact he hasn't called in to work is, uh, troubling."

"Well," he says in this clipped Maine-kind-of voice, making it sound more like *whelp,* "that leaves work. I'm wondering if Spencer quit and that nice Kate Weston just didn't get it. He gets rash sometimes and maybe he didn't fully explain. I know for a fact that CEO they've got there makes him kind of mad."

"Andrew Rushman?"

"That's the one. He talked about it on Sunday, what a jackass the fellow is. 'Course, as I say, Spencer can get kind of rash, sometimes."

I'll say.

And then Mrs. Hawes gets on the phone and pushes me into a conversation about how good she thinks I am for Spencer even though "I understand you don't think it can work in the long run."

My interest picks up. "How do you understand that?"

"Spencer called me from California. Tuesday morning. You know, the morning you two broke up."

I hear Mr. Hawes say in the background, "You didn't tell me that."

She whispers back, "It was a conversation he wanted to have with his mother."

"You talked to him on Tuesday?" I say. "I didn't know that."

"Yes, he called. He was upset." Pause. "I think my son was going to ask you to marry him."

I cannot possibly describe all that I have felt over the course of this phone call: fear, guilt, astonishment, flattered, tempted to try it again with Spencer, annoyed, angry, scared.

Scared. What I have always vaguely felt when I was with Spencer. Like any roller coaster, the relationship always had a scary part looming ahead, and I have no doubt but that it heightened our sex life for at least a while.

I call Kate back and relay what the Haweses have said. "That's it," she says, "if I don't hear from him by tomorrow, I'm filing a missing-person report."

I promise to check his apartment when I get off tonight and let her know if I find anything.

A half hour before broadcast time, Alexandra catches me in the newsroom and pushes some copy into my hands. "The weather's a mess. Fix it, will you?" I scoot over to an empty terminal and call the piece up. She's right. Whoever wrote this is not big on grammar or comprehension. The weatherman, Gary Plains, saunters in, looking for me. "You're editing my piece?"

"Have a seat," I tell him.

"I wrote it myself," he says proudly.

I smile. "It's very good, but we need to simplify it a bit."

He talks to me while I type and sentence by sentence I am able to maneuver Gary into reworking the order, the syntax and the meaning of just about everything he's written. Within twenty minutes, it's not a half-bad explanation of why ice storms keep hitting what should be warm climates in the south. And perhaps more important, Gary feels he's still the writer of the segment. (What do they do with him usually? I wonder.) We insert the copy into the main news script and print out a hard copy for Gary. Ten minutes later, all is dark but the sets in Studio A and *DBS News America Tonight with Alexandra Waring* is on the air.

"Thank you for salvaging the weather," Alexandra calls to me from her dressing room bathroom after the newscast.

"Yeah, but what happens Monday?" I ask.

"Zooey should be back. He usually watches over Gary's stuff. He took the week off. Feels like a month." The bathroom door opens fully and the anchorwoman comes out, dressed in blue jeans, a turtleneck and sweater.

"Hey, you look great," I say, having never seen her so informally dressed.

She looks at me. "Why does this surprise you?"

I shrug. "I don't know. You look normal. I mean, jeans suit you."

"I did grow up on a farm, you know." She walks over to her dressing table chair and sits to put on some socks and Bean Brother's boots. "And I'm going to my farm now."

"New Jersey?"

Bending over. "Jersey." She finishes tying her boots and sits up. "Can you be here on Monday? Plan on putting in next week, too? Until we figure out what we're about?"

"Sure."

She studies me a moment. "Do you think you could live in New York?"

"If I were working here?" I say quickly. "Are you kidding?" My heart is starting to race. Oh, my God, could I really get a job here? Maybe as that weekly crime-and-punishment reporter?

"What I'm thinking about," Alexandra says, standing up, "is trying you out as assistant managing editor."

Alexandra is the managing editor so this means she wants me to be her assistant.

My hopes crash. A thirty-year-old assistant managing editor? When Alexandra was thirty, she became a national news anchor.

"You're disappointed," she observes.

"No, I'm grateful," I have the sense to say.

"Look, Sally," she says, taking a step closer. "You are completely new to this game. You've got a lot to learn. On the other hand, you've got a lot of talent, particularly in writing, and heaven knows, we need another good writer around here."

"Who's the other one?" I joke.

"Me," she says, not kidding. "And I think by working with me you'll learn an awful lot. I know you want to go on air—"

"I never—"

She holds up a hand to silence me. "You've got the bug, Sally, I saw you Wednesday night. You loved being on the air—you loved it when we did the magazine story on your dad five months ago. And the camera likes you. But with your kind of talent, you can't go out there half cocked. You need to learn the business. So when you come in Monday, I want you to come in knowing whether or not you can work for me in that capacity. And whether or not you can move to New York—because you'd have to be here."

I think of Scotty. And my big yard. And Abigail! At Mother's. I'd have to leave Scotty with Mother. *No.* No way, I couldn't. It would break my heart. But keep Scotty in an apartment?

"The salary we'll talk about," she continues. "I think you'd want to hang on to your place in Connecticut. Personally I'd go nuts if I was in here all the time. And we should be able to see the money is enough for you to swing both." She picks up her bag. "So let's talk on Monday," she concludes, moving toward the door. "Oh—and I'm afraid it would mean giving up your job at the paper."

"What a hardship," I say, following her down the hall toward the garage. People pass us, saying hi. When the corridor is clear again, Alexandra turns around. "I'm creating this job especially for you," she says quietly. "And I'm doing it because I believe in your talent, but most of all, I believe in you. So if you consider joining my 'merry little band,' make sure it is a place you really want to be."

I've got a lot to think about. I really want to go home to Castleford and talk things over with Mother, but I promised myself I'd check Spencer's apartment. Make sure something's not— Well, whatever. To check.

The greeting I get in the lobby of Spencer's apartment building is embarrassing. The night concierge wants to know where we've been, when is Spencer coming home? "The cat sitter will be glad you're back."

"I completely forgot about the cat! Someone's been feeding her, right?"

"The kid in 10-E, but he ran out of food day before yesterday and his mother's complaining she has to buy all this stuff and her son hasn't been paid, and it was only supposed to be three days."

I promise to take care of it. Then he asks me if I want Spencer's mail, explaining the mailman brought it to the desk because his box is full. He hands over a small Godiva shopping bag, which is surprisingly heavy since it's only been six mail days since Spencer left. I stop at his box and take out even more mail. Then I go upstairs and let myself into the apartment, where Samantha, his little cat, throws herself at me in desperation.

This reduces me to near tears. In the past five months I have made myself completely at home in this apartment, and, to be honest, I learned more about my body here than in the preceding twenty years. I have had more orgasms in this place than—

But that's not why I feel like crying. It's because the kitty's so lonely and Spencer's missing and I don't know what has happened to him.

I don't know how or why I've become such a total detractor of Spencer. A week ago, he was flawed, but mine. He's not very practical, but he is poetic. And what does that mean? Instead of ordering pizza, he loved to cook for me. Instead of simply turning on the TV to watch something he wanted to see—usually the news, a talk show or sports— he would first capture me and drag me to lie down alongside of him on the couch while he watched and I usually read something.

And the sex thing. Was it *sex?* Or was it gently exploring, pushing this, touching that, looking—feeling—for that combination that would make the tumblers click into place, even when I thought my body was beyond feeling?

This sounds odd, I know, but there was something about Spencer that worked at me. It was not physical, not mental, exactly. It was a kind of *knowing,* a psychic zeroing in on desires I did not know I even had.

Sounds ridiculous. Particularly now. But I know I can never be safely alone with Spencer Hawes, not without that pull working at us to be as physically close to each other as possible, and then once that is achieved, feeling almost desperate for something much more than that.

I shake off these thoughts and try to pull myself together by dumping Spencer's mail on the table in order to make a neat pile.

I am shocked by what the envelopes indicate.

Don't get me wrong, I have bills, and I can't pretend I haven't missed payments all over the place in my younger days. So I know the kind of envelopes bills come in, and I know the envelopes that angry collection agency notices come in. And what I see in this pile of mail is a pile of both kinds of envelopes. They are from banks (not statements, those are a different-size envelope), department stores and collection agencies.

I am looking at someone's mail who is deeply in debt.

But how can that be? He must make at least a hundred thousand.

On the other hand, he rents and doesn't own any property.

He leases his car. He couldn't lease his car if he has bad credit.

Citibank AAdvantage, Chase, First Union, Barney's, Bank One, Saks...

The strange thing is, in the five months I've known Spencer I've never known him to use anything other than his corporate American Express card, accepting without question his explanation that it accrues general account miles and he pays Bennett, Fitzallen & Coe back for personal use.

A few minutes later I'm beginning to think he uses the corporate card because it's the only one that gets paid.

A notice from the building management that his February rent has not been paid. Notices from a Mazda dealership, Comp USA, a ConEd late notice, a red-bordered Nynex envelop, a mailgram from Time-Warner cable, bills from Brooks Brothers, Larsen Florist, Madison Avenue Bookshop, Kinney Parking, Columbia House, East Side Pets, Max's Gym, Paragon Sports...

This is a nightmare. What the hell is the matter with him? Where does his money go?

I pick up Samantha, kiss the back of her head and hold her close to my chest, thinking over what I should do. Or whether I should do anything.

Samantha starts to purr and I remember that her master is missing and that I'm worried that something has happened to him. If it has, then sooner or later I will have to call his parents, and then this mess will be theirs and I know they don't have much. On the other hand, maybe Spencer will be home shortly and can straighten it out.

Samantha purrs, angling her nose up under my neck.

"It's okay, baby," I tell her, "I'll make sure someone takes good care of you until your daddy comes home."

And then, standing here, I realize Spencer may have killed himself. Because looking at this pile of mail, I think maybe that's what I would do.

People will call me a fool, but I can't leave things like this. I walk over to Spencer's desk to see if I can find an envelope to put a rent check in. I intend to drop it off at the rental office on my way out. I pull out one drawer and then another, and then open the double drawer on the bottom right, the contents of which take my breath away.

It is jammed with *un*opened bills.

I feel sick. "Okay, Sally," I say aloud, "let's just take care of the basics." And so I go back to the table and look for the utilities. I open the ConEd bill and find he hasn't paid them in three months—$142.15. That's not bad. I write a check. Nynex is a whole other category, two months and more than six hundred dollars in long distance. Who the hell has he been calling? I look and see calls to all over everywhere, but most of all, the bills are from talking to *me* in Connecticut.

I write a check to Nynex for $638.98. I write the rent check, $2,162. I open the Mazda envelope. Hasn't paid his car lease for two months, either. It's $299 plus penalties, total $619.96. Okay that's it.

But then I see an MCI bill and open that. Hasn't paid his phone card bill in three months. I pay this in case he wants to use it to call home! It's $223. And lastly, I open a bill from Kinney Parking in the basement of this building where the Mazda is parked. That hasn't been paid since November and the car is going to be impounded. I write a check for $1,085.

Great, that makes $4,871.09 worth of checks I've written, and $1,800 of that is on a credit line at eleven percent.

There goes every "extra" bit of money from my old WSCT salary.

He'll pay me back. He better pay me back!

It is nearly four-thirty in the morning when Samantha and I reach my house in Castleford. As wiped out as I am, I still go out to the shed to retrieve her litter pan and food and set her up. While she's eating, I fix myself a couple of soft boiled eggs and toast. I glance through yesterday's paper and consider listening to my messages. I vote against it for the sake of sleeping a few hours first.

So I brush my teeth and fall into bed, and Samantha and I drift off.

I dream about Spencer.

CHAPTER ELEVEN

I awaken Saturday morning to find Samantha curled up on my bed in a small patch of morning sunshine. I offer her a sad smile, touching her head with a finger.

There really is something wrong with Spencer. All those bills, all that spending. His spending habits are evidently equal to his sexual compulsiveness.

Still, he makes a great deal of money. It's one thing to be short, or maybe he's been helping his parents out or something, but if that were the case, wouldn't he have cut back on something? I didn't have to open those envelopes from Brooks Brothers and Barney's to know that's where his suits and shirts came from. Spencer is an immaculate dresser, wearing only the finest clothes, fitted to a T, but now that I know the secret behind this accomplishment it only makes me feel sick.

I drag myself out of bed and walk into the kitchen to put coffee on. Then I turn on my answering machine.

Kate Weston. Did I find anything at Spencer's apartment?

I call her immediately and tell her no. "Then I'm calling the police," she announces. "At least we'll find out if he's in a hospital or jail or something."

With a heavy heart, I tell her I think it's a good idea.

After hanging up, I resume listening to my messages. There is this weird one from my jerk-off boss at WSCT. Happily, ex-boss. "What the hell is this, Sally?" he says. "Are you changing careers or what?" Laughter in the background. "Well, if we're any judge, we think you should go for it."

How could he know about DBS already?

"By the way, what are you doing Saturday night?" he adds. More laughter in the background.

Jackasses. I'll be glad not to have to see any of them again.

I call Mother's but there's no answer. I leave a message that I'm home and have lots to talk about.

I get dressed and go into the office.

"What's the matter?" I ask the Saturday receptionist-operator at the Castleford *Herald-American.*

"Nothing," she says, staring at me.

I pause, taking a closer look. "Do you feel all right?"

"Yeah," she says tentatively.

"Okay, then," I say, moving on.

Somebody in the newsroom whistles as I turn into my cubicle. I turn around. Nobody's owning up. "What's up?"

One of the guys laughs. Another reporter, a young woman, swears under her breath and walks away. Then she comes back my way to hang on the wall of my cubicle.

By now I'm humming at my desk, looking through my in-box. Things are looking up. I may be able to quit soon.

"Sally," the woman says. I look up. She looks pained. "There's some kind of tape floating around."

"What of?"

"You. I don't know exactly what it is," she rushes on, "but it has something to do with you."

I glance back at the pile in my box. "Where's the tape now?"

"Royce went somewhere with it. I saw him."

"Huh. Okay, thanks for the tip." Tape of what? I'm wondering. The only damaging tape I can think that might be floating around is something from the Tokahna Casino, that somehow my explanation of who Royce's Raiders are had somehow been captured on film.

In the bottom of my in-box I find a large bulky manila envelope. The notation on it says it was delivered by hand yesterday to reception at 2:00 p.m. It is simply labeled Sally Harrington.

Inside is a Jiffy bag addressed to Reverend Millar, First Congregational Church, 145 Main Street, Castleford, CT. A note is Scotch-taped to the bag.

Dear Sally,
This is exactly how this was sent to Reverend Millar. I realized what it was and am giving it to you. He has not seen it. Nor has anyone else here.
I'm sorry, but I thought it best to get it to you.

It is signed by a friend of my mother's who volunteers in the church office.

Something tells me I might not want to watch it here at the office, but I want to know what it is. So I make my way to the conference room, lock the door behind me and cue up the video.

It is clearly me, leaning toward the camera, lighting a bedside candle. I am in a loosely tied silk robe, one breast nearly falling out of it. I am sitting on the edge of the bed and rotating my neck, like I always do after a day of writing. I bring up my hand to press parts of my neck, trying to get a kink out.

A shadow passes over the camera and Spencer is crawling over the bed to kneel behind me. He is absolutely buck naked and has a full erection, which, as he nestles closer to me, rests on my lower back. He starts massaging my neck and I start making moaning sounds about how good it feels. He leans to kiss the side of my neck and resumes massaging. Suddenly I laugh and say, in a hollow-sounding voice (the audio is not good), "Good heavens, Mr. Hawes, could that possibly be what I think it is behind me? I thought you were exhausted."

"Of everything but you," he whispers, kissing my neck, rising slightly to drag himself against my back.

"Oh, God," I sigh, closing my eyes and curving my back into it.

He continues to kiss my neck and slides one hand down under the robe to hold my breast. I murmur something and he begins feeling my breast, and my head rolls forward, lost in the sensation of what he is doing under the silk.

This goes on for quite some time, the only sound being my breathing and my murmurs, which are growing louder. After a while, he eases me onto my back, my legs still hanging over the side of the bed, and he kisses me full on the mouth, pulling my robe open to hold both of my breasts, massaging them, breathing heavier himself. Then he pulls the robe open completely and straddles me, sitting on my hips, his swollen self lying on my stomach. I laugh quietly, stroking his thighs.

And then I slip my hands around him and pull his body forward, making him slide up to my chest, where I then use both hands to close my breasts over him, holding him there. Spencer's eyes close and his back arches and he moves a little, making a quiet gasping sound, and I can see that my legs have begun to twitch in excitement, one foot starting to arch. In a few moments Spencer is moaning, rubbing himself between my breasts, back and forth, back and forth, while I dutifully hold him in place—only my lower body has begun to twist in earnest.

He stops suddenly and opens his eyes, and takes my hands away. I whisper, "No, let me," and try to guide him to my mouth.

"No," he whispers hoarsely, pulling away, sliding down to kiss me.

Unceremoniously he plunges his hand between my legs and I nearly throw us both off the bed. "Just as I thought," he whispers, and it's obvious from the sounds coming from below that I am utterly slick with desire. He's working his hand between my legs and my body stiffens, my back locking, and I am obviously climbing toward climax. But he pulls his hand away and sits up, moving between my legs.

"Oh, Spencer, please," I beg.

He is on his knees between my legs, and holds himself in his hand, rubbing the end around the outside of me. I nearly go through the roof. *"Please,"* I cry. And then he rolls over onto his back and laughs, saying, "Come and get it," and I need no urging at all, and in a moment I am sitting up and moving on top of him. I hold him in my hand, directing him into me. I easily slide down on him and for a moment I seem to lose the rhythm of things, but then the passion comes roaring back and I start to rock.

I cry and whimper, rocking on top of him, lost in the sensation. His lips are stretched back over his teeth as he tries to hold on, as I continue to thrust and push and slam my way to what is finally an orgasm that leaves me frozen on top of him, like an arched statue, and now it's Spencer's turn to gasp *"Please,"* and suddenly he just slams me over on my side and we roll over and he starts wildly thrusting, panting, while I'm shaking all over, past orgasm, and then he's up on the palms of his hands, crying out *"Yes,"* pushing me up the bed a few inches. And then, abruptly, he collapses on me.

The tape fades to black.

CHAPTER TWELVE

"Yep, you're right," my high school friend, Detective Buddy D'Amico says, coming back into his office at the precinct. In his left hand is a plastic evidence bag with a video in it, in the right, a plastic bag holding a Jiffy bag. "The chief got one, too."

I drop my face in my hands.

"So," he sighs, dropping the bags on his desk and sitting down, "that makes me, the mayor, Al Royce, the chief, Reverend Millar—"

"Don't forget the Masonic Lodge," I add from behind my hands. "Buddy," I declare then, "I'm going to die."

"Come on, Sally—" Buddy begins. But then he realizes what I know already, that not all the men around town are going to be like him and shut the tape off as soon as they recognize who and what it is, but to the contrary, will watch it and no doubt pass it on. "I will find out who did this, I swear to you."

I drop my hand and he meets my eyes for only a moment before averting them. Who the hell can blame him? He's seen me in my most private moments. How do you ever look at anyone the same way again?

"I don't know what to do about Mother," I say, my eyes falling to the floor. "I don't even know what to say."

Suddenly the rage takes over and I find myself slamming my hand on Buddy's desk, making the cup holding pens and pencils spill over. "Goddamn it, Buddy, it's my family's life! I just can't believe it!"

I start crying and cover my face again.

The tape is all over town. The paper got it, the police chief, the mayor's office, the board of ed, the country club, even the public library. Someone left a message at my house that guys were watching it in the waiting room of the local Jaguar dealership.

Mother. I have to do something. I can't let her go around town without her knowing.

"Come on, Sally, let's pull it together here," Buddy says gruffly.

He's just trying to help. I don't have to do this alone. He's my friend, he'll help me. I look up, wiping my face with Kleenex and then blowing my nose.

"Okay, first off," Buddy begins, "where was this film shot?"

I am so close to breaking down again. "New York," I croak. "It's Spencer's bedroom."

He makes a note and without looking up, asks, "And you were taping this for your own use?"

I snap out of it. "No! I wasn't taping it at all!"

Buddy looks at me. "So Spencer was taping you without your knowledge."

I am one step away from killing myself. "I don't know." Buddy doesn't say anything. "Maybe," I say.

"And Spencer's missing."

"Since Tuesday morning. In Los Angeles."

"Did you guys have a fight or anything?"

I nod. "Yeah. We had a fight. I broke up with him."

Buddy bites his lip. "A tough question, but I've got to ask

it. You dumped Spencer, he's hurt, he's angry—could he have sent these tapes all over town?"

I shrug. "I guess he must have." Then I frown. "No, I don't believe it. It's just so out of character."

Of course, setting me up for a three-way was out of character, too.

"But you broke up with him," he repeats.

"But if he did, then where the hell is he? I was just in his apartment last night. He hasn't been there. How could he send all of these out when he hasn't even been home?"

Buddy is making notes and I cringe, knowing what he's thinking. How could I get involved with someone like this? Particularly when Buddy himself had been sweet on me in high school and, Mother thinks, is still a little bit now. But Buddy is married with a little daughter and I've been going out with some kind of pervert. Bankrupt pervert.

I can't believe I paid those bills last night for him. What kind of idiot am I? I don't have two nickels left to rub together.

"Can you still get into his apartment?" he asks next.

I nod. "I've got the key."

"Okay," he says, throwing his pencil down, "we go in tomorrow morning and see how the tape was made."

"You mean—" I begin. "You'll go in with me?"

"Absolutely," he declares. "But listen, Sally, you gotta go and talk to your mom. It's not fair if she doesn't know."

"Have you seen the tape yourself?" Mother says calmly, putting another log on the pile in the fireplace. Her boyfriend, Mack Cleary, is coming over and she was laying a fire when I arrived.

"Yes."

Mother glances at me, pressing her lips into a line. "Is it explicit?" she asks, reaching to rearrange the logs for something to do.

"Yes," I say quietly. I swallow. I don't know how to handle this. Mother has lived in Castleford for more than thirty years. My father and his parents, their entire lives. While it's true the Harringtons have had their scandals—my grandfather systematically blew the family's fortune and then killed himself—none, that I know of, have involved watching one of the Harrington women on film screwing her brains out.

"You thought you were alone, unobserved," Mother continues, now simply looking at the logs.

"Yes."

"And did you do anything you later regretted?" She glances up again. "I mean, regretted even if you hadn't been taped?"

I know what she means. Was I doing something freaky with Spencer that I hated; was I drunk and submitting to something creepy.

I didn't consider Spencer rubbing his penis between my breasts freaky, but then, I didn't know my minister and half my hometown was going to watch him do it.

"No." I'm having trouble breathing, I feel so trapped. "Mother, I'm so sorry. I'm just sick about it." I turn away. "There's just no way I could ever imagine Spencer doing something like this."

"Spencer?" Mother says sharply. She is getting to her feet, a little stiff. "You think Spencer is responsible for this?"

"Well who else could it be?" I practically wail.

Mother is getting angry. "Sally Goodwin Harrington," she admonishes me. "Are you telling me that you have spent five months thinking you're in love with some kind of mentally deficient deviant? Some kind of monster who would take delight in humiliating your entire family? Are you trying to tell me that that young man wants vengeance against me, by showing people in town my little girl making love with him?"

I am at a loss for words.

"Sometimes you're so smart you're positively a fool," Mother mutters, walking into the kitchen. On the way she whirls around and points at me. "Think." In the kitchen there is a heavy thunk against the sliding glass doors. Then a second thunk. It's Scotty and Abigail, having heard something in my mother's voice to alarm them. They've come charging up the stairs and are jumping up against the sliding glass doors to see if everything's all right. Mother lets them in and tells them to cool it. She closes the door, hand still on the handle. "If Spencer did film you, I'm sure he did it only as a way to keep his focus on you."

"I'm sorry, I don't get it."

Mother gives me a warning look, as if I don't know how much longer she can put up with my stupidity. "From what I've gathered," she says, "he's been quite a ladies' man. So if he wanted to make a life with you, Sally, maybe he made the tapes to keep him company on the lonely nights you were in Connecticut." And in case I don't get that, she adds, "To keep him from getting into trouble with other women."

Dear God. Mother's telling me that maybe instead of cheating on me while he was in New York, Spencer would watch tapes of us. And what, masturbate? Oh, God, get me out of here! I am not hearing this from Mother! I'd rather bolt the country, jump from a plane without a parachute.

Scotty's making little whining noises of concern, licking my hand.

"*Sally,*" Mother says sharply.

I look at her.

"Leave the issue of who made the tape to the side, and tell me who you know would bother saturating Castleford with it. Who do you know that would know exactly who to send it to in order to humiliate not only you, but me and your brother.

I'm slow, but I'm finally getting it. "Mr. O'Hearn?"

Phillip O'Hearn, the man to whom my father gave his start in business? Phillip O'Hearn, who was directly connected to my father's death?

Since I did go on national TV to call him a murderer, I guess Mr. O'Hearn might have a grudge against me. And Mother. And Rob.

But the gall. Hadn't he done enough? He'd killed my father! Mother's husband! And so he's taking revenge on us?

"But how would he make the tape, Mother? Somebody would have had to—how could Mr. O'Hearn get into Spencer's apartment? It makes no sense."

"That's for you to find out," she tells me.

CHAPTER THIRTEEN

"Sally, it's Alexandra Waring calling," the anchorwoman says as if I might not have ever heard of her.

Buddy and I are on the outskirts of Manhattan in my Jeep.

"Hi, thanks for calling me back," I say. "I'm on my way into the city with Buddy D'Amico."

"The detective," she says, "I remember him. So what is this tape you're so concerned about?"

"It's a videotape of Spencer and me having sex in his bedroom," I say. "And before you ask, no, it was not filmed with my knowledge, no, I don't know who taped it, and no, I don't know who has sent it to everybody in Castleford, to say nothing of WSCT."

"I see," she says. "Well, listen, I have a call in to Wendy Mitchell. Give me the address of Spencer's apartment, will you? I'll have her meet you there to work on this."

"Thank you."

"I'm also sending someone to check on the executive mail," she adds. "To see if anyone sent a tape to us."

I don't say anything, just keep driving. That's all I need, my new boss watching me.

"We'll get this sorted, Sally. Just keep yourself on an

even keel. It's nothing to be ashamed of, you didn't do anything wrong."

Right. Except getting involved with Spencer in the first place.

I unlock the door to Spencer's apartment and half expect him to be there.

He's not. The apartment is empty, silent but for the traffic on Third Avenue below. Wendy and Buddy quickly move past me to the bedroom.

"There it is," Wendy says in a matter of seconds, pointing to the headboard. The bed is made of carved cherry and as a courtesy to his neighbors, is bolted to the wall. (Anyone who has ever been to bed with Spencer knows why.)

Wendy points to a dark, shaded curve in one carved flower. I bend close and she shines a penlight on it. Good Lord, there it is. A round, dark glass lens maybe a quarter-inch big.

Wendy and Buddy go to work with the tools they brought and unbolt the headboard from the wall. When they pull it away, a small, thin wire comes out of the wall. Wendy lightly knocks all around the wire and looks at Buddy.

"In the next apartment?" he says.

She nods. "I think so."

We go next door and knock. A young Black woman in warm-ups and a T-shirt opens the door. I introduce myself, saying I know it sounds odd, but we're having an electrical problem next door and could we look at her side of the wall?

She looks us over, no doubt speculating on the odds that we're a classic New York robbery gang.

"You can call down to the front desk and check us out," I offer. "I'm Spencer's girlfriend." I nearly choke on the words. "The guy next door. I'm registered at the desk and everything."

She frowns slightly. "Did he come back finally? That cat's been meowing for days."

"I took the cat home late on Friday," I say, hoping this will help our credentials.

"Where do you have to look?" she asks next.

"On that side of the wall," I explain, pointing toward Spencer's apartment. "About four feet out from the window."

She turns around to look over her shoulder. "But my mirror's there."

"We'll move it out and then back," I offer.

"It's not that kind of mirror," she says. She pulls the door open wide and leads us in. "Come see yourself."

"Oh, no," I say, walking into the woman's living room. The wall next to Spencer's bedroom is covered with mirrors. On top of that, a ballet bar has been installed.

"Have you lived here long?" Wendy says.

"Four months."

"Did you put the mirrors up?"

"They were put up for me," she explains, "before I arrived here from Chicago."

Wendy and Buddy are examining the mirror panels at close range, no doubt trying to figure out if we can remove some of them.

"Are you dancing here in New York?" I ask politely.

"I'm on a special fellowship with Julliard," she says modestly.

"Wow. And Julliard provided you with this apartment?"

She thinks a moment. "I think it's a private deal. I think some company donated it for the fellowship. It's only for a year and a half."

"Ah," I say, nodding, as Buddy walks back to us.

"Do you know what company donated it?" he asks.

She shakes her head. "The building might know. I don't even see the rent bills."

Buddy is taking out his wallet. He opens it to show the woman his Castleford Police Department badge and credentials. She looks at them and hands them back. "Aren't you a little far from home?"

He smiles. "Yes. But we have a police matter that involves the apartment next door. Actually, that involves the wall between this apartment and that one. And I want to ask you, as a personal favor, if you would allow us to remove a panel of the mirror. Perhaps two."

"I promise we'll replace it exactly the way it was," I say quickly.

"We have to see what's back there first," Buddy cautions me.

The dancer squints, swinging a hip to one side and planting a hand on it. "You think you're gonna pull my bar out?"

"Well," Buddy says, looking over his shoulder at it.

"I don't think you should do anything until I get the super up here," the dancer wisely announces, walking over to the door to pick up the in-house telephone. She lifts the receiver and buzzes the desk. "No offense," she says to us, "but it's not my apartment. I can't just go tearing it apart."

It's the super's day off. The building manager, however, who evidently lives in the building, comes racing up to find out who we are and what we're doing. Buddy takes her by the elbow to a corner of the room to quietly talk to her. Still, I can hear her saying, "No. Absolutely not. It's not your property. It's not her property."

"Well whose property is it?" Wendy finally asks. "Can't we call them?"

"No," the manager says. She has decided to hate us, I think.

"Nobody owns this apartment, do they?" Wendy continues. "They're just renting, right?" She looks at the dancer. "You've been here four months and you say the whole lease for you is only eighteen, so..." She looks back to the manager. "So my guess is, someone leased this apartment for two years, but used it only two months before fixing it up and offering it to Julliard." She smiles. "And you're upset," she says to the building manager, "because no one asked for authorization to install all these mirrors and the bar, aren't you?"

"And who the hell are you?" the building manager demands.

"Wendy Mitchell, head of security for the DBS television network here in New York. And I'm one step away from calling the police and a news crew and getting them over here to find out how it is that your building has been participating in a felony."

The manager looks downright astonished. Then her face twists up and she cries *"Felony!"* and immediately I have to wonder what the parent company who owns this building might have to hide.

It goes on like this for a while, Wendy promising horrible things, the manager saying, go ahead, so what? until Buddy asks me to call 911 on my cell phone.

"All right, wait a minute!" the building manager says, relenting. But first things first, she has to call down to the front desk to make sure I've been signed in with Spencer's apartment in the first place. Yes? Yes. A minute later the super, who is supposedly nowhere to be found, has arrived, by which time the dancer has made herself some tea and is locking herself in the bedroom.

The manager finally agrees to let us, with the super's assistance, take down the end of the bar and two panels of mirrors to see what's behind it, but first, of course, all three of us have to go to the management office to sign a bunch of damage waivers and promises to repair.

Actually, the waivers were a smart idea because back in the apartment Buddy and the super find out that the panels are not only bolted into the wall, but are glued as well, so when they try to pry off the first panel, it pulls part of the plaster off and then breaks in half.

"Oh, no!" we hear behind us. It's the dancer; she slams the bedroom door closed.

It *is* a mess and getting worse. More plaster falls. The second mirror panel comes off, pulling another huge wedge of plaster out, exposing a steel beam. Wendy is on her cell phone to DBS, telling maintenance to get a crew over here, fast.

They have to get a third panel off, which, mercifully, doesn't break, and when this one comes down we can see inside the wall. Next to another steel beam there are two thin wires hanging down, at the end of which is some sort of a socket. Wearing plastic gloves, Wendy picks up the end to look. "Plugs into a video camera." She looks at Buddy. "It was definitely filmed from *this* apartment."

"Oh, shit, what's this, what do you mean 'filmed'?" wails the manager.

"We definitely need to have a chat about who leased this apartment and when," Wendy says.

"Maybe you're out of your mind," the manager suggests.

"Well," Buddy says, "it's as we thought—a felony. I guess I better call in the locals."

"All right, all right," the building manager says, giving up. The super stays in the apartment while the three of us accompany her to the management office.

The apartment was leased by a Peter Reingold, a financial analyst who, it says on his application, commutes between L.A. and New York. The rent was paid for two years, in advance, by his company, Valcromiter Technologies. A quick security check through DBS turns up that there is no such thing as Valcromiter Technologies (the number belongs to a very irate lady named Mrs. Spiñola), but there is a Peter Reingold, and yes, it is his social security number and address on the application. But Wendy reports that he does not know anything about any apartment in New York because he hasn't been east of Denver in the four years since the car accident that left him in a wheelchair.

Buddy and I ride home to Castleford, leaving Wendy at the apartment with a crew dispatched from DBS to fix the dancer's wall.

"When we find out who rented the apartment," Buddy says, "we'll know who made the tape." He looks over at me. "Any possibility Spencer rented that apartment as well?"

I give an ironic laugh. "No way. He couldn't even make the rent on the one he's got."

"You're kidding. I thought he made a lot of money."

I feel a pang of disloyalty to Spencer, telling Buddy his business. "He doesn't manage his money well."

After a while, Buddy says, "I'll find out who's behind this, Sally, I swear."

"I hope so" is all I can say.

It's long after dark when I drop Buddy off at his house. Then I head for Mother's. The lights are not on. I pull up, hear the dogs barking inside and wonder where Mother has gone. A motion detector turns the light on over the front door. I walk up and let myself in, petting the dogs as I do. When I close the door behind me, I nearly jump out of my skin when Mother says, "You're back."

"Golly, Mother," I mutter, turning on the light.

Mother is blinking against the light. In her hand is a highball glass.

Mother never drinks.

But she's drinking now.

I walk over and go down on one knee next to her chair. "I'm so sorry."

She looks at me as if she doesn't quite recognize me. And then she smiles slightly, putting her glass in her left hand so she can touch my hair lightly with her right. "You're my baby," she tells me.

A tear falls on my cheek.

"No one should be able to hurt my baby."

"I'm going to get to the bottom of this," I murmur.

She frowns. "Phillip did this. I know he did. He killed your father and now he's coming after you." Her chin trembles slightly. "Well I won't stand for it, Sally, I won't!" She puts her glass down on the table with a thump. "I won't." She gets up and goes into the kitchen.

"Mother, please, you're tired."

She picks up the telephone and starts to dial.

"Mother, no!"

"I'm going to tell him I'm going to have him killed, see how he likes it," she declares.

I grab the phone from her; she resists. I get it and slam down the receiver. "Mother, no! You're drunk!"

Her mouth falls open, stunned at the tone of my voice. And then her face crumbles and she falls to my shoulder, weeping as though her heart is breaking.

And I have no doubt but that it is.

CHAPTER FOURTEEN

Mother is better this morning. I stayed over and she's up and at it like nothing happened last night. She drives off to school and I am off to my house to shower and change and throw some clothes together. It's Monday and I've got to get into DBS by noon.

While I'm packing, I call Rob to see if he can come home.

"It's high ski season," he tells me. "Unless Mother's on her deathbed or something, I just can't leave. What is going on?"

I tell him. And he's suitably freaked out. "What the hell are you going to do about this!" he demands of me. "You can't go into New York and leave Mom there when everybody in town's watching you fuck on a video!"

Somehow I catch on my little brother is not going to be a big help with this. I try to explain that I am in the process of negotiating a job at DBS News and need to be in New York, to which Rob replies, "What are you going to be, Sis, the next Jessica Savitch or something? Have your messy personal life make the bestseller list after you're dead?"

I count to three before answering and borrow a line from

Spencer's repertoire. "How do you know who Jessica Savitch is? There's no comic book edition about her life yet."

"Ha, ha. Listen, Sally, take a piece of advice. Cool it with these hip lovers of yours?"

We hang up, both of us angry.

I steel myself to make the call I wish I didn't have to. To Mother's beau, Mack Cleary. I catch him just as he's leaving for campus.

I like Mack very much, don't get me wrong. It's just so strange after all these years to think that Mother is not only seeing, but having sex with a mild-mannered retired scientist who's teaching at Wesleyan. She's my *mother.*

I tell him about my job prospects at DBS. "So I've got to go into the city," I explain, "but I don't want to leave Mother alone."

"Is this about the tape?" he says.

"Oh, you know," I say.

There is a pause. "I was sent a tape, too, Sally. Of course as soon as I realized what it was..."

I don't hear much else for a while. Finally I come back to my senses. "Did you tell Mother?"

"Of course not. But she called me yesterday and told me about the other tapes. To tell you the truth, Sally, I've been mustering up the nerve to call you." Pause. "It's not the kind of phone call I want to make to you. Or anyone. I simply mean—gosh, Sally, your mother thinks the world of you and I do, too, and please just tell me what I can do to help."

It's interesting, I think, that Mack doesn't ask me for an explanation of where the tape came from. I give him one, anyway, briefly covering the facts that someone had illegally taped Spencer and me, and someone had duplicated the highlights and sent them to basically every person or organization that knew my family well.

There is a very sad, tired-sounding voice coming from

Mack. "I don't suppose I need to ask who would do such a thing to hurt you."

"Mother is convinced it's Phillip O'Hearn."

"She might very well be right. Oh, Sally, I'm so sorry. No wonder your mother—" He pauses. "There must be something I can do."

"Mother just left for school but I know she's not herself. And I've got to go into New York. I mean, I could stay—"

"Say no more. I will simply come over this evening whether your mother likes it or not." He hesitates. "She shouldn't have shut me out on this, Sally."

"It's difficult for her. Because, you know, it's about Daddy." I wince. Come on, Sally, be generous. "You know she loves you, Mack. But it's that lack of resolution where my father's death is concerned that makes her put a wall up."

While I'm talking to Mack, the damn call-waiting starts clicking (my telephone company keeps imposing it on me in the misguided hope I will someday want it) and I get off with Mack to find myself talking to the New York Police Department about Spencer. Kate Weston at Bennett, Fitzallen & Coe has filed an official missing person's report.

I tell them everything, give them names, dates, addresses and the fact that for some reason they will not divulge, the LAPD thinks Spencer went to Honolulu, although DBS security has checked the passenger lists and has not found his name.

After I finish with the police, I run back to Mother's with Samantha in a carrying case (poor Mother, it's getting like a zoo over here), let the dogs go out for a quick run, make sure they won't kill the cat when they come in (fortunately, they know Samantha and merely lick her head a couple of times and leave her alone), and leave a note for Mother that Mack is swinging by this evening. I put a key under the flowerpot out back for the handyman who comes in the middle of the day to let the dogs out. I grab a cardboard box from Mother's shed and hop into the Jeep.

I waltz into editorial at the *Herald-American* and people turn to look at me. I try to be brave and smile, carrying my box into my cubicle. I put it down on my chair and start putting my personal things into it. I don't worry about my Rolodex of names and numbers. (Journalism 101: duplicate your new Rolodex information weekly.)

Someone is standing behind me. "Oh, no. You're not quitting, are you?"

I recognize my colleague Joe Bix's voice.

I nod. "I think maybe I've had it in this town." I turn around. "Can you imagine anyone being able to keep a straight face while I'm interviewing them?"

Joe looks so sad. "Nobody watched it except Al."

"Yeah, right," I say, picking up a picture of Mother, Rob and me and packing it away.

"I didn't," he says quietly.

I straighten up to look at him. "Thanks, Joe." I take a couple of steps over to give him a hug. He's not the best writer in the world, but he improves daily. Perhaps more important, Joe is finally learning to stand up to Al, which may or may not have something to do with Joe recently learning that the stock options his wife earned at her job at Priceline.com in Norwalk are now worth in excess of five hundred thousand dollars.

"Sally, I can't stay here without you," he sighs, hugging me back.

"Sure you can," I tell him.

After a moment, we release each other. A little crowd is gathering around my cubicle. "You can't quit, Sally," someone says. "We'll die."

"So who do you think did it?" Joe asks me.

I glance at the crew. "Who do you guys think?"

"O'Hearn," they say almost simultaneously.

"That's what my mother thinks, too." I turn my back so I won't start crying and collect my little windup toys off the bookcase, and then take down the old *Oxford* dictionary that had belonged to my father.

"Your poor mom," Joe murmurs.

"Tell me about it." I continue to pack. When I'm finished, I turn around to find most of Editorial still standing there with long faces. "I'll be seeing you," I promise.

Suddenly people are kissing and hugging me, while I'm just standing there like an idiot with my arms around the box.

"Stay in touch, Sally. We'll miss you."

"Call me for lunch!"

Another reporter elbows his way through. "I think Al may have made a dupe," he whispers. "I saw him take the tape out Saturday and he came back with a bag from Vackett's." Vackett's was a nearby video production service.

"Where is he?" I ask.

"In his office," people say eagerly, hoping for a scene. I don't blame them. The frustration around here has to get vented somehow. Most family-owned papers these days have the good sense to put talented editorial directors at the helm, while the owners choose the best-suited family member to establish the general stance of the paper and oversee it as a business. Not the *Herald-American*. One has the vision of the Royce siblings pulling each other's hair out behind closed doors at their annual meetings, resulting in the one with the least hair, Al, winning his way to call himself editor.

I bring my box down the hall and set it down outside Al Royce's office door. Then I knock and go in. He is on the phone and looks startled. "Gotta go," he says, hanging up. And then he just sits there, looking at me as if I'm a ghost.

"Sally," he finally says. His face is blushing red and I

know he has watched that tape, all right, probably more than once.

"Suffice it to say, Al, I think it's best if I move on."

Now he is beet red and doesn't seem to know what to say.

"You got a tape," I prompt.

Another silence. And then he nods.

"I'm going to find out who did this," I tell him. "And not only am I going to ruin him, but I am going to destroy him. Do you understand that?"

Sputter. "I had nothing to do with this!"

I take a wild shot. "What about what you said about me? I heard what you said about me, Al," I lie.

"About the sock? I meant it as a compliment," he says quickly. "You know, a kind of joke, a compliment. You know how we fight all the time, I just meant you were very attractive and if I put a sock in your mouth you'd be the ideal woman."

"I see," I say, walking closer to the desk. "So are you going to put anything in the paper about this?"

"Absolutely not," he says quickly. "I would never do that to your mother."

At least on this point I believe him. He's been in love with Mother for about thirty years, and that is the only reason we have ever been able to work together. Call it a transfer of affection. But I see something new in his eyes where I am concerned and it makes me sick.

"Anyway, it's best I move on," I say.

"It's been coming. You've got bigger fish to fry."

"Maybe." Right now I feel like a call girl without a phone. "Listen, Al, there is something else I want to let you in on."

His head cocks to the side, but his eyes travel down to my mouth briefly and inwardly I shudder. "What's that, babe?"

Babe?

"If anyone gets in between me and Phillip O'Hearn they're gonna feel it."

Al and Phil are on the golf committee together at the Castleford Country Club. For years the erudite Royce family had nothing to do with the déclassé O'Hearns, but things have changed over the years. The Royce fortune is not what it once was and the O'Hearn fortunes have skyrocketed. I have no doubt that it has been an extremely expensive proposition for the O'Hearns, but at least this one Royce family member, Al, has welcomed them to the city's small ranks of golf-playing philanthropists.

Al's mouth presses into a line and he nods once. "You may be right. It could have been Phil. He was really pissed about that DBS story."

"Do you have the envelope the tape came in?" I ask, slowly circling his desk.

"Buddy D'Amico already stopped by for it." He swallows, his eyes flitting to my chest and then away, embarrassed, nervous.

"He took just the envelope?" I ask, now even with him behind the desk.

"And the tape," he says quickly. "And the tape," he says again.

"What about the duplicate? Did you give him that?"

He tries to meet my eye. "I don't know anything about any duplicate."

"Where is it, Al?" I say, feigning tiredness when what I feel is rage.

"I don't know anything about any duplicate," he insists.

I lean slightly forward and whisper, "And I don't know anything about you screwing the advocate from the Libertarian Town Committee, either."

He looks positively gray. "What the hell are you talking about?"

I smile, slowly descending to squat next to his right-hand set of desk drawers. Eyes still on him, I ask, "Do you want specific times and places?" With my right hand I softly knock on the lowest drawer. "Is it perhaps in here?"

He swallows, pissed, maybe a little unnerved that I might somehow have been in this particular locked drawer before. (Which I have; I merely watched over the shoulder of Al's sister a month or so ago when she broke into his desk to look for a copy of their mother's will.) He leans over and yanks the drawer open. Next to a bottle of Johnny Walker Black, a fireproof deed box and a pearl-handled Colt, there is a black plastic videotape case with a Vackett's sticker on it.

I reach in, hand first hesitating over the gun; I raise my eyes smiling, daring him to move. Then I reach down and take the tape. "Thanks," I tell him, standing up.

"Let me know if you need a reference," he says, and I realize, with enormous satisfaction, that Alfred Royce Jr. is actually frightened of me. I hope word travels fast.

I drop Al's extra copy of *Sally Does Spencer* with Buddy, and am on the road to New York at the perfect time of ten-fifteen, when traffic patterns are relatively light. I've got a lot on my mind. Too much. I have to fight to concentrate on driving.

I'm not sure what I've witnessed with Mother last night, whether it was a meltdown of some kind, and whether this is good or bad. Is Mother finally allowing herself to express the anger she must feel toward Phillip O'Hearn? Is this part of a healing process? Or is it a whole new rage that she cannot deal with? And if the latter is the case, that it is a new rage, how might it manifest itself in her otherwise peaceful life?

I hope it does not come between her and Mack. When it comes to Daddy, Mother can get distant.

No, Mack will help her through this.

I hope she lets him.

In the meantime, I know I've got to tell Doug about the tape. He has to know, it's his hometown, too.

I pick up my cell phone to finish this whole morbid exercise.

"I don't even know how to tell you this," I begin, holding the wireless phone between my shoulder and chin while I change lanes on the Merritt.

"You don't have to," Doug says. "My boss got a videotape on Friday."

My foot goes off the accelerator and I feel close to retching. Finally, "I don't know what to say."

"Don't worry, I have no intentions of watching it."

Thank God.

"But I'm just about the only one in the office who hasn't," he adds.

"Oh, God," I mutter, glancing over my shoulder to try to get over to the right lane. I can't drive. Once I'm safely exiting the Parkway, I sigh. "I'm so sorry, Doug."

"Oh, I don't know, everyone seems to think I should go out with you again."

I don't know if he's trying to be funny or trying to kill me. What does it matter, it feels the same.

I pull over on the side of the road.

"You must have had to look long and hard to find such a creep to go out with," he says.

"I don't think it was Spencer who filmed it," I say quietly.

"Oh, great, you had other people film you having sex?"

His anger is starting to ignite mine. "No," I say with exaggerated care. "As a matter of fact, I might find out today who leased the apartment next door to spy on Spencer's apartment—"

"Oh, come on, Sally, the guy's a pervert, admit it!"

"Mother, and even Al Royce, seem to think it might be Phillip O'Hearn."

Silence. And then, "How the hell would Phillip O'Hearn know how to do it?"

"Well he certainly would know who to send the tapes to, wouldn't he?"

Silence. He's thinking. "Possibly."

"So let me ask you, Mr. Assistant D.A.," I say, "has Mr. O'Hearn broken any laws by sending that tape everywhere?"

"Depends if the tapes were made without your knowledge—"

"Oh, for God's sake, Doug, cut it out!" I snap. "It was not done with my knowledge or any remote concept of permission!"

"Well, if he knew that, then yes, he has broken the law. Because the tapes were made illegally and he knowingly distributed them. But if he didn't know they were illegal—if he was told that you and your boyfriend taped them for your own pleasure—"

I resist yelling.

"Then maybe there's a violation of privacy—"

"Oh, *maybe*," I say with a sneer.

"Hey, look, it's your problem. I'm just answering the question."

I am half a step away from telling Doug that maybe he should watch the tape because he might learn a few things that would have kept his ex-wife and girlfriend in line over the years.

But of course I won't ever say anything like that. Because, well, I love him. And I've completely humiliated him. I can't even imagine the anger and jealousy and outrage he must feel over having his colleagues see another man making love to the woman who was supposed to have belonged to him.

When I arrive at DBS the receptionist tells me that Cassy Cochran, president of DBS, wants to see me as soon as I come in. When I get up to her office, her long-time assistant, Chi Chi, jumps up, saying, "Go right in, she's waiting," and then she opens the door calling, "Here's Sally, I'm calling Wendy."

Cassy Cochran is sitting on a couch reading some kind of report. The office is gorgeous, one full wall of glass, floor to ceiling, looking out onto the park that exists in the middle of the U shape that is the West End Broadcasting Center. Beyond is the sparkling Hudson River.

"Hi," Cassy says, closing the report. "Hang on a sec." She makes some notes on a legal pad and gets up to walk over to her desk, where she puts the folder in a drawer.

Cassy is rather famous in the world of television, not only for being the first woman president of a network, but because she is blessed with great blond, blue-eyed beauty that anyone else would have used for a career in front of the camera. She is a complicated person. She has also been my meal ticket of late. An assignment to do a profile of her for *Expectations* magazine is what gave me the opportunity to work with DBS in the first place.

The fact that one of the most loved people in broadcasting had a bombshell secret in her past would have made headlines, had I written the article as it had been assigned. But I chose not to for a number of reasons, the foremost of which was that I too came to see Cassy as a figure of goodness in this miserable world, a person who did not deserve more pain than life had already inflicted on her.

The editor of *Expectations* magazine, Verity Rhodes, however, was furious I didn't write the exposé as she had envisioned. The whole assignment had been a setup, a plan to use some bumpkin from central Connecticut (me) as a means of hurting not only Cassy, but her husband, Jackson Darenbrook. Darenbrook (as in Darenbrook Broadcasting Company) is the CEO of the family media empire and he is not without enemies. It has been my experience, however, that enemies of Jackson or Cassy are individuals I would do almost anything to avoid. As Mother would tactfully say, "They're just not our kind of people."

Cassy closes the desk drawer and comes back around her desk. "You've certainly had a time of it, my friend."

"Which current hell are we talking about?" I ask her.

She offers a sympathetic smile, gesturing for me to sit. I sit on the couch, she takes a chair. "Alexandra told me about the video. I'm sorry."

"Thanks. I'm sorry, too."

"Alexandra was sent one as well, you know."

I can't help but grimace. "So does she think I'm telegenic?"

Cassy doesn't laugh and nor do I. It was a stupid thing to say but I feel so stupid, so vulnerable, so utterly a mess. The idea that my prospective boss, a lesbian one at that, has been watching me have sex with Spencer doesn't particularly thrill me. It's a hell of a résumé.

"I wanted to tell you," Cassy says, "that I'm putting Wendy Mitchell on this full-time until we get the straight dope on what happened. And who's behind it."

"Thank you."

"Um," she continues, twisting her mouth a bit before speaking, "as soon as Wendy told me about it, and the timing on all this, I..." Her eyes meet mine. "I couldn't help but wonder if this doesn't have something to do with Verity."

Verity. Verity Rhodes. It was through Verity, incidentally, that I first met Spencer. Verity introduced us. And then Spencer and I got involved—

"Wendy, great, you're here," Cassy says, waving the security woman into a seat. "I was just telling Sally that you're going to work on this full-time until we figure out what happened."

"I'm getting a pretty good idea already," Wendy says. "First off, I've got the dates on the apartment all laid out.

And according to the leasing office, Sally, not only was the apartment next door to Spencer Hawes's apartment leased two months before you even met him, the previous tenant was paid almost forty thousand to move to another apartment in the building." She looks at me. "So the first question is, who do we know that's got that kind of money?"

"Certainly not Spencer," I say.

"No?" Cassy asks.

I shake my head. "No."

"But he must do very well," Cassy says, frowning.

"It's a long story," I say, waving it off, "but trust me, the money did not come from Spencer."

"Well that's interesting," Wendy continues, looking at her notes, "because according to Julliard, the eighteen-month lease they gave the dance student so she could live there rent-free as part of her fellowship was donated by the publishing house of Bennett, Fitzallen & Coe." She looks at me. "Isn't that the publishing house Spencer works for?"

"Yes, but—"

She holds up a hand. "Hang on. I called the editor-in-chief, Kate Weston, to check this out with her, and so her office referred me to Corporate, and not even an hour ago a spokesman assured me the firm hasn't the slightest knowledge of any such arrangement. In fact he said, and I quote, 'No offense to the world of dance, but if we were going to give an apartment away, we would have given it to a deserving young person in book publishing.'"

Cassy looks at me. "Are you getting the same feeling I am, Sally?"

I shake my head. "No, I'm sorry. I must be on overload."

"If we're looking for someone who would rent an apartment next door to Spencer to spy on him—before he even ever met you—I think we need to look at who was in Spencer's life at that time." When I don't speak, she continues. "Who would treat forty thousand dollars as small change, if it meant finding out who was sleeping with Spencer?"

"Verity?" I say.

"Corbett," she says. Corbett Schroeder, Verity Rhodes's husband, an older, powerful, vindictive, immensely wealthy corporate raider who chose Verity as his second wife.

Wendy looks confused. "Verity Rhodes? Corbett Schroeder? I don't get the connection with Spencer Hawes."

Cassy calmly turns to her. "Corbett's wife, Verity Rhodes, was having an affair with Spencer."

"Before he met me," I add.

Wendy looks rather astonished. "But wasn't she the one who assigned you to write about Cassy for her magazine?"

I nod.

"You started a relationship with a guy who was having an affair with your boss at *Expectations?*" She lets out a small whoop. "Girl, you're a lot more interesting than I thought!"

"Enough, Wendy," Cassy says out of the side of her mouth.

I'm still trying to think this possibility through, that Corbett had someone filming Spencer's bedroom. Would Corbett do something like that?

Yes!

But why? There was the child, Corbett and Verity's son. Would Corbett use the tape against Verity in a divorce? Or to prevent one? Or to get custody?

And then I met Spencer, and within days there I was making love in the same bedroom where Spencer and Verity had had so many afternoon trysts.

Or could Verity have set up the surveillance next door? To make sure he wasn't cheating on her?

No. She wouldn't. Verity is too proud—too cocksure of herself. I remember when she found out about me and

Spencer. Her reaction was not so much *How could he?* as it was *How could I have misread this man's taste so badly?*

No. It had to have been Corbett. He was well known for his corporate and industrial espionage. It would have been a snap for him to redirect some of his resources to keeping tabs on his glamorous wife.

Oh, brother. So this is what life is like for those who act compulsively, who get themselves into one mess after another. Like me.

"Could you update Buddy D'Amico?" I ask Wendy. "He's working on the Castleford end of it, trying to find out who sent the tapes to everybody." I look to Cassy. "Popular opinion has it the local distribution of my film debut came from Phillip O'Hearn."

Cassy's face grows dark. "The same man who...? Your father's friend? I mean, former friend?"

"Yep, that's the one. Mother's convinced of it."

"Good Lord," Cassy says.

There is a rapid-fire knock and then the door bursts open and Will Rafferty appears. "Sorry, Cass," he says in a rush, "but we've got problems." His eyes move to me. "You've got to come with me to Legal. Now."

"Why?" Cassy says. "What's happened?"

"NYPD's here. Remember that guy who came in with Sally, Lilliana Martin's boyfriend?"

"Cliff," I say. "Cliff Yarlen. What about him?"

"You were the last person seen with him. When Alexandra took you out to the airport last Wednesday night. The cops are grilling her right now, wanting to know why you guys went out to JFK and if you know where Yarlen was going."

"He was going back to Los Angeles," I say. "He was waiting for the weather to clear." And then I have a thought. "Oh, no, don't tell me he's missing now."

"Worse. He's dead," Will says. "Somebody shot him

twice in the back of the head with a .22. They found his body in an air-cargo crate at JFK this morning."

I look down, trying to take a breath.

"Alexandra wants you to get one of the lawyers and go downstairs and talk to the cops," he says, coming over to literally take me by the arm and pull me toward the door. Before I can assume this plan was formed out of concern for my welfare, he adds, "If I can get the cops tied up with you, then maybe I can get Alexandra on the air to break the story."

Ah, such is the life of news.

PART
THREE

CHAPTER FIFTEEN

The police won't let me leave New York City for two days because I am, right now, the only suspect in the murder of Cliff Yarlen. They don't have a motive, nor do they have the weapon, but they can place me at JFK with Cliff. They also know that Cliff was the last person to see Spencer Hawes outside Lilliana's house in L.A., and that Spencer is missing. And now that Cliff is dead, that makes me the last person to have seen Spencer alive as well. To top it off, I am supposedly Spencer's *ex*-girlfriend, and so they are very curious as to why I have been paying his bills. "To delay the search for him?" one police detective offers. They're also fascinated that I recruited a Connecticut cop to tear down the wall of the apartment next door to Spencer's.

I was amazed they identified me so quickly as the last person to see Cliff, but the driver told them he had driven me and Cliff to Manhattan earlier in the day and my description fit the one given by Cliff's attendant at the Admiral's Club.

For two days now headlines on the East Coast and West Coast have been screaming mob hit. For two days NYPD has been combing my record to see if I have mob ties, or if I have ever been part of a blackmail sex racket, since I seem to be featured on a tape that's been circulated all over central Connecticut.

The management at DBS has been wonderful. Cassy Cochran bumped me up to a small suite at the Sheraton; her husband, Jackson Darenbrook, has made sure a crackerjack lawyer has been present every time I've talked to the police; and Alexandra has tried her best to suppress her irritation that she can't get me off to Los Angeles. Lilliana Martin has surfaced and an ABC camera crew taped a brief statement from her. Hiding behind dark sunglasses, with a scarf tied over her head, Lilliana looked as though she had been caught leaving a liquor store. "He was a fine person," she said, voice sounding hoarse. "I am deeply saddened, and I have nothing more to say."

Alexandra hit the roof that ABC scooped us. "I thought no one could find her!" she ranted in the newsroom. "Looks to me like they simply walked up to her in the middle of the street! Why are we the only ones who don't know where she lives?" I have described Lilliana's house in Cold Water Canyon to our L.A. affiliate until I'm blue in the face, but they insist that Lilliana does not own, rent, nor is she staying in any house in the canyon. "Knock on the damn doors and look for her!" I yell, getting into the current spirit of the newsroom.

Sources at LAPD say Lilliana was interviewed by them in her lawyer's office in Century City and they don't know where she is staying. The lawyer's office is not commenting on anything and her agent has run away somewhere, no doubt in fear.

"As soon as you can leave," Alexandra instructs me, "I want you to go to California and find Lilliana and lock up an interview with her. It doesn't have to be now. It can be later, but you've got to talk her into talking to us first. When you've found her, let me know, and I will fly out to see her myself. But it seems to me, she likes you, Sally, so... Play on it."

Play on *what?* I want to yell at her. Every guy that goes near this woman disappears, and so I'm supposed to do what, exactly?

But who are any of us kidding? Bottom line, all one journalist has over another is his record and his charm. And the fact is, the most charming one is the one who usually gets the exclusive.

I try to be my most charming to the police, pleading my case that perhaps I can be of help if only they'll let me go to Los Angeles.

The police give me their bottom line. I cannot leave until midnight Tuesday night, by which time they will have absolute confirmation from a vacationing Riga Royale desk clerk that at one-thirty in the morning I was checking into the hotel and not shooting Cliff Yarlen in the back of the head at JFK. Since there are no commercial flights to Los Angeles available after midnight, I find myself being chauffeured to Teeterborough to board the private jet of Darenbrook Communications. We literally, I kid you not, sit on the tarmac until midnight, at which time a transit cop signals we can leave.

I've got my instructions. Find Lilliana. Call into NYPD every day at noon. And, if I have time, figure out what happened to Cliff and find Spencer.

I spend most of the flight reading up on Cliff Yarlen and Lilliana Martin.

"Yes, I know that of course Attorney Sedorg can't reveal Lilliana's whereabouts," I say at nine o'clock to the legal secretary. After arriving at my hotel room in Century City sometime after 3:00 a.m., I'd finally slept—for five whole hours. "I just need to leave a message for Lilliana—to tell her where she can find me. Because I'm here in Los Angeles and she thinks I'm in New York."

The secretary has, no doubt, taken hundreds of these kinds of messages since the actress went into hiding.

"She'll want to see me," I tell her.

"Uh-huh," she says.

"Just make sure you get the number right," I stress to her, "and that she understands I'm here, in Los Angeles, and will come over as soon as she wants to see me."

That seems to get to her. "Who are you with?"

"I am a personal friend," I say firmly.

"All right," she agrees. "If she calls in, I'll give her the message."

That done, I jump in the shower, take some care with my hair and makeup and don a simple black Donna Karan dress I pulled from DBS wardrobe. I add Grandmother Harrington's strand of pearls and pearl earrings and I am respectability itself.

While back East Cliff's family is waiting for the release of his body to hold a proper funeral, this morning his West Coast union brethren are holding a memorial service in his honor.

I am familiar with the location of the service, a large New Age pseudo-Protestant church in Beverly Hills that caters to disenfranchised Christians and Jews who have definitely lost the way. In other words, it's an "in" house of worship that plays down the Christ angle and raises a lot of money for liberal causes.

At any rate, the church is on Santa Monica Boulevard and I have to drive through a barricade where a couple of press people are hanging out. Near the front of the church, a car valet takes my rental away and two large men in black suits walk over. One holds a clipboard. "Name?"

"Sally Harrington," I say. "You won't find it on the list because I just got in from New York. I was with Cliff the day he died, and the police only relented last night to let me come to the service."

The two men step away to confer, looking at me. I open my bag and take out a newspaper clipping from the *New York Post*. I unfold it and point. "See?" I say, pointing to my name.

One guy examines the article while the other glares at me as if I'm the one who no doubt murdered Cliff.

Finally, they let me go in.

The church is nearly full and I take a seat in the very last pew. There is an enormous photograph of Cliff on the altar, resting on a velvet-covered easel. A minister opens the service with some prayers and I remember from the DBS notes that Cliff was brought up Catholic and spent the first twelve years of education at a parochial school in Brooklyn. I wonder if he ever came to this church, or did the union pick it because they knew this institution wouldn't discriminate against the mob.

A number of union men get up to say nice things about Cliff, and after a while it seems odd to me that there doesn't seem to be any spokesperson for his family. I can't see if Lilliana is here or not.

The most touching fellow is an older man who is suffering from cancer, who explains how Cliff personally straightened out his health benefits and saved the quality of life for his family.

There are not many women here, but those who are, are crying. I'm not.

I often wonder if the fact my father was killed while I was a child has, in some way, made me less affected by funerals. We're all going to die and I learned that lesson early on and firsthand. It's easy for people to say *We're all going to die,* but much harder for them to really get it. *I can die at any moment NOW.*

Since I link my own death with a chance to see my father again, death does not feel like the worst thing that can happen to me. I believe the spirit goes on to a new phase of existence somewhere; yes, I believe Cliff Yarlen has moved on; and yes, I believe in the prayers I said after I learned Cliff had been murdered, asking God to watch over him.

Self-deluded or not, that's how I feel, and I trust that Cliff is in a better place.

Cliff's past, taken in the right context, I suppose, is rather straightforward. I have read the available background information on him so many times I now practically know it by heart.

Clifford Mark Arlenetta was born in Bensonhurst, Brooklyn, in April 1962. He was the fourth of five children. His mother, Gina, was a housewife, his father, Joseph, an executive with a hotel linen-supply business controlled by the Genovese crime family. Cliff's maternal grandfather, Rocky Presario, was a boss in the Gambino crime family.

Cliff graduated from high school and earned an accounting degree from St. John's University in the name of Clifford M. Yarlen. He received his CPA certification for New York State and earned an MBA degree at night at NYU while working as an accountant for a midtown Manhattan hotel. He married once, at twenty-two, but the marriage was annulled the following year. He had no children.

Cliff's father was sent to prison in 1980 on murder and racketeering charges in connection with his attempted "corporate expansion" into Atlantic City. Ironically, it was Joe's own brother-in-law, Frankie Presario, who turned state's evidence against Arlenetta, before disappearing into the federal witness protection program. Cliff's oldest brother, Nick, took over for his father in absentia. In 1986 Joe died of a heart attack in prison. In 1988 Cliff was brought into his maternal grandfather's arena of northern New Jersey to serve as chief accountant for the American Federation of

Technology Workers, a new union that was formed after the breakup of a major telephone company.

Cliff Yarlen had no police record. His résumé spelled out that he was simply a well-spoken, well-educated third-generation mafioso. His oldest brother, Nicky Arlenetta, has a record a mile long and the feds have been after him, to no avail, for over a decade.

In 1993, Rocky Presario's baby, the AFTW Union, got a foothold in the Silicon Valley in California and began to grow. In 1996 the union reached Los Angeles, but faltered when it tried to recruit members from other unions. In 1998 Cliff Yarlen was sent to Southern California. Although he was never a technology worker, his distinguished service to the union as head accountant allowed him to run, and win, election as AFTW president. In 1999 he announced the union's first major Hollywood contract, with a major studio heavily invested in special effects, animation and computer merchandising: Monarch Studios.

Cliff's profile soared. So did the stature and caliber of the union membership. His crowning achievement, it appears, was to have been dating Lilliana Martin at a time her star was ascending at Monarch, too. Brooklyn boy makes good, dates famous actress from the Midwest.

The man next to me has taken off his glasses to mop his face with a handkerchief. It is getting very warm in this church.

On the altar, they have saved the biggest gun for the last speaker and my eyes widen in surprise when I recognize my old admirer from the Malcolm Kieloff party, Jonathan Small.

"My name is Jonathan Small," he says, "and I am the production head at Monarch Studios." This announcement causes a few whispers in the congregation. "I'm here today to pay tribute to my very good friend and colleague, Cliff Yarlen."

For a studio guy, he doesn't seem to know much about pacing his presentation, because within minutes he's got us all bored to tears. He's lecturing us on progress and innovation and "men among men." I haven't a clue what Jonathan is talking about. "The goodness of progress and re-creation of the norm is what a good life is all about," he is saying.

Huh?

"And my friend Cliff was such a man. And I shall miss him."

People start clapping, and I think how weird this is until I remember that I am in Beverly Hills, after all, and Jonathan is the production head of one of the biggest (solvent) studios in town. (They clap for everything out here. I took my college roommate to an AA meeting once and at the end, they rolled credits— "Coffee by Muffy D., herbal tea by Lula F. and cookies presented by Joe S."—and everyone applauded.)

The minister closes the ceremony with a prayer and then announces there will be a reception at the Beverly Hills Hotel, courtesy of Monarch Studios.

I slip outside and park myself next to a pillar of the church so that I can view rather than be viewed.

Interesting. I don't think there were more than a dozen women at the service.

No Lilliana, either.

Jonathan comes out of the church like the new bantamweight champion of the world, slapping backs, shaking hands, exchanging serious but nonetheless slightly jocular banter with the guys. I don't know how, but somehow he senses something and turns around to look directly at me. "Sally," he says a bit breathlessly, coming over. His smile reaches wide and he kisses me on the mouth and hugs me, while I just stand there. "I can't believe you're here," he says, holding my arms.

"Jonathan!" a woman's voice calls. I look past him and see that it belongs to a tall blonde whom I have no doubt is "talent" at the studio.

"I need to see you," I tell him seriously.

"I need to see you, too," he tells me.

"I mean—" I start, but he's being pulled away by an unhappy-looking man.

"Where are you staying?" he calls.

"Century City Towers."

He makes the gesture that he will call me.

Great. Jonathan, I guess, thinks I am badly smitten. But then, perhaps this is a good thing. Being charming is, after all, my new line of work.

CHAPTER SIXTEEN

After I retrieve my car from the church (call me cynical, but honestly, car valets at a church?) I cut up Beverly to where Sunset Boulevard meets Cold Water Canyon, and head up into the mountains, searching for the road Spencer and I turned onto with Lilliana last week. I have to turn around twice, but I find it. (What kind of idiots are at this affiliate, I wonder, that they couldn't find it?) And sure enough, just as I described over and over again to anyone who would listen, Lilliana's house is toward the end on the left. Yep. Same split-level, circa 1940s, same gray limestone I described, same white gravel drive, same brick inlay walk. In the driveway is parked a battered Volvo sedan and a Hummer, one of those $80,000 armored jeep vehicles that made its name in World War II and has made a comeback with the rich and the restless. Somehow I doubt either one of these vehicles belong to Lilliana.

I park my rental, march up to the front door and ring the bell. Some young guy answers it. He's maybe sixteen, has a ring through his forehead, long blond hair—secured into a ponytail—and hasn't shaved for a few days. He's actually very cute.

"Is Lilliana in?" I ask.

He looks a bit confused. "I—maybe you should come in and talk to my parents."

Parents? Do I have the right house?

I am ushered into the living room and it looks like the same house to me, the same piano, same bookshelves, same art. There is the couch I sat on, there is the rug where Lilliana sat at my feet, sipping cognac. The young man leads me into the kitchen, where said parents are making what look like banana splits. But this is California; I can see on the carton that the main ingredient is frozen tofu.

"Hi," the father says, looking up in surprise. He is an older version of the boy, only with gray streaking his ponytail, no ring in his forehead, he has shaved and he is wearing wire-rimmed glasses.

"Hello," the woman says, smiling cautiously. She looks sort of like the skater Dorothy Hamill, that kind of brown hair and eyes. She's attractive, around fifty, I think, and looks like the boss.

"This lady's looking for Lilliana Martin," the boy says.

This lady, I wince.

"Ah," the wife says, "another one. Are you police or press?"

"I'm a friend who is very worried about her." I gesture to the house around us. "She brought me here last Monday night. I've just come back from New York and am trying to find her. So I came back here."

The wife looks at her husband for a long moment. "I think maybe you need to make a phone call."

He makes a *hmm* sound and nods but doesn't move. He licks the spoon instead.

She looks at me. "We've been in Turkey for six weeks. My husband is translating the sacred text of Ghalla."

How translating whatever the heck the sacred text of Ghalla is means they can afford a two-million-dollar house in Cold Water Canyon is beyond me.

"The son of a friend of ours was house-sitting for us," the translator explains, "and I am assuming Lilliana Martin was a friend of his. For obvious reasons, we have thus far denied she has anything to do with us."

"Why is that?"

"The press. The cops. You're not the only one who's been here."

"Was your house-sitter by chance Cliff Yarlen?" I ask.

The grown-ups exchange looks again. "No," the husband says, shaking his head. "I've never heard that name before."

"I have," the wife says, thinking. "How do I know that name?"

"He was murdered in New York last week," I supply.

They stare at me. "And what does he have to do with our house?" she asks.

I decide it is in my best interests not to freak them out, not to tell them a dead mafioso had been living here while they were away. "Nothing that I know of. Lilliana knew Cliff and I know she's very upset. I knew him as well and I'm looking for Lilliana to tell her what happened. To make sure she knows he did not suffer."

"Is he the guy in the crate at JFK?" the son asks.

I nod.

"And you knew him?" the mother asks me.

"Through work," I lie. "We met through a movie at Monarch."

This seems to make them feel better, that I might actually be somebody, not just some shady broad who murders people in their houses. The father carefully writes out the name and number and address of their house-sitter, also providing me with directions to where he lives, which is only about a mile away on Mulholland Drive.

On the way, I check my voice mail. Nothing except an irate message from a detective of the NYPD. My first day and I forgot to call them. I call Attorney Sedorg's office to see if anyone's spoken to Lilliana yet. The secretary is out to lunch, the switchboard doesn't know. I try Lilliana's agent and am told he is out of the country. I call the home of my college roommate's parents to see if they're home, but they're not. Morning's father is a big name in these parts and I'm hoping he might be able to turn up Lilliana's whereabouts for me.

I approach the house-sitter's house and immediately assume he must live with his parents. The house is very large with utterly spectacular views (but where I could never live, not hanging off a cliff), and I figure people hire the owner's kid because the owners are obviously so rich they can handle any damage their kid might do.

"Hi," I say to the Hispanic lady who comes to the door, "I'm looking for Jeremiah."

"I'm sorry, but he's not here."

"But this is his house?"

"This is the residence of Mr. and Mrs. Sadler," she says. "Jeremiah is their son."

"Ah, I see," I say, not understanding the need for such distinction. "But he lives here, right?"

"I don't..." She gives a shrug.

"So he's here in town?" I offer my credentials, that I am a friend of the translator of the sacred text of Ghalla and his wife. This reassures her and she admits he is house-sitting for some friends and I gradually wheedle an address out of her. It's just down the hill off Benedict Canyon. Back into my car I go and drive on.

At this next house—one of those weird flying-saucer houses that had one second of popularity in the seventies— it is not Jeremiah, but a teenage girl who comes to the door, a rather lavish creature who is big into Goth. Her dark hair is long and teased big. She is extremely heavy-handed with the black eyeliner. The top she is wearing is made out of black netting with two patches of black fabric over her nipples. Her black jeans are worn and heavily patched. "Jeremiah's not here," she reports. "He's house-sitting in Malibu."

"Oh, so, is this your house?"

"No, it's the Morgans'. They're away."

"And you're what—sub-house-sitting?"

"Sort of." She offers a crooked smile, as if she doesn't want to break down and be in good humor. She may try to make herself as ugly as possible, but this girl cannot hide the perfect orthodonture of her teeth and the healthy glow from a lifetime of wholesome food. This has been one well-taken-care-of kid.

"I bet you're Jeremiah's girlfriend."

"Who *are* you?" she giggles.

"I'm Sally Harrington, a friend of Lilliana Martin's from Connecticut. I stayed with her last week at the Cold Water Canyon house. I came into town unexpectedly tonight and I was looking for her."

"Oh, yeah," she confirms, "she was there awhile. Hang on, I've got her number somewhere." She disappears into the house and I peer into the foyer. It's difficult to believe people would pay money for a kooky house like this. Every room looks out at every other house on the hill. She comes back and hands me a piece of paper with a telephone number and address.

"Thank you so much," I tell her.

She smiles despite herself, shrugging a little in shyness. "Did you want me to tell Jeremiah anything?"

"How old is he, anyway?"

"Seventeen."

"Only seventeen and he has this big house-sitting business going, huh?"

"He's like, into making money, you know? Being independent. I guess 'cause his dad's so successful and all."

"That's nice," I say. "And now you're helping out."

"Well, you know, my parents are kind of a drag. Jeremiah and I go to Lyttleton Academy and, you know, like my parents think it's okay for me to house-sit and, like—" She giggles again. "I think like it's better not to have to live with them."

Man, if this were my daughter, I would pull her home by the hair, wash her face, put her in jeans and T-shirt and lock her in her room for a year.

I guess the kid in Cold Water Canyon was right to call me "lady."

Before I start the car I try the number the girl gave me for Lilliana and, no surprise, I hear a recorded message that this number has been disconnected. Okay, I can still try the address. So I start the car and head back up Beverly Glen to Mulholland and take it all the way over to the Hollywood Hills. I zero in on the address and find, again, no surprise, there is no such number as 16 Hillstrom Place. There is 2, 4, 12 and 22 and I get out of the car to knock on the door of each bungalow to make sure Lilliana Martin is not here somewhere.

"You think I'd come to the door if I had Lilliana Martin here?" one man says to me. "I'd be banging her in every room of the house!"

"Oh, charming," I say, lip curling in disgust.

"Fuck you!" he cries, slamming the door.

Another dead end. I decide to head back to Beverly Hills and take Mulholland to Beverly Glen. I know this area pretty well because there is a little shopping center up here where we always had a spy or two from the magazine hanging out, hoping for leads while watching celebrities picking up prescriptions, dry cleaning, renting videos or eating scrambled eggs. I was sent only once because when I came back I said I had learned nothing and my boss thought I was lying. (I was. But whose business is it if someone has herpes or has gained twenty pounds between films or has a crazy mother driving them nuts?) At any rate, I drive to the little shopping center and go into the luncheonette to get a bite to eat.

I am halfway through my eggs and bacon and freshly squeezed orange juice when my cell phone rings. I cannot believe it when I hear Lilliana's voice saying, "I hear my close personal friend, Sally Harrington, is looking for me."

"Oh, my gosh, it's you!" I can't help but blurt out.

"Yes, indeedy, 'tis I. What do you want?" Pause. "Besides an interview?"

"Oh, no, Lilliana, it's not like that." I turn to the wall so people won't overhear. "There's just so much that's happened and I don't think you know about it."

"Maybe I don't want to know any more, Sally," she says, sounding tired. "Maybe I just want to be left alone."

No response.

"I was the last person to see Cliff," I tell her. "He came to my house in Connecticut last week, he was looking for you. We went into New York together. We spent a lot of the day together."

"Oh, no," she says, upset.

"Please, Lilliana, I need to talk to you."

"Sally, please—"

"There are things I have to tell you," I say. "I can't over the phone."

Silence.

"I'm not like other reporters," I say. "I'm not like that. I know you know that. I would never compromise you."

She likes you. Alexandra Waring's words come back to me. *Play on that.* So here I am, part conniver, but truly, mostly just a scared person who wants to know what happened to Spencer. And to Cliff Yarlen.

Still she has not responded.

"If you trust your instincts at all," I stress, "you know you can trust me."

"My instincts?" she says. "I was *drunk,* Sally."

"That's not what I mean," I say.

After a moment she says, "You were with Cliff?"

"Yes," I say softly.

"And he thought I might be with you," she sighs.

I remain silent.

Lo and behold, she tells me where she is.

CHAPTER SEVENTEEN

I turn off Beverly Glen onto Skyview Drive, a quiet, winding street whose houses are built into the curves of the canyon, trying to afford both privacy and views on as little as a half acre. The address I'm looking for is at the end, emblazoned on a large iron gate embedded in two stone pillars. The gate is closed. I can't see the house from the road.

I press the button of the gate intercom. "Yes?" It's Lilliana. She sounds out of breath.

"It's Sally."

The gate buzzes open and I wind up the paved driveway. When I clear a corner my mouth falls open because I can't believe any actress of Lilliana's early stature could possibly afford this property. It is a real stone house, not just a stone facade, a genuine 1920s Bel Air mansion. I hear dogs barking inside. I park in front and walk up to the front door. I can hear Lilliana talking to the dogs. The front door swings open and two dogs, a large mutt and a German shepherd, are sitting on either side of the actress, panting, peering out at me with hungry eyes.

"It's all right," she tells the dogs, and they stand, cautiously edging toward me. I hold out my hand. One sniff and they turn tail and trot back down the hall.

"So you're here," she says, looking me over as if trying to remember why she allowed me into her life. She is perspiring heavily, dressed in a half T-shirt and sweatpants, the former soaked with perspiration, and a hand towel slung over her shoulder that I bet she had just used to wipe her face. Frankly, she looks great. "I was working out."

"Thank you for letting me come," I say quietly.

She hesitates, looking uncomfortable, and then reaches to touch my arm in a friendly gesture. Without booze in her system, I can tell she might actually be a bit shy. She smiles a little. "I'm sort of glad you called. It's nice to see you again. I felt badly about the other night."

"Don't." I step forward. "Listen, I'm so sorry about Cliff."

She nods, turning away, motioning for me to follow.

We walk down a hallway, past a large sunny living room on the left. This house, in contrast to the one in Cold Water Canyon, is English in feel. Dark wood, Oriental carpets, oil paintings, what looks like a stained hardwood staircase curving up to the second floor.

As we enter a kitchen, she turns around. "Would you mind if I finish?"

"I'm sorry?"

"Working out," she says, holding out her hand to guide me down another hall ahead of her. "I was on the Stair-Master, I've got to finish or I won't do it."

"Please do," I urge. I have entered a marvelous room, what I guess might have been a solarium converted into a gym. It has hardwood floors, exercise mats and various pieces of exercise equipment. And lots of plants. She tells me to put my bag down on the corner sofa unit (an overstuffed, cheerful chintz) and directs me to go around the white-wood bar to help myself to whatever I would like in the refrigerator back there. While Lilliana punches some data into the StairMaster and starts moving again, I take a look.

Yogurt, apples, oranges, grapefruit. Saratoga water, diet tonic water, Fresca (golly, I haven't seen that for years) and grape juice. I ask her if she would like anything— "No"— and help myself to a glass of Saratoga sparkling water with a big dollop of grape juice.

How Lilliana can afford this place is beyond me. Nothing in her middle-class Ohio background indicated money, and her career thus far couldn't possibly have generated even the down payment. But then, for all I know, this isn't her house.

"This is one of the most beautiful houses I've ever seen in my life," I say, moving to sit on the couch.

"Thank you." She is across the room, facing me, making the StairMaster look easy the way the truly fit always do. I like to run, but I don't like StairMasters. I look like an exhausted duck, whereas Lilliana resembles a vaguely equestrian creature gently soaring her way up to where the gods hang out.

I sip my cold drink. "I went to the house where we went with you last Monday," I tell her. "And I met a man who is translating something called the sacred text of Ghalla."

She laughs a little, giving a toss of her head to look up at the ceiling, hands on her hips, legs pumping away.

"I gathered it's not your house."

"No," she says, eyes on the ceiling, legs moving.

"I got the impression the other night that it was."

She doesn't say anything for a while. Finally she brings her head down to look at me. "We stayed there awhile. It was Cliff's idea." A moment later, her breath getting a little shorter (thank heavens, she's human) she asks, "What's the sacred text of Ghalla?"

"I haven't the slightest idea, but I think it must pay extremely well."

She laughs and the machine whines into higher gear. I don't envy her. I also don't want to bug her while she's trying to work out. "Do you mind if I look around? Until you're finished?"

"Be my guest."

I leave my grape juice here in case I trip or something. What I am most curious about is whether or not she really lives here. And with whom. Or what. In the kitchen I am met by the dogs. They're simply standing in the far doorway, which looks as though it leads into the dining room, but the dogs make me too nervous to explore in that direction.

The kitchen is very nice in this house, too, though it is not as modern as the one in the Ghalla guy's house. There is a lot of counter space, a large gas range, double refrigerator, trash compactor and dishwasher. A small TV sits on the counter. There is a small breakfast nook that looks out a bay window into the backyard, where there is a lovely pool, beautifully landscaped with stone, flowers and shrubs. In the nook, instead of one shelf of cookbooks as in the other house, there is an entire wall of them. I take a closer look. The classics are all here, some in as many as three editions—*The Joy of Cooking, Fannie Farmer Cookbook, Craig Claiborne's New York Times Cookbook,* et cetera—and numerous specialty cookbooks, from bread to pasta to seafood to vegetarian dishes.

I move away from the bookshelves and the ears of the German shepherd twitch forward. Murmuring sweet nothings to him, I opt to go back the way we came in, back down to the front hall to look around in the living room.

The furniture is not as old as I first thought, mostly Empire, mostly mahogany. I pause by a low mahogany bookshelf and peer in. Classics. But not a matching set. No, these were lovingly selected or collected one by one. A ragged Modern Library edition of *The House of Mirth,* a small Oxford hardcover of *Barchester Towers,* a creased orange spine of a Penguin edition of *The Ambassadors,* a book club edition of *War and Peace,* a gray Scribner's trade paperback of *For Whom the Bell Tolls,* a battered Doubleday hardcover of *Of Human Bondage.*

I pull out a Viking *Portable Dorothy Parker* and peak inside the front cover. Scripted in light pencil is *Lilliana Martin.* I check the inside of a Delta trade paperback edition of *Slaughterhouse Five* and find *L. M.*

Huh. She didn't finish at Ohio State, but nonetheless seems rather well read. It is also the first indication she actually lives here.

Strange, though... I have never been in any celebrity's house where there are no photographs of themselves. Interestingly, now that I look around, I see there are no photographs of anyone.

There are two couches on either side of a large fireplace and a single large portrait is hanging over the mantel. It is not old, but then it is not recent, either. It is a fine oil of a dramatic-looking young woman in formal pose. What's so unusual about it, though, is that it's a portrait not unlike the kind Reynolds or Romney might have painted in the eighteenth century, portraying their subjects in a classical or mythical setting, sometimes as a muse, sometimes as a goddess. The woman's dark hair is loosely piled on her head, her large brown eyes are deep and expressive, her cheeks are rosy, her lips, hinting a smile, are deeply red. She is wearing something that looks like a toga that dreamily fades into the bottom of the picture.

"That's my mother," Lilliana says from behind me.

I start, feeling a bit caught.

Lilliana steps up to stand next to me, looking up at the painting, patting the perspiration off her face with a towel in one hand and holding an open bottle of Evian water in the other. "She died when I was nine."

"She was an extraordinary-looking woman," I murmur. "And it's such an unusual portrait."

Lilliana is smiling up at her. "It's a lot like she was. Born in the wrong century, born in the wrong place at the wrong time." She takes a swallow from her bottle and looks at me. "I don't look much like her, do I?"

I look up at the painting and then back down at Lilliana's face. This is actually the first time I've had a good look at her without makeup on. Yes, I can see the resemblance. I also assume, as I had when I first met her, that the blond part of Lilliana's appearance is not natural. But I still don't think she's as dark as her mother was. The mother's eyes were completely different, too, deeper set, whereas Lilliana's are bright, open. My eyes travel to her mouth.

"Here," I say, touching my own mouth and chin, and then touching my cheekbones. "The lower half of your face, the bone structure. That's all your mother."

Lilliana smiles appreciatively. "Yes, you're right." Then she seems to snap out of wherever she is, mutters something about cancer and her mother, and suggests we go into the kitchen.

"I went to the memorial service for Cliff today," I say on the way.

"You said he came to your house in Connecticut," she says without turning around.

She hops up to sit on the kitchen counter and gestures for me to take a seat at the breakfast table.

"I don't know why," I say, "but he seemed to think you might have come to Connecticut with me."

She's drinking water and, I guess, has no intention of responding to this.

"You can imagine how surprised I was to find him in my front yard."

"Yes, I suppose you were."

She doesn't, I notice, really even have a stomach when sitting like this with her half-shirt on. Unbelievable.

"So, um," I continue, "I told him you obviously weren't there, and he was going into New York and I needed to go there, too, so I rode in with him. Later he heard from you, or about you, or something. At any rate, he knew you were all right in Palm Springs, so he was going to fly home. I saw him at JFK—it was sleeting and he was waiting for a flight to get out." I wince slightly. "Evidently he was killed not long after I left him."

She nods again, biting her lower lip and looking out the window.

"I'm very sorry, Lilliana. It must have been quite a shock."

"Yes." Her eyes are still directed outside. After a while she clears her throat and sips some water. "So," she says quietly, "how are you after all this? How's Spencer?"

I look at her. "You don't know, do you?"

She turns her head slightly in question.

"Spencer disappeared the morning after we were at your house. Tuesday morning. The last person to see him was Cliff. Outside the house in Cold Water Canyon."

It takes a minute for her to absorb this news. "You mean you haven't seen or heard from him at all?"

I shake my head.

"Oh," she says. "And so you thought he was with me in the Springs. That's why you left that message with Richie— to tell Spencer to call work or something."

I nod. "Yeah. At first, I thought he might be with you."

"Oh, boy," she says next, on an intake of breath, sliding down from the counter to sit down in the chair next to me. "I'm so sorry," she says, lightly resting her hand on my arm. "I wouldn't have wanted you to worry."

After a long moment, I say, "You know something about his disappearance, don't you?"

Her eyes don't waver. "I don't know where he is, Sally. I swear to you. Until this moment I didn't even know he was missing."

I narrow my eyes. "But you know someone who might know, don't you? And before you deny it, remember I know—the whole world now knows—that Cliff Arlenetta was in the mob."

She takes her hand away and backs off slightly, eyes still on mine.

"Last Monday," I say, "when Spencer and I took you home, after we left, we had a fight. I threw him out of the car. He walked back up to your house—what I thought was your house—to use the phone. He said your car was in the driveway, your front door was wide open and you were nowhere to be found."

"That's true," she says quietly. "I had left."

"How? Your car was there."

"I had a lot to drink," she said evenly. "I got a ride."

"And left the front door wide open?"

"Yes."

This is like pulling teeth. "So where did you go?"

"What does it matter?"

"It matters because I need to figure out what happened," I tell her. "Lilliana, we met you the night of the party, we took you home, and the next thing I know, you and Spencer both disappear, your ex-boyfriend, who's in the mob, shows up on my doorstep three thousand miles away in Connecticut, and then that night in New York he's murdered. I don't know how you can pretend there's no connection here with you."

Her expression finally breaks. She averts her eyes and brings up one hand to her forehead. "The reason why I left had nothing to do with you or Spencer. If Spencer walked into something—" She stops herself and drops her hand.

Her eyes show worry. "Did you say Cliff actually *saw* him? At the Cold Water Canyon house?"

"Yes. The next morning. After Spencer and I spoke at the hotel. He went back to the house to see you. Cliff said he found Spencer waiting there." I pause. "Waiting around for you to show up."

"What did Cliff do?"

"Nothing. They introduced themselves and Spencer said he and I had met you the night before. Spencer said he was just checking to make sure you were okay, that we had all partied a lot the night before." I shrug. "Cliff said he left him there."

Lilliana is staring down at the table. "That's weird." She looks up. "How did Cliff find you? Back east where you live?"

"I have no idea," I say honestly. "All he said was that he assumed you had come back to Connecticut with me. I got the distinct impression he thought maybe you and I had, um—" This is embarrassing. I flick my hand through the air. "You know, had gone off together."

She rises from her chair, thinking, turning away from me. Then, as if she is unsure, she slowly walks over to the wall phone and picks it up. She holds it on her hip and turns around. "I have to make a call. It'll just be a minute." She moves past the dogs into the hall beyond, muttering, "Just let me do this."

Thankfully, the dogs follow her so I can get up and move to stand in the doorway.

"It's Lilliana," I hear her say. Several moments go by. "The morning after you picked me up, there was a guy here, his name's Spencer Hawes." Pause. "He's Malcolm Kieloff's editor!" she yells. "He hasn't been seen since!" Pause. "Yes!" Pause. "Cliff saw him standing in the drive-way, looking for me." Pause. "No. Nothing at all." Pause. "By God, you better!"

I am sitting at the table again when she comes back in and slams the phone in the cradle, making it bounce out and clatter to the floor. She kicks it across the room into the refrigerator and then goes over to pick it up and checks to see that it's working. She hangs it up but remains standing there, her back to me.

I wait.

She turns around. "If I hear anything, I will call you."

"That's it?" I say incredulously.

She looks as though she might cry.

"You owe me some kind of explanation, Lilliana."

She shakes her head. "I'm sorry. No. I can't."

"What do you mean, no?" I say, getting mad.

"You're the press, for God's sake!"

"Do I look like the goddamn press? Do I have a camera? Do you see a notebook? A tape recorder? Don't you get it, Lilliana? Nobody knows I've even found you! I was sent out here to find you, and I've found you, but I haven't told a soul. Why is that, do you suppose? I'll tell you why. It's because I sense you may be in some kind of very bad trouble and that's why you're hiding out. Well, I can't help you unless I know what is going on."

"No, no," she says, shaking her head. "No, Sally, just leave it. I'm fine. I'll try and see if I can somehow help to find your friend, but you've got to get out of here, leave me alone. *Please.*"

I walk over to her. "I have to find Spencer. I am scared to death he's lying dead somewhere."

"I don't think so," she says, turning away.

I grab her arm and whirl her back around to face me. "You don't *think* so? How is it you would know enough to know that?"

"I don't, Sally!" she wails. The tears finally come. "I swear I'll call you if I can find out anything. *Please,* you've got to trust me. You've got to leave now and let me find out what I can. But God, you *cannot* tell anyone where I am. Not now. Whatever you want—later. I'll give you what*ever* you want, I swear to God. Only leave me alone now and wait for me to call you."

I stare at her, trying to regulate my breathing. "Just tell me," I say quietly, "why you brought us home after the party. Did you *want* Cliff to find us there? Were you trying to hurt him? What the hell was going on?"

She drops her head, shaking it. "Please go. I'll try to find out about your friend." She sniffs, wiping her eyes and turning away.

I decide to let her off the hook. For the moment.

"I can't wait long, Lilliana. Spencer's in trouble, I've got to find him."

"Please go," she whispers, crying.

I get my bag and I do go, letting myself out the first door.

I wonder if she will really call me or if she'll disappear again.

CHAPTER EIGHTEEN

After leaving Lilliana's I realize I am more baffled than ever. Her story is all so strange, so implausible.

She, an actress, he, a mobster, were going out. Cliff moves into a house where a seventeen-year-old is house-sitting and Lilliana moves in at least part-time with him. They decide to break up, *so she stays?* He piles his belongings in the front hall to take them away, so Lilliana picks up Spencer and me at a party and brings us back to that house to have sex?

No way. There's something missing here. Something about their relationship.

Okay. That night, we left the Cold Water Canyon house around eleven. We fought. I threw Spencer out of the car. Let's say it took him a half hour to hike back up the road to her house. He arrived and found that Lilliana was gone. Someone came to pick her up between eleven and eleven-thirty, leaving the front door wide open.

Why?

Maybe she went home to the stone mansion. Okay, suppose she did. Who took her? And why, if she went home, couldn't her agent find her there the next morning? And why did he frantically call the crew from Bennett, Fitz-allen & Coe to find out if anyone knew where she was?

Where did she go?

Okay, the next morning, Cliff went to the Cold Water Canyon house. To pick up his stuff? Maybe. He found Spencer hanging around, saying he met Lilliana the night before and was checking on her. Cliff said why? Spencer said we had been partying quite a bit. Who is we, Cliff wanted to know. My friend Sally. We gave Lilliana a ride home but she went out or something, she left. Cliff said where did she go? I don't know, that's why I stopped here this morning, to make sure she's all right. Cliff said she's not here, Spencer said he'd wait around a little longer, and then Cliff left. Presumably Cliff called Lilliana's home and found out she was not there, either. He called their friends, she was nowhere to be found. He talked to the agent, who presumably gave him my name. He discovered I had checked out and was on my way home to Connecticut.

Now, why did he think Lilliana would be with me? He knew she didn't leave with me the night before. He knew she left the Cold Water Canyon house with someone other than me. And yet the next morning he got on a plane to Hartford to track me down and look for Lilliana.

Meanwhile, Spencer vanished. His rental car was found in an airport parking lot, the police think he could have left on a flight to Honolulu. A missing-person report was filed in Los Angeles Tuesday night for Lilliana and on Wednesday she was spotted near Palm Springs. She called her agent and her lawyer and the LAPD to tell them she was not missing, simply needed to get away. Upon hearing the news, Cliff went to JFK to catch a flight back to Los Angeles, but someone shot him twice in the back of the head and hid his body in an air-cargo crate.

I pull over on a small sandy lot on the valley side of Mulholland and call the newsroom at DBS to reach Will Rafferty. "Did you find her?" is his first question.

"I'm getting close," I say. From the background noise, I can tell the news group is in full tilt to go on the air in two hours. "What I need, though, is whatever we can get on a family named Sadler and their seventeen-year-old son, Jeremiah," and I give him the parents' address. I'm dying to ask him to do a check on the address of Lilliana's house, but I don't dare. Not yet. I don't want to lead anyone else to her, not until I understand what is going on.

"Alexandra's on her way to Taiwan," he tells me.

As overwhelmed as I am, I still find myself wondering who will anchor the news tonight in her absence. I think I wish it was me.

"She should be through there by the weekend. She wanted you to know she's stopping in L.A. on her way back."

No doubt to check up on me firsthand. It's good news, though. It means the anchorwoman's focus has swung back to the other three hundred fifty-nine degrees of news, and for the moment I am relatively free to play Lilliana my own way without interference.

Will promises to have whatever research he can turn up faxed to the hotel. "And listen," he says, "have you checked your messages? Half the world has been calling for you."

I admit I haven't and promise to take care of it.

"And what about the affiliate?" he asks. "They say they haven't seen you yet."

"They will when I can help them."

He gives a knowing laugh. "Don't like anyone looking over your shoulder, eh? Boy, does that sound familiar. Okay, be good, get something good, stay safe." And he hangs up.

I sit there awhile, looking out over the valley, listening to my messages. They are pretty horrendous. Buddy D'Amico to say another video of me having sex with Spencer turned up at a local high school. Mr. and Mrs. Hawes shyly calling from Maine, asking do I think they should be worried about Spencer? The police have been at their door. Personnel director from the *Herald-American* telling me we have to settle how many vacation and sick days I have left before he can cut my last check. Also, what about my pension fund? An L.A. affiliate news producer named Glen asking where the hell am I? He wants a camera crew tagging my movements. My brother wanting to know what is going on, Mother sounds horrible. Kate Weston touching base, any news? Crazy Pete Sabatino, resident conspiracy theorist of Castleford, regarding the battle of George W. and George Bush and the inner circle against the angry aliens. ("This doesn't have anything to do with your untimely departure, does it?" he whispers.) Wendy Mitchell touching base. Mack calling to say he is watching carefully over Mother, keeping her busy. My lawyer yelling I didn't call the detective at the NYPD as I promised. Frankly, unless they really think I killed Cliff, I don't know why they're demanding to keep such close tabs on me.

And then the last message, God bless him, Doug. To apologize for "flying off the handle about the videotape. I was way out of line with what I said. But you know, it's because there is a part of me that still can't believe you left me to be with him." He clears his throat. "You know, the other times we broke up, somehow I thought we'd always get back together."

Yeah, right, I can't help but think. *The first time, I didn't see you for nearly ten years! You got married to someone else!* But I know what he means. For the last two years there seemed to be an inevitability we would end up settling down together.

"And with, uh, therapy and everything, sometimes I wonder what you saw in me at all." There is a trace of humor in his voice. "Except an ability to ignore the fact you work all the time because I'm working all the time." He clears his throat again. "Truly, I am so sorry I got so angry. You must be out of your mind with this video thing, you must be worried about Spencer, I didn't mean to add to your worries."

I know Doug's dying inside. I know he's still angry and hurt and feels totally humiliated in his office, that sacred place he always hoped to keep his messy personal life out of.

"Call me, Sally, if you can." Pause. "Things are really fucked up—"

Unfortunate choice of words, I am inclined to think.

"But I can't bear the idea of not being in touch with you again. You know, being totally cut off." Pause. "Well, see how you feel, but I hope to talk to you soon."

I feel incredibly relieved by his message. Happy, even. He's not letting me off the hook, but he is willing to take some responsibility, willing to feel awkward and hurt and angry and relieved and all those things I could hear in his message.

I have been in love with this man since I was seventeen years old.

But I just don't know. I can't imagine him ever getting over all this. I don't think I could. I'd be too proud. *Ha! Pride goeth before the fall,* I think. Would I ever learn?

I am thirsty. I look around, realizing I don't have my usual bottle of water. It's getting late, I'm wiped out. I decide to head for the hotel, return some calls and wait for the Sadler information from DBS. I'll order dinner, watch the DBS news. But my thirst can't wait and I choose to swing back toward Beverly Glen and hit the delicatessen at the mini shopping mall to purchase a bottle of water.

On my way out of the parking lot, I check my rearview mirror and for the hell of it, take another turn around the whole lot and park again. I wait a minute, drinking my water, and then back out and take a whole other swing around the lot the other way, cruising past a maroon Taurus. The man at the wheel doesn't even glance at me. When I reach the road I take a left and then immediately speed up into a driveway. Moments later, I see the maroon Taurus come zipping out of the shopping center lot and zoom down toward the light. I wait a minute and then back out into the road again. At the Beverly Glen light, I turn right. About a quarter mile down, the Taurus is waiting for me on the side of the road. This time, though, I can slow down enough to get the license plate. Then I continue to the hotel, ignoring the fact I am still being followed. I turn my car over to the valet, go upstairs and call DBS to run the license number.

I can't help but wonder if anyone in the mob drives a Ford Taurus. I doubt it. So who was following me and for how long? Had they followed me from Lilliana's?

I don't know, and until I get more information, I don't want to care.

While soaking in the tub, I study my file on Lilliana Martin for some kind of clue.

Lilliana Rose Martin. Father, John Paul Martin, born Columbia, Missouri; mother, the former Bernadette Daily, born Peoria, Illinois. The lady in the portrait. Lilliana Rose, born Elizabeth Mason, Women's Hospital, Charlotte, North Carolina, April 8, 1974 ("possibly 1969," it says). *(Ah-ha! Knew it!)* Only child.

Family moved to Gainesville, Ohio, in 1980 after Bernadette died of cancer. Father remarried 1984 Dorothy Phelps. Lilliana graduated Gainesville High, 1990 (cheerleader, yearbook, literary magazine, lead in class play), attended Ohio State, dropped out 1992 for modeling jobs in New York. Role on *One Life to Live* 1994 to 1996, moved to L.A. for supporting role *Roommates.* In 1999 offered first movie role in *The Long Road,* studio lobbying hard to get Best Supporting Actress nomination.

Current California driver's license. The address is old. Organ donor.

Registered Independent. Always pays taxes and parking tickets. Address on last tax return no longer applicable. No record of real estate holdings.

I turn my attention to the father's page. No college. A career in sales. Radio and then pharmaceuticals in Missouri, a Mercedes car dealership in Ohio. Very boring, by the looks of it. Not much on the mother, either. Worked at Bennett's Department Store until she married Martin. The second wife, who knows.

I hear the fax machine in my room come on and grab a towel to see what's being sent. The phone rings at the same time.

"Sally, it's Will. Got a read-back on the license plate you called in."

"And?"

"United States Department of Justice."

"The feds," I say, swallowing. "Well, I guess they still think I killed poor Cliff."

"Probably," Will agrees.

I pull the first sheet out of the fax. "So what is this you're sending through?"

"Not much on the kid yet, Jeremiah Sadler," he says. "This is what I have right now. I thought you'd want it."

He's right it isn't much. Parents paid three million six hundred thousand for their house in 1996. Father's a record producer.

Disappointed, I turn my attention to the room service menu. I call down and order a steak and a salad and a bottle of Amstel Lite. I return to my bath, adding hot water. I put a washcloth under the back of my head and close my eyes.

Five minutes later there is a knock at the door. I quietly curse—they said it would be forty minutes—as I get out of the tub and slip on the terry-cloth robe the hotel provides. I should look through the keyhole first but I don't.

"Hey," Jonathan Small says, walking in and trying to slide his hands around my waist.

"Hey!" I protest.

"What?" he says, sounding amused, gently pushing me farther inside and kicking the door closed behind him with his foot. "You look good," he says, looking me over.

"I'm taking a bath."

"Great," he says, taking off his suit jacket. "I'll help."

"Jonathan!" I say in my strictest voice.

He looks at me as if I'm nuts. "What?"

"Slow down," I tell him.

He chuckles, walks over and throws himself down in a chair. I bring the telephone to him. "I just ordered room service. Order something for yourself."

"Thanks."

I turn CNN on the TV for him, grab some underwear, jeans and a shirt and go into the bathroom and lock the door. I hastily get dressed, *don't* put any makeup on (don't even brush my hair), and stash the files I was reading in the stack of towels. When I come out, my heart skips a beat because Jonathan is standing next to the desk, reading my notebook. "Should have taken shorthand," he laughs, tossing the book down. "Then maybe I could find out what makes you tick."

"Be careful what you ask for," I say. I'm not waiting for room service. I open the minibar and grab a beer. Jonathan passes on the offer. I pour the beer and take a healthy series of sips before I turn my attention back to him. "That was a beautiful service today," I say, trying to make him less jovial. "Your tribute was very moving."

"Thanks." He is more subdued. "He was a good guy. I'll

miss him." He saunters away from the desk to sit on the edge of my bed. I frown.

"Did you know him a long time?" I ask.

He nods, absently scratching his cheek.

I don't know what it is about Jonathan, but I find him totally physically repulsive. Maybe it's those little round glasses. Maybe it's his personality, that inferiority complex mixed with bravado. Or maybe it's the air of heavy-handed money, the promise of *If all else fails, I'll pay you?*

There is a knock on the door and it is room service for real this time, my dinner, two Amstel Lites and a bottle of Dom Pérignon on ice. I have lost my appetite for food, but not for champagne of this caliber. I tell the waiter not to set up the table yet but go ahead with the champagne, and gratefully accept a glass after Jonathan samples it and gives his approval.

After the waiter leaves and we are settled, Jonathan on the edge of the bed, me in a chair, I say, "Were you friends with Cliff for a long time?"

He swallows, shaking his head. "Couple years."

"Were you the one who brought the AFTW their first contract at Monarch?"

He looks surprised.

"I spent some time with Cliff," I tell him. "The day he was killed, as a matter of fact."

"So I understand," he says quietly. He certainly doesn't seem so cocky now.

"He said that contract was really the big move forward for his union," I lie. Cliff and I didn't talk about any of this. "So is that why you got promoted? It worked out well for Monarch?"

He takes another sip, studying me over the rim of his glass. "Yes," he finally says. He lowers his glass to his lap. "So how did you meet Cliff?"

"Through Lilliana."

"I thought you just met Lilliana last week."

"Well," I say diplomatically, "I guess maybe you should ask her about it. Cliff was her boyfriend."

"Speaking of which," he says, bringing one leg up to rest his right ankle on his left knee, "I hear your boyfriend's MIA."

"My ex," I say without thinking.

"Ah," he says knowingly, nodding. He drains his glass and leans to put it down on the bedside table. "So maybe there was a trade." He smiles. "I hear Lilliana can be like that."

"Like what?"

"She takes yours, you take hers." He raises his eyebrows and lets them fall. "And I can see Cliff going for you."

"Well," I say, looking down into my glass, "that's not it. There was nothing of the kind." I meet his eyes. "If I had to hazard a guess, I think Cliff's work finally caught up with him. And I find it interesting you are so closely tied to it."

I see a flicker of something in his eyes. He stands up. And then he smiles as he moves closer and leans over to rest his hands on the arms of my chair, bringing his face within inches of mine. "I think you're a drama junkie, that's what I think." He kisses me.

I pull away.

He puts his hand behind my head and tries to pull me toward him.

I put my hand on his chest. *"Stop it,"* I say, trying my best to sound like Mother.

The fax machine comes on and both of us turn to look at it. "Secret messages from more secret admirers?" he taunts.

I try to get up, but he purposely blocks my way. "Come on, Jonathan," I protest.

"Make me," he says, smiling, trying to kiss me again.

"I mean it, stop it." I put both my hands on his chest and shove him away. He totters back a couple of steps. I get up quickly and move to the fax machine; I sense him coming up behind me; I twist away and back across the room toward the door. "Jonathan, stop it, this is stupid."

He catches me by the bathroom door and pulls me toward him. Not for the first time I realize how, even when slighter and shorter, a man is always surprisingly strong. "Come on, Sally," he murmurs, pulling me into him by the small of my back and sinking his mouth onto my neck.

I count to two and then yank myself away, stepping into the bathroom. He seems to be slightly confused, standing there, blinking, clearly not understanding the rules I play by. I lunge for the door and throw it open with a crash. Then I stand inside the threshold, crossing my arms over my chest, and loudly announce, "If you want to go out with me, ask me out. Don't ever, *ever* try to manhandle me again."

He laughs, rubbing his eye. Then he walks over to the bed to pick up his jacket and slip it on. "Okay," he says, sounding surprisingly good-natured about it. He holds his hands up. "Fair's fair, I'll call you later and ask you out." He walks past me but pauses in the door, and I bring my hands up in apprehension. He looks at my mouth a moment, smiles and continues out. "It's not like I don't have anything else to do," he says over his shoulder. He turns around, walking backward down the hall. "Or anyone else to do." He turns back around, waves a hand over his head. "Call you later, pretty girl!"

I close the door and lock it. Then I call downstairs, demanding to speak to security, or whoever was responsible for letting some man get my room number and come up here and accost me. The desk clerk is nervous and very apologetic about it, but then when somehow it comes out that it was Jonathan Small, the desk clerk tells me that Mr. Small is an executive with Monarch Studios, and Monarch Studios owns forty percent of this hotel. "He's like an owner," he says weakly.

"He's like a lawsuit waiting to happen," I declare. "And you know what Century City's like, all I have to do is yell 'I need a lawyer!' and twenty thousand windows will fly open."

Apologies, apologies.

"Just make sure nothing like this happens again during my stay." He doesn't promise armed guards at my door, exactly, but something close to it.

This week has simply been too much, I think, hanging up the phone. My eye travels to the fax machine. I almost forgot about the faxes that came in.

It's more information on the Sadlers, the house-sitter's parents. My eye is drawn to Jeremiah's mother, who runs a nonprofit charity. Will has circled her name and drawn an arrow to the margin, where he has written, "What's interesting—her sister, Mary Howard, is personal secretary to Jonathan Small at Monarch."

Huh. So the house-sitter in the Cold Water Canyon house has an aunt who works for Jonathan.

Small world.

CHAPTER NINETEEN

"Listen, man, Jasmine told me you were coming but I've got to get to school," Jeremiah Sadler tells me at the door. This house-sitting job of his is in Malibu, looking after a large, modern, glass-and-cedar house built on a rock cliff overlooking the beach. If I'm not mistaken, Barbra Streisand's old place is just a hop-skip away. "If I'm late again, my ass is kicked, *bad.*"

"I'll write you a note," I promise, taking out my wallet.

His hopeful expression crashes when he examines my ID. "DBS? What good is that in this town? We're taught to run away from you guys."

Jeremiah's light brown hair hangs in dreadlocks to his shoulders. He is wearing a maroon-colored T-shirt, a string of painted wooden love beads and baggy gray Dockers. I love rich kids. My roommate, Morning Rubinowitz, had been a little like this. When she arrived in our dorm room at UCLA that first day she had no hair at all, she had shaved it off. I can only imagine what a lovely couple Jeremiah and Jasmine-big-into-Goth will be at their prom.

"I was a friend of Cliff Yarlen's," I tell him. "And you've heard what happened to him."

"I don't know anything!" he cries, backing away a step.

"I don't mean you killed him," I say in such a way as to imply that yes, I do think he probably killed him and will prove it. "I just want to know what your arrangement was."

"Arrangement about what? I don't know what you're talking about."

"The house."

"What house?"

"In Cold Water Canyon." I recite the name and address of the owners.

His face takes on a decidedly nervous look.

"I'm not here to broadcast your name on the news," I say, making the threat implicit. "Your parents are very nice people. I wouldn't want them to be disappointed in you. Or embarrassed. Or humiliated."

His eyes plunge to the ground. "What?"

"I know you let him stay there. I just wondered how he came to know you. How did you meet him?"

"My aunt. She works at Monarch and I think she knows him."

"Are you sure it wasn't your aunt's boss, Jonathan Small, who arranged it?"

He shrugs. "I don't know. Aunt Mary just asked me to let him use the house. I think maybe Mr. Small used it, too."

"How much were you paid?"

He looks at me.

"This is not to broadcast on the news or anything," I say again.

"Five thousand. He only used it for like a week."

Five thousand dollars. I had forgotten what this town is like.

"He had an awful lot of stuff there for a week," I comment.

Jeremiah shrugs, making his love beads rattle. "He didn't break anything. He cleaned up." He sighs, looking off. "Nobody would have known anything if—" He looks at me with renewed interest. "Are you the one who sent all those reporters there? Man, I almost got killed by the owners. They were going to tell my parents."

"You mean your parents didn't know you weren't staying there?"

"I got a lot of houses, I got a business, they understand that," he says nonchalantly. He looks at his watch and groans. "Shit, I've got school. I've got to go."

"In a minute," I caution him. "Was this the first time your Aunt Mary asked you to do this?"

He sighs again, looking bored. "No," he admits. "It was for the same guy, Yarlen. Or her boss. One or the other. It always worked fine until this time."

"You're telling me that Jonathan Small had—rented—a house you were house-sitting before?"

"Yeah."

"What for?"

He nearly sneers in my face. "Come on."

"What for?" I repeat.

"You know, women and stuff."

"I see. And how many of these houses were there?"

"I don't know."

"I'm not going to tell Jonathan Small what you told me," I say, using another threat.

"Six," he answers.

"Jeremiah, why do you think Cliff Yarlen and/or Jonathan Small needed to borrow six different houses?"

"I told you, I assumed it was for girls. Aunt Mary says Mr. Small's got a lot of girlfriends. I figured he was doing them there. Look, I gotta go," he stresses, dancing around like it's the bathroom he's talking about, not school.

"One last question—when did your Aunt Mary first ask you to 'rent' a house to them?"

"Last summer. But it was Mr. Yarlen's gig, he's the one who always paid me."

I scribble a note on DBS News letterhead saying that

Jeremiah had been assisting in an important investigation and if the school authorities wished to verify it, I could be reached at my hotel.

I sit in my car and watch in amazement as Jeremiah puts on a white Oxford button-down shirt over his T-shirt and beads, dons a blue blazer with the school crest on it and slings a tie around his neck, all while slogging along to his car. With the Oxford shirt open and tail out, and his baggy pants, he looks like a pile of clothes moving to the cleaners.

I wave, listening to my voice mail on my cell phone. No word from Lilliana yet.

Jeremiah fires up what I know is at least a sixty-thousand-dollar Porsche, lays a patch to speed five yards to me and rolls the window down. "If you ever need a place to stay," he says, holding out a card to me, "let me know."

Jeremiah B. Sadler
Residential Security

Good grief, what a world.

My college roommate, Morning, is still parasailing in the Amazon and "handling PR" for the rain forest. While I love Morning dearly, I'm afraid she's not much of a provider and has drifted into several kinds of "careers" touching on show business. To be honest, I don't think she could get a job if it weren't for her father. She's been a writer (who never wrote a thing but had an office at a major studio for three years), a producer (who got a show for her actor boyfriend, who dumped her the second it was canceled), and in recent months has moved into PR, something that evidently constitutes a great many parties in a great many countries. I don't know what kind of party she's throwing in the rain forest, but trust me, if there's a way...

Let's face it, if you're one of two children of a man who's worth more than three hundred million dollars, who cares what you do? The point is, she'll be getting half of it in the end. I only hopes she lives long enough to receive it. (She is extremely generous, my friend is, and I have an ongoing short list of charities I push on her to hit her parents up for. When she gets her part of the family fortune, I'm hoping for additional influence.)

They all have strange names in Morning's family. The mother's a flower. Daisy. Her brother's a car—Corvette, aka Corey. And Papa's Old Testament, Leviticus. To make matters worse, their last name is Rubinowitz. That's what you look under in the phone book to find them, Leviticus D. Rubinowitz, but beyond the close-knit circle of good friends and family, he is known as Levi D. Rubin, executive producer of some of the most popular prime-time TV dramas for the past forty years.

The Rubinowitzes' home is high in the Hollywood hills, complete with fences, a massive iron gate and a twenty-four-hours-a-day guard. Daisy has told me to come up for lunch, Levi's coming home, and whatever questions I have he'll be happy to answer, it would be wonderful to see me. So I have arrived and we're sitting in the sunroom, having a glass of ice tea served by Tita, who I've known, I am amazed to remember, for twelve years now.

Daisy and I catch up on our families. In the summer of our junior year, Morning was in so much trouble in so many places that she came to live with me and Mother and Rob for the summer. She got into trouble there, too (got caught giving some guy a blow job in the parking lot of the mall; backed Mother's car into a pond; made an unwanted pass at my brother), but Mother has a way of sorting things out, and it included inviting the

Rubinowitzes east for a visit, the highlight of which was to see their daughter making milk shakes at McDonald's. (She had been demoted from the counter because she was rude to customers.)

At any rate, Daisy likes my mother a good deal and always asks after her. ("A true lady, through and through," she says every time I talk to her, "just like my grandmother from Germany.")

Despite the immense amount of money they possess, the Rubinowitzes have not been unscarred by tragedy. I think that's why Morning and I became friends, because we shared that. There had been another brother in the family, the eldest, Utah. (He was the state.) When Morning was twelve and the family was vacationing at their home on Lake Tahoe, Utah was killed in a motorboat accident. Morning says her mom has been kind of out of it ever since, and suspects she is addicted to tranquilizers.

Levi arrives home from the studio and we hug and sit and chat. Then Tita announces lunch is ready and we go outside under the terrace canopy. It is surprisingly warm and sunny today, a welcome relief, Daisy says, from all the rain they've been having.

Daisy is blond (not for real, naturally, but she looks it), trim and works out a lot. She still smokes cigarettes, however, and it does not agree with her lungs. Her attractiveness is marred by coughing fits and her face is getting that slightly lopsided look that old face-lifts can offer in later years.

Levi adores her. A lot of guys in Hollywood have played around, but for all his money and success, he's remained gaga over his "princess." They've been married forty years and he never seems to notice anything wrong, not even if, as I saw once, Daisy starts watering silk flowers.

It's so funny because so many people in the industry are scared of Levi. I couldn't be. Behind his gruff manner and bearlike presence, he is too warm, too caring. He is also one of those men who loves women.

"I wondered what you might know about Lilliana Martin, Levi."

"She's going to win an Oscar for *The Long Road,*" Daisy says matter-of-factly. "Levi saw a rough cut. She was terrific."

He murmurs agreement. "Come a long way from the soaps."

"She was going out with that crook, Cliff Yarlen," Daisy adds, looking to her husband. "Who murdered him?"

I am thunderstruck by the casualness of her statement.

"Who knows," Levi says, sounding tired, sipping some cold cucumber soup, "they're all interchangeable."

"Can we slow down a minute?" I ask. "Cliff Yarlen was a crook, everybody knew that?"

"He wasn't an outright crook," Levi says, "he was the point man forced onto the union. The American Federation of Technology Workers is a relatively new outfit. I don't know, I think it was the Gambinos who cooked it up in Jersey. Then they made their way out here, got into a couple special-effects labs upstate, and, uh, then brought people out from New Jersey. I think Yarlen was out of Jersey. Now, let's see." He shakes his head. "No, I got it right, Genovese was New York. Jersey's the Gambino unions. Or was. Anyway, they sent Yarlen out here and railroaded him to president. He was a bright guy. A personable guy." He nods. "He did okay out here. Smooth talker."

"And he got the union into Monarch Studios?" I ask.

"Yeah. They got into Monarch, but I think that's still their only major studio. For example, we wouldn't touch them. At least not yet. But who knows, the way things are going." He looks thoughtful a moment. "They really only need Monarch. Because Monarch's buying up everything in sight."

I continue to grill Levi over soup and salad and toasted French bread and am amazed at his cavalier attitude about Cliff Yarlen's role in organized crime.

"What do you mean he was put in place to make sure the right bosses are on the job?"

"They need the right boss to file the right data," he says. "Who worked, how long, the nature of the job. The guy in that seat can say whatever he wants."

"You mean it's a license to steal," I say.

"Well, to be fair, it's not like the old days. Production can get an overseer in there now, but if the studio exec is bad, his guy's going to be in on it. So the whole exercise is moot."

"But suppose the boss on the floor is honest about billing," I say. "What other crime could there be? I mean, if Cliff was an organized crime figure, what was the illegal part?"

"Well," Levi says, "it could be any number of things. To start with, whenever I see a new union manage to wriggle into this town—and that's tough, trust me—I always assume the studio has some less-than-sterling financing they need to use. Money that might go undetected awhile longer if it is funneled through a new organization."

"Are you talking money-laundering?"

"All right, let me explain," he says, pushing all the dishes away from him.

"You must be getting old, Levi," his wife says. "For forty years you've been saying there is no organized crime in Hollywood."

"Well this is off the record, right, kiddo?" he asks me. "I mean you're not going to finger your old pal Levi, are you?"

"Of course not. I'm just trying to understand what might have happened to Cliff."

His expression grows concerned. "He was a friend of yours?"

I shake my head. "I just met him, back east. The day he was killed, actually."

"He was in with a bad crowd. Nice guy, but bad crowd," he says gravely. "I'd never let him near my family." He clears his throat, reaches for his dirty plate and plunks it back down in front of him. "This is Monarch Studios, created in the 1930s, in large part the brainchild of Frank Nitti, heir to Al Capone."

"I thought they were Chicago," I say.

"Chicago took Hollywood, kiddo," he says. "Anyway, they established a procedure. They took their illegal booze and cigarette and prostitution and gambling monies and funneled it into Hollywood and then back out again through the unions they controlled." He shrugs. "It's a fact of the business to this day. Who cares where the cash comes from as long as you get to make your movie? It's just the way it is, we need megabucks."

"You used to say organized crime never existed, Levi," Daisy says again, sounding increasingly annoyed.

"So," he continues, taking my plate and setting it down, "this is the Chicago mob." He connects the mob plate to the studio plate with a fork. Then he takes Daisy's plate and sets it down above the other two. "Here's the unions." He connects that plate to the studio with a fork, to the mob with a knife, forming a triangle. "Now they got it coming and going, everybody's happy. And then the fifties come." He puts a soup bowl on top of the Monarch plate and points to it. "TV." He looks at me expectantly. "See?"

I shake my head. "Sorry."

He points to the stacked studio and TV plate and bowl.

"You got twice the production load here, but not enough financing."

"What about the box office?"

He looks at me as if I'm a moron. "Trust me, there isn't enough financing for everybody who wants to make a movie. Never has been, never will. Everybody wants to make a movie, everybody's looking for money. So we get New York pushing its way into Hollywood. And then we get all these international assholes falling in line behind the studios. Old Nazi money coming from Switzerland and South America. We got crazy Arabs. Asian heroin rings. You name it. And then in the 1970s..." He stands up and walks away a few steps, looking around for something. He comes back and plunks down a big plastic bucket on the table. "This is the cocaine money arriving."

I look at him. He nods vigorously. "Yeah. And look what happens. A whole slew of new TV production houses and independent film studios pop up around *that* money." He crowds our water glasses and coffee cups around the bucket. Then he lays two pieces of silverware, end to end, to connect the union plate to the cluster of smaller studios. Then he puts a saucer on top of that connection and points at it. "That's our new born-and-bred California mob. A whole new generation with fancy names and Ivy League educations and manners, the works. Okay," Levi continues, "so we've got more money, more jobs, more product than ever in Hollywood." He looks at me. "So who's gotta problem?"

I point to the Monarch plate and the Chicago mob plate. "The original syndicate and studio," I say. "They've lost their market share and control over the unions."

"Precisely," he confirms. He looks at Daisy. "Smart girl, I always said so." He sits back slightly, gesturing with his hands. "So what can they do? *Go to the new technology.* Those special effects. All those computers.

The lasers, the digital art, the CDs, the Internet, all that stuff... The syndicate says we'll create a whole new union, pull talent out of the old Bell Labs, MIT, Silicon Valley, build it up, bit by bit, and then come a-calling to an ailing movie giant."

"And the offer is?"

Levi tears off a piece of bread—"This is the AFTW"—and puts it down between the studio and the original unions and the cocaine money with the independents around it. "We'll give you a break on labor costs if you give us work."

"The original unions must have gone crazy," I say.

"Oh, yes—but the feds say," Levi continues, "hey, your workin' class fellas can haul cable scenery and drive trucks, but they can't design computer programs. So the new union specializes in all these gimmick productions, Monarch tries them out on a series of special-effect and animation flicks, then throws them more work as they acquire a cartoon studio, Internet companies, video houses, all that stuff. I haven't even gotten to the music industry yet." He picks up a fork and holds it like a figure standing on the plate representing organized crime. "And then your friend Cliff came in with the crowning achievement. He negotiated the first long-term agreement with Monarch, and worked the AFTW into some of the independents."

"And?"

He throws the fork representing Cliff over his shoulder. It bounces off the concrete into the bushes. "Somebody got rid of him."

I sit there for a moment.

Daisy gets up, muttering she liked it better in the old days when organized crime didn't exist, and goes into the house.

"Who got rid of him?" I finally say.

He sits back from the empire on the table. "Hard to say. I've heard he was a target for other unions. I've heard the feds were about to nail him with indictments, left and right." He turns his head to the side slightly. "And I heard that his big brother, Nicky Arlenetta, has been muscling in to try and take control of the AFTW."

I take a moment to absorb this information. "His own brother would kill him?"

He shrugs. "Or have somebody else do it."

I think about this. "But they're from the same family," I say. "I mean the same crime family, aren't they?"

He shakes his head. "No, Nicky's New York, part of the old Genoveses. Cliff was Jersey." He gives a hardy heh-heh-heh, as if recalling some memory he can't share with me. "After Atlantic City got rolling, who the hell knows what's what anymore back there."

"What about Malcolm Kieloff?" I ask, referring to the CEO of Monarch. "How involved is he?"

Levi laughs. "Malcolm doesn't care about anything except looking good and making people happy. He's a terrific businessman. Genius, actually, I believe that. And a decent guy."

How many times have I heard that about the superrich? "Yeah, but he must be a part of this," I insist.

Levi shakes his head. "No. Not really. He just hires who he thinks are the right people and let's them do their thing. As long as the product is good, business is good, people are happy and stockholders are proud."

"Do you know Jonathan Small?"

He frowns. "Ugh, that pip-squeak. Yeah, I know him."

"He was just made the head of movie production at Monarch."

Levi nods. "He's the one who brought the deal with the AFTW." He flashes his palm in the air, as much as to say, *ta-dah.* "What a surprise he was given production."

"What do you think of him? As an executive?"

He offers a tired laugh, shaking his head. "I've seen fifty Jonathan Smalls come and go in this town, and he will not be the last. But I'll tell you this, no trail will lead back to him, not if they got rid of the evidence efficiently."

"What evidence?"

"Cliff Yarlen," he explains.

CHAPTER TWENTY

With my new lesson in movie-making under my belt, I head back across town to see Lilliana. I've got a ton of angry messages on my voice mail, not the least of which is one from the NYPD because I'd forgotten to call in again. I call Will Rafferty because on his message he says it's urgent and I believe him.

"They found Spencer Hawes this morning! He's alive, he's down in Long Beach."

"Oh, thank you, God," I say, eyes tearing. "Thank you, God."

Will gives me the address of the hospital. Spencer was dumped at the emergency room entrance this morning and a press guy heard the radio call to the police. That's all he knows for sure.

Three hours later, I have gotten as far as the waiting room outside ICU where two police officers have instructed me to sit until they get back to me. The nurse, at least, tells me that Spencer is resting comfortably.

Two hours pass. I'm about to give up, when another police officer comes around the corner with Mr. and Mrs.

Hawes. They rush to embrace me. They are terrified, baffled and hopelessly out of their depth in something like this.

I don't know them well at all. I spent one weekend up at their house in Maine, and was somewhat shocked at how "country" Spencer's parents were. They did not like movies and did not read much. They enjoyed game shows, motor boating, fishing, square dancing and were active with their church.

Spencer's mother is a small, strong woman with many lines in her face from the sun. His father is tall, heavyset, with deep lines in his face as well. He smokes cigars all the time, and when he can't, he chews them. He's chewing one now.

"How is he?" Mrs. Hawes asks, clutching my hand in both of hers.

"The nurse says he's resting comfortably." I glare at the two officers. "They won't let me see him."

"Of course, we'll all go together," she says, turning to the policeman who escorted them up. "She's practically his wife."

Mr. Hawes, looking very tired, puts his arm around his wife's shoulders to steer her to follow a nurse. I trail behind the policeman, who whispers, "You've got a lot of people looking for you, Sally Harrington."

"Not as many as were looking for Spencer."

"Don't be so sure about that."

"Can I please just see Spencer before we get into this?" I plead.

I am relieved when we actually leave the ICU area and enter what looks like a normal ward. The nurse explains it's post-op for orthopedics.

Spencer might be going to be all right, but nothing could prepare us for what we see.

My handsome Spencer is monstrous-looking. His lips are cracked and broken, his hair shaved off on one side where there are several black, horrid-looking stitches. He is asleep with his eyes open, the whites of his eyes exposed, his puffy lips slightly open. He is, we're told, heavily sedated. His right arm is bandaged and slung in a trapeze, his right leg is in a cast to his hip. He has an IV in his left arm and a larger tube disappearing down the front of his hospital gown.

Mrs. Hawes leans over the bed to gently close his eyes, and then lifts his upper lip. We all gasp, because there are only bloody stumps where his front and eye-teeth had been. With a wail, Mrs. Hawes runs out of the room with Mr. Hawes following. I can hear her crying hysterically in the hallway.

"It's okay," I whisper, taking Spencer's free hand in mine. His nails are broken, but clean. He has no idea I'm there. I lean close to his ear. "Everybody's safe, so are you, every-thing's going to be all right."

"He's going to be fine, you know," the nurse says brightly. "Everyone looks bad right after surgery."

"What *are* the extent of his injuries?"

"The elbow's going to give him the most trouble," the nurse says. "He's going to have to have more surgery, but the doctor will tell you all about that. His leg looks worse than it is. It's broken in two places, but it's clean. They had to put a pin in there, but it'll be stronger than before."

I take a deep, shaky breath, trying to regain my compo-sure. I can still hear Mrs. Spencer crying, "Why, why, why?"

"This is a feeding tube?" I ask, pointing to the tube down his gown.

"Until his mouth feels better."

"And this?" I point to the IV in his left arm.

"For dehydration. He was badly dehydrated when he was found." She points to his mouth. "Obviously broken teeth, but he's lucky, no evidence of jaw fracture." She grimaces. "It's like he got hit in the mouth with something."

"A tank, perhaps," I say dully.

"Oh, I know, it is distressing, isn't it?" the nurse says. "But they think he fell from a height onto some kind of hard structure. His injuries, his elbow and his leg—it would be consistent with falling, for example, twenty feet in an elevator shaft or something."

I look at her. "Is that what they think? An elevator shaft?"

Her eyes move to the door behind me. I turn around. There is a man in his late thirties or so, good-looking, dark hair, dark eyes. Very preppy. His expression for some reason makes me suspect he's FBI or something. That or an escapee from a Ralph Lauren ad.

My beeper goes off. I look at it. Will Rafferty. Eyes on the man in the doorway, I extract my phone out of my purse and call in. "Rafferty," Will says.

"It's Sally."

"Thank God. Listen, we got a crew outside in the parking lot. Can you get out there and do a quick report?"

"I'll get back to you."

"Sally!"

"I said I'll get back to you," I say forcefully, clicking off. I walk toward the door. "Excuse me," I say to the stranger. "I need to talk to his parents, give them the score. They're very upset."

Wordlessly he steps to the side to let me pass.

I can hear Mr. Hawes trying to calm his wife down. I follow the sound and see that they are huddled together in a small conference room. I can't imagine what the other patients think is going on. I take a breath, throw back my shoulders and try to bounce into the room. "Good news!" I exclaim.

Mrs. Hawes stops in mid-sob to look up.

"He's going to have to have dental implants," I say, "but

he'll look better than ever. No jaw damage, no permanent marks on his face, the leg is a simple break—two places, but should heal in six weeks. The elbow is a little trickier. He'll have full use, of course, but might have to have a little more treatment."

I sit next to Mrs. Hawes to take her hand. "I swear to you, he's going to be fine. They think he fell somewhere. But he's all patched up now and they're loading nutrients in him through that one tube under his gown, and hydration in that IV in his arm. They just want to make sure he rests now, and that he starts to heal, and while he's sleeping, you see, they're building him up." I look up at Mr. Hawes. "The doctor should be coming to see you very soon."

Spencer's mother wipes her eyes with a little ball of Kleenex. I search my bag and find a paper napkin and give it to her. "He looks so scary, like someone I don't know," she says.

"Mmm." I nod in sympathy. "But he is your son and he is going to be all right and he will be himself very soon. You'll see a tremendous change in him by tomorrow." God, I hope so.

My beeper is going off again. I excuse myself to look at it. Will again. I know what he wants.

"My suggestion," I tell Spencer's parents, "is that we wait with Spencer until the doctor comes to talk to us. Then I will get you settled in a hotel nearby and you guys can eat and get some rest. And come back in the morning."

"The police said they have a place for us to stay," Mr. Hawes says.

"Good, well, I'll just make sure you get settled."

"Thank you," she says, squeezing my hand. I stand up and help her up.

"Okay, bright faces, now, he's going to be all right," I prompt, moving them along. "I think maybe you might

want to whisper to him that you're here," I add on the way.
"Then he'll know everything's all right. Even in his sleep."

My beeper goes off again. This time I take the batteries
out of it and shut off my cell phone. Then I follow Spencer's
parents into the room and they do much better this time, and
talk to their son. I relax a little, leaning against the windowsill. Then that man appears at the door again, signal-
ing for me to come outside.

"Sally Harrington?" he says quietly, taking something
out of his pocket. He flashes some credentials at me, which
I take from him to carefully study. Schyler Preston, federal
prosecutor, United States Department of Justice. Looks
legit. I hand them back to him.

"Why don't you come this way, where we can talk."

He leads me back to that same little conference room. I
take a seat and he closes the door behind us. He sits down
across from me. "I'm very interested in your connection to
Cliff Yarlen."

I cough a little and cover my mouth. I drop my hand.
"Spencer has been missing for over a week and is dumped
half-dead at this hospital and you are interested in my relationship with Cliff Yarlen."

"Yes."

He wears a wedding ring. Of course.

"Well, guess what? I have no real connection to Cliff
Yarlen."

He pulls out a notebook from his inside blazer pocket and
turns some pages. "The day he died he had been at your
house in Castleford, Connecticut. Then he drove you to
DBS headquarters in Manhattan. Later you met him at the
Admiral's Club at JFK, where you kissed him. On the
mouth."

"He kissed me," I say quietly. This must be someone
else's life. Has to be. I straighten up in my chair. "What happened to Spencer?"

"I'm sorry," he says.

"So am I, but what happened to him?"

"We're working on it."

I look around. "You know, my network wants me to go outside and do a live report on Spencer being found." I check his reaction. None. "Why don't we just go outside and then you can listen as I explain to America what's going on. Who is where, including the fact that you're here—"

"Don't do it," he warns me.

"I'm going to have to tell them something."

"No, you don't. You could slip out of here, they'll never know."

"I have to take Spencer's parents to a hotel."

"We will look after Mr. and Mrs. Hawes."

I sigh, trying to get my thinking straight. "Well, I'll tell you this much. I know you were about to indict Cliff."

No expression from the prosecutor.

"And what I say is true, I have no connection with Cliff except that I met him on what turned out to be his worst day." I swallow, trying to choose my words carefully. "I know he was a key executive for an organized crime syndicate out of New Jersey. I know his brother, Nicky Arlenetta, wanted to take over his union. I also know he had an arrangement with a seventeen-year-old rich kid who house-sits, that Cliff spent time in six different houses since last summer, and that his activities in those houses involved Jonathan Small and Lilliana Martin."

At last, the slightest tightening of his jaw. I think he's starting to be a little impressed. "What is your connection to Jonathan Small?"

I have to laugh out loud. "What my connection is with everybody in this mess! Supposedly sexual."

It was not the answer he expected.

I dismiss my answer out of the air with my hand. "It's finally beginning to dawn on me that there's been an awful lot of unexpected sexual interest in me of late, and I'm not sure how much of it was real. Is real."

"Was Jonathan Small sexually interested in you? Is that why he went to your hotel room last night?"

So he knew that, too. "That's what I thought."

"What do you think now?"

"I think he was trying to find out the same thing you are. What my connection was to Cliff." I laugh to myself again, shaking my head. "Good grief, I thought he was there to try and make love to me." I look at him. "Now I think he was probably there to figure out whether or not I should be killed, too."

I notice that my right hand has a slight tremor. I hide it under the table.

Preston's flipping through his notebook and stops at a page, finger tracing some words. "How close are Spencer Hawes and Malcolm Kieloff?"

"They aren't. Spencer just rewrote his book in English for him. He didn't even sign it up. The CEO of Bennett, Fitzallen & Coe acquired it and dumped it on Spencer."

He nods. Turns a page and looks up. "What about this surveillance camera on Hawes's apartment in Manhattan?"

"Oh," I groan, looking away. "Look, that has nothing to do with this, although if you guys want to look into it, fine. I'd appreciate knowing who completely destroyed my mother's peace of mind in Castleford."

"I think Wendy may have some information for you on that," he tells me.

I blink. "Wendy from DBS?"

He nods.

"You sound as though you know her."

"I do," he says simply. He's pulling a phone out of his pocket. "And I'm going to call her now and she's going to talk to you."

"About what?"

"About a deal."

Within moments I'm listening to Wendy explain that if I agree to keep quiet on everything I know, after the case breaks the feds promise the exclusive to DBS.

"Who brokered this deal?" I ask.

"Alexandra," Wendy replies.

"Well, she better talk to Will, because he's hounding me on another line to go outside and make a statement."

"Perhaps it's not in the best interests of the network for a whole lot of people to know about this," Wendy suggests.

"So why do you?"

"Because I'm the head of fricking security, Sally! And Alexandra's your boss! So tell Skye Preston what you know and get the hell out of there!"

"But how do you know this guy?" I persist, meeting his eyes over the table. "Sorry," I mutter to him. Back into the telephone I rephrase. "How do you know Federal Prosecutor Preston?"

"When I was in private service," she says, "I helped him break up a money-laundering operation. It was also a murder case. Herbert Glidden."

I remember that case. A couple of years ago a TV producer, Herbert Glidden, was murdered in East Hampton, Long Island. It turned out he was laundering money for a group of overseas investment institutions and they got sick of him. It was initially a tremendous scandal, exposing one major American bank, a famous clothing designer, a fashion magazine, a leading architectural firm, a winery and even a new country club in the Hamptons.

I wonder if this case is connected in some way or if Preston merely specializes in glamorous money-laundering facilities.

"Sally," Wendy says, "Skye is also a friend. His wife is

an extremely close friend. You can trust him. And you *will.* Got it?"

"Got it." I hang up and hand the phone to him. "So what do you want to know?"

"I'm not trying to clip your wings," he says seriously. "I'm just trying to find out exactly why one man is dead, who murdered him, and who nearly murdered your friend in there."

"I bet you already have a good idea," I say.

"Tell me, how did you find Lilliana Martin?"

"Who said that I did?"

"You were with her from three-twenty to nearly five-thirty yesterday afternoon."

"Is that where your tail picked me up yesterday?"

He ignores the question. "How did you find her? It's important I know."

"She called me."

He frowns. "She called you? Why?"

"I left a message for her with her attorney and when she called in, they relayed it, and she called me."

"What was the message you left?"

"That I was here, in L.A."

"And she called you and said, come on over, just like that. With everyone in Los Angeles looking for Lilliana Martin, she just said, come on over, this is where I am."

"I had to convince her. And she trusts me. Which is why I'm not sure you should be dragging her into this. She's had a big shock with Cliff's death. Maybe you should just leave her alone." I try another approach. "I suppose you know that Spencer went back to the Cold Water Canyon house last Tuesday morning to check on Lilliana. But she was gone. The house was empty. Cliff was there and he didn't know where Lilliana was, either."

He takes a pencil out of his breast pocket and makes a note. "What time?"

"About ten. Cliff left him there. No one saw Spencer after that. Not until this morning."

A light seems to dawn on the prosecutor's face. "I see what happened."

"I don't." I try to look trustworthy. "We have a deal, Mr. Preston, and Spencer is my boyfriend."

"Ex-boyfriend," he counters.

"So you know that, too. Okay." I sigh. "Still, I've agreed to your conditions. Surely you can at least tell me what significance that information has?"

"That on Tuesday morning Hawes might have been mistaken for an associate of Cliff Yarlen's. He may have been picked up to be used as some kind of hostage."

"Someone mistook an executive editor with Bennett, Fitzallen & Coe as an associate of some mob boss?" I say sarcastically. "Who could dream up that one?"

He looks down at his notebook and then back up. "What did you talk about for over two hours with Lilliana Martin yesterday?"

"Who says we were talking?"

He gets this ever so slightly startled look.

I laugh. "What do you *think* could have occupied us for over two hours?"

The faintest amount of color comes into his face.

"Lilliana spent half the time working out in her gym while I amused myself," I confide, leaning on the table. "Looking at her books and stuff. Then we just talked about the fact that Spencer had disappeared. She didn't know that. Nor did she know he disappeared right after Cliff saw him."

The prosecutor is nodding.

My next realization I keep to myself—that yesterday Lilliana had raced off to call someone about Spencer and today Spencer was dumped here. I'd rather ask her about the connection between the two events myself, prosecutor be damned. He's got enough to do.

Soon I've been excused, and after going in to see Spencer, the police help me slip out the service entrance of the hospital so I can duck my colleagues waiting outside.

CHAPTER TWENTY-ONE

Last night I went back to my hotel and spotted press people hanging out in the lobby, so I drove out to Santa Monica and took a room at the Miramar. I walked over to the mall to buy some clothes and a few things and then went back to change at the hotel and take a run along Ocean Boulevard. (Lots of people run with sunglasses on at night in this neck of the woods.) To be honest, the night was wonderful. I ate and slept like there was no tomorrow, resting in the knowledge Spencer would be okay.

Now that he's back, and I know he has been victimized, it's amazing how my very thoughts about him have changed. Yes, he is a charmer, in the past a hopeless womanizer, and obviously he has some kind of problem with money.

But you have to know him. See how loyal his colleagues are to him because he is a very talented editor and a fair and strong and dynamic business leader. He is respectful of everyone, from a janitor to a CEO. He almost always gives the benefit of the doubt to people, really only wanting to encourage people to sharpen and hone the talents and skills God gave them.

He enjoys women as equals. Unfortunately most women

find his glamorous life-style, talent and good looks and attentiveness almost irresistible, and he, equally unfortunately, has a bit of a problem saying no.

I have to say, though, that until the Malcolm Kieloff party I had never doubted his sexual or emotional allegiance to me. That's why I got so upset. It simply never occurred to me he would violate our privacy. Or pact. Or whatever it is you have when you think you're in love and are trying to clear out the ghosts of the past to make room for a future together.

Even his affair with Verity Rhodes was sincere. At the time it was going on, no one, save his friend and colleague Kate Weston, knew about it. And it went on for quite some time. The one question I never really got an answer to was whether Spencer got involved with me because he genuinely fell head over heels, or because he could no longer put up with the small part of Verity's life he was allowed to share with her. He did say, when we were talking once, late at night, after we had made love on a friend's boat (never left the dock, mind you), something like "You don't know what pain and loneliness are until you visualize the person you love lying in someone else's arms—and choosing to be there instead of with you."

I thought he was talking about all the nights Verity spent with her husband. But then Spencer said something about understanding how Doug felt about me, how painful our relationship must be for him.

Funny, but now that I think about it, it was after that night our sex life started falling apart. It was as if we both had truly realized, had truly felt, for the first time, the level of pain we had inflicted on people who had cared very deeply for us.

It was after that night the doubts started.

This morning I drive down to Long Beach and sneak into the hospital to see Spencer, but I'm told he's in another part of the hospital for some kind of tests. I wait and wait, two hours go by, but he isn't brought back, and no one knows where Mr. and Mrs. Hawes are.

I call Kate Weston in New York, who tells me Bennett, Fitzallen & Coe is paying to airlift Spencer to New York to be treated there, and so his parents can live in his apartment. *At least the rent's paid and the phone and electric are on,* I think.

Finally I give up.

I leave the flowers I've brought on the windowsill and lay my card on his pillow. I really would like to see him, but I look at my watch. It's going to take me at least an hour and a half to get back to Bel Air, and it's time to wrap this up. I can't avoid DBS News forever, not if I want a job.

I check one more time with the nurses' station and they tell me the same thing, they'll bring Spencer back as soon as the tests are done. I make my way back to the service elevator. As I turn the corner, I nearly collide with a police officer escorting a glamorous-looking woman. It is Verity Rhodes. The magazine editor of *Expectations* does a slight double-take at the sight of me but quickly recovers. "He's been asking for me," she says simply, breezing past.

As I approach Los Angeles, checking my rearview mirror every five minutes, I vow to stop thinking about Verity Rhodes and feel progressively more nervous about the car I'm driving. I have no way of knowing how many people know it by now and I don't want anyone to follow me to Lilliana's.

I pull off 495 in Torrance and swing into a Taco Bell. I go inside, walk out the other side and hike over to a mall, where I call for a car. A navy blue Lincoln Continental pulls up fifteen minutes later and I get in, directing the driver to head for Bel Air.

* * *

"Buddy, hi," I say to my old friend and detective pal back in Castleford.

"Sally, where the hell have you been?"

"Busy," I say, glancing ahead at Lucas, the driver.

"I heard about Spencer on the news. How is he?"

"Very badly banged up, but he's going to be all right. They're taking him back to New York."

"What does he say about what happened?"

"Nothing yet. He was out of it when I saw him last night and this morning I couldn't see him." I want to get off because anyone with a radio-receiving band of 900 or more can listen in on cell calls. (How do you think the media ever learns anything?) "I don't have much time," I tell him.

"Okay, so listen," Buddy says, "we're ninety-nine percent sure we know who had Spencer's bedroom under surveillance. Do you know if Spencer ever fooled around with anybody connected to Corbett Schroeder?"

"Oh, yeah," I say easily. "His wife. Verity Rhodes. I just left her at the hospital. She said he's been asking for her."

Buddy hesitates.

"It's all right," I assure him. "Please, truly, it's all right."

"That makes sense then," Buddy continues. "Wendy finally got an ID on one of the guys who was in that apartment. There were two who came and went—"

"How did she do that?"

"The guy loaned the night concierge a couple of computer magazines. His name and address were on them. Anyway, he's a freelancer for a security company that does work for Corbett Schroeder—"

"What kind of work?" I ask, curious.

"As far as I can tell, industrial espionage."

"Now, that makes sense," I declare with satisfaction. Corbett Schroeder has a veracious appetite for taking over companies, stripping their assets and dumping the carcasses. (It pays better and saves time over building good businesses and developing employee and customer loyalty.)

"So we got this guy cornered. He swears he didn't watch anything. He sat in the apartment for his shift, and when a light started flashing, he was to pop in a new videotape. The camera was set in position and was activated by motion."

"What did he do with the tapes?"

"Left them there. Someone picked them up each day. I guess they took them to Schroeder."

"Charming profile of a marriage, isn't it? Schroeder watching his wife with another man."

"So why would Schroeder be pissed off at you?" Buddy asks me.

"Remember that *Expectations* piece I wrote on Cassy Cochran?"

"Yeah."

"That wasn't the version he wanted. It was a setup job. Verity wanted me to hammer Cassy to humiliate her husband, Jackson Darenbrook. Schroeder hates him and he was counting on me to deliver. And I didn't."

"That article was extremely flattering, as I recall."

"And well it should have been," I say. "Buddy, I've got to go. Just tell me, do you have a link between the tapes and Phillip O'Hearn or not?"

"Possibly. We know a woman got the tape duplicated in New Haven. She used a fake name and paid in cash. We've got a good description from the post office, too. They remember her because she insisted no return addresses were needed on the Jiffy bags."

"Five eight, blue eyes, about forty, thin, pretty, light brown hair streaked with blond, drives an older red Mercedes," I guess.

"How did you know?"

"It's O'Hearn's current girlfriend. She lives in Wallingford."

"What's her name?"

"Doesn't matter," I tell him. "Buddy, this is really all I need to know, that it was Schroeder and O'Hearn and I'll take it from there. The girlfriend's first husband beat the hell out of her and she's got two kids under ten and O'Hearn's the only chance those kids have got, so leave her alone. I'll take care of him."

"What are you going to do?"

"I don't know, but if what I decide ends up being murder, I'll let you know." And I hang up.

I direct the driver to exit 495 to take the Mulholland way to Lilliana's. By the time we are descending into Bel Air, however, my mind is drifting back to Verity Rhodes. I think I am jealous.

When we pull up to Lilliana's gate, a man appears at the driver's window. He's got to be security or a cop, who knows which?

"Ms. Sally Harrington," the driver announces as if he's my butler.

The guy looks into the back seat at me. "Sorry, but Ms. Martin is not having any visitors today."

"You better call Ms. Martin and make sure of that."

"I am sure of it," he says. He points up the road, telling the driver where to turn around.

I get out of the car. "Get on that intercom," I command him, "and tell Lilliana I'm here. Sally Harrington."

"She's not seeing anybody," he repeats.

"Fine, I'm calling 911," I say, getting back into the car. His hand is around my wrist in a second and I am astounded at how easily he's pulled me back out of the car. I look at him directly. "Get your hand off me."

"You want me to call Ms. Martin? I'm calling Ms. Martin," he says, keeping his clamp on me and snapping a walkie-talkie out of his pocket with the other. "Yeah, I got a lady jumping up and down out here who insists I call Ms. Martin or she's callin' 911."

Squawk. "Who is she?"

He pushes the button down and extends the walkie-talkie to me. "Sally Harrington," I say.

"Hang on." *Squawk.* A minute later, "Ms. Martin says for her to go back to her hotel, she'll call her."

"Let me have that thing," I say, reaching for it. I push the talk button down. "Tell Lilliana she can either see me now, or wait until after I testify for Schyler Preston."

Now there is a silence of at least three minutes. The guy and I are eyeing each other and my driver looks like he wants to be anywhere but here.

Finally, *squawk.* "Bring her up."

"You," the guy says to the driver, "turn around up there and then park down here where I can see you. Other side of the street. Keep your windows rolled down." He wheels around suddenly, calling, "They want her up at the house!" Another man appears, walking down the drive toward the gate. He is big and dressed in a suit.

I'm getting the decided impression these guys are not the feds.

He unlocks the gate and holds out his hand, as if he's the second on a relay team. My guy hands me off, the second one holds me firmly just above the elbow.

"Very touchy-feely group, you guys," I comment, walking up the drive.

Parked in front of Lilliana's is a new silver Cadillac De-Ville and two gray Buicks. I am hand-delivered to the front door. It is opened by Lilliana, dressed in gray Champion sweatpants and a cancer-cure walkathon T-shirt. "What are you doing, Sally?" she sighs, leaning against the door frame.

"What am *I* doing?" I say. "You should see Spencer. All of his teeth are broken, his leg's been broken in two places, his elbows smashed, he's nearly dead of dehydration and you're asking me what *I'm* doing?"

"I'm glad he was found."

"Found? Seems to me it was more like you ordered him, like a cheeseburger. Serve up one Spencer Hawes, please, and then the next day there he is." I look around. "I must say, you've got interesting company. Where are the dogs?"

She doesn't answer.

"So are these the guys who killed Cliff?"

"Go away, Sally," she half pleads.

"How can I go away? I've got the mob killing people on one side of me, the feds on the other, Spencer is nearly dead, and the only one who knows what's going on is you. So I'm sticking with you until this is cleared up."

There is a low whisper from behind the front door. "All right," she whispers back to whoever it is. Then she rubs her eye and looks back at me. "Are you going to leave?"

"No."

"Okay, you win, you're in," she says, reaching to pull me in by the arm.

The front door slams behind me and is locked by this enormous wrestler-looking guy standing there. He, too, is in a dark suit.

"I win," I repeat, "and am in what?"

"Deep doo-doo, girl," the actress says over her shoulder, leading me to the kitchen. "We've got to go downstairs."

"We are downstairs," I point out.

"Into the basement." She turns around to address the guy behind me. "Can I just get some orange juice?"

"I'll get the orange juice," he tells her. "Come on, Lilliana, get down there, will you?"

"Come on," she says to me, opening a door.

We go down a set of wooden stairs into a small cement basement. There is a wine rack and a lot of outdoor stuff. In the corner there is a workshop table with a lot of tools hanging from a Peg-Board. Lilliana points to an old red-wood chair and cushion next to the water heater for me to sit on. A single light bulb is on, and the two small rectangular windows are blocked with what look like old folded-up gym mats. I sit down.

"We can play checkers or croquet," she says, falling into a redwood lounge next to me. She takes a deep breath, looking up at the floor joints over our heads. "Golly, I haven't done this in a long time."

"You've done this before?"

"Once, when I was a kid," she says quietly. "No, twice."

"And what is it, exactly, that we're doing?"

She turns her head to smile, bringing her arms up to hold them on top of her head. She's posing, for Pete's sake. "We're playing it safe."

The big guy comes downstairs with two glasses of orange juice. He hands her a glass and then me.

"Did you sample it, Joey," she says, "to make sure it's not poisoned?"

"Yes, as a matter of fact," he replies, trudging up the stairs. The door closes behind him.

Lilliana raises her glass. "Cheers." She sips a little and puts the glass down on the arm of the lounge, as if she wants to wait for it to settle in her stomach so she can make sure there's no arsenic in it. I don't touch mine at all, but put it down on the floor.

"So what's going on, Lilliana?"

"A meeting. Supposedly." She looks at her watch. "In about forty minutes we should know how it went and what's going to happen." She looks at me. "Until then, we've got—"

She stops talking because we hear the sound of some kind of motor. "Oh, no," Lilliana says, starting to get out of the lounge.

There is a weird whistling sound and then a tremendous

explosion that jolts our chairs and sends a cascade of plaster down over us. There's another whistling sound and another explosion, flipping our chairs over as the staircase comes crashing down, taking part of the kitchen floor with it. There is a horrible metal squeal and the refrigerator from the kitchen smashes down on top of it.

Lilliana has grabbed my hand and is pulling me back into the corner, under the workshop table. There are men shouting. Can that be gunfire?

This is crazy. Black smoke has started sinking from the kitchen. The house is on fire. Water is spewing like a fountain on the other side of the basement. The smoke makes me cough and I start to move out from the table, but Lilliana yanks me back. "Keep down on the floor," she commands. There is a tearing sound. "Hold this over your nose and mouth." She's pressing a piece of soft fabric in my hand. The stove falls down from the kitchen, snapping the detached staircase in two. I smell gas. Lilliana runs over to the cyclone cellar doors, slides the bolt across and throws open the door, the outside light partially blocked by smoke and dust and floating debris. Then she runs back, grabs me and pulls me into a crawl space up behind the water heater.

"Keep down no matter what," she whispers.

"Lilliana!" yells a male voice from what's left of the kitchen.

I wait for her to call out, but she doesn't.

"Go around to the back," the male voice says.

We don't move. The smoke is bad. Water is pooling across the floor, the charred debris drifting down from the kitchen hisses as it hits the water.

"Cellar doors are open, she's gone!"

"Check the pool house!"

Someone passes in front of the cellar door. We cringe, trying not to cough.

"Fuck it, where is she?"

"Shit," the first voice says.

We hear the whine of a siren.

"All right, come on, let's get out of here."

I long to cough, but curl down even farther, practically stuffing the cloth in my mouth. We're not going to last long, not with the amount of smoke coming down.

I hear more sirens. "Sally Harrington!" I hear someone yelling outside. "Sally Harrington!"

"Who's that?" Lilliana says.

"Who cares? Come on," I say, grabbing Lilliana and pulling her to get down out of this crawl space. We both double over, coughing. "Here!" I try to yell, leading the way to the cyclone doors, but I can't breathe. Stars appear before my eyes, I'm swooning. Lilliana has stumbled to her knees behind me. I drop the cloth and pull her with two hands. My lungs are burning, I can't see, I trip and fall, try to get up.

A pair of hands grab me and pull, and I pull Lilliana. The heat is horrible but the smoke turns from black to gray and embers and soot are flying everywhere and I hear sirens and cries and then, suddenly, we fall on the lawn and the air is sweet and I cough and gag and Lilliana does, too, and I see that the guy who pulled us out is my driver and all he is saying is "God, oh God," like a whimpering child, "Jesus God."

I close my eyes. More hands are on me, turning me over. Something over my face. It feels cold, good. I open my eyes.

"Oxygen," the firefighter says. Lilliana has a mask on already and it crosses my mind they gave her one before me—ah, celebrity.

I roll over and squint at the house. For a stone house, the damage is tremendous. The cedar roof has a large jagged hole, the edges of which are burning, the windows are all blown out, and part of the back side of the house is simply missing.

Lilliana pulls off her mask. "Where's Joey?" she croaks.

"I don't know, ma'am," the medic says.

"Joey!" she screams, trying to get on her feet.

"He must have been the one in the kitchen," someone says, and Lilliana starts running and I get up and go after her, and the driver runs after me. A fire truck has just rammed the gate open and is coming up the drive. Lilliana has stopped, her eyes wild. She grabs my arm. "We've got to get out of here."

I have learned to believe this woman.

I look around to the driver. "Where's the car?"

"You got to go to the hospital," he says.

Ladders are going up, another fire truck swings in. Hoses are running up the drive.

"Get us out of here!" I tell him.

"Down the hill," he says, pointing. We run down the driveway. Cops are there. "Hey, you, stop!" one of them cries.

"We're going back to our house next door!" I yell, as if I am a neighbor. "They told us to get out of the way!"

We hurry down the drive. The car is parked quietly on the far side of the road, heading downhill. Lucas runs around to the driver side and we jump in and he takes off. We pass more emergency vehicles screaming up the road. "Where to?" he says into the mirror.

"Palm Springs," Lilliana tells him.

He steps on the gas and looks at me in the rearview mirror. "You know this is going to cost extra, right?"

CHAPTER TWENTY-TWO

I feel more than a little like Thelma and Louise, except we have Lucas, the poor guy, stuck driving us and I don't know who it is we are fleeing. All I know is I'm the only one who has any cash on them because, thank God, I left my pocketbook in the car. This was Lucas's first fare of the day and Lilliana only has on a sooty athletic bra and her sweatpants, since it was her T-shirt we used against the smoke.

We stop at a Mobil Mart near the airport and I slip into the ladies' room to take a sorely needed whiz and to examine the scrapes and bruises. While Lilliana sneaks into the ladies' room next, I continue into the store to buy a medium T-shirt that says California on it, two pairs of sunglasses, three quarts of water, three cartons of yogurt, three coffee cakes, a bag of low-fat potato chips, bubble gum, sugarless gum, a chocolate bar, a bag of popcorn, three apples, a carton of orange juice, a bag of strawberry twists and a pack of Marlboro Lights. And last but not least, I have the cashier throw in a state lottery ticket because if I'm not the luckiest person alive in the world today, no one is.

I return to the ladies' room to give Lilliana the T-shirt and sunglasses, and make my way back to the car to find Lucas listening to the all-news station. "They said something about it!" he says, excited.

"As curious as I am about what is in Palm Springs," I say to Lilliana when she gets back in the car, "I'm thinking maybe I should find Schyler Preston." I hand Lilliana the cigarettes. "You do know who he is."

She makes a small sound of disgust while opening the cigarettes. "Yes." She kicks her head back in the direction of Bel Air. "Great job he did, huh?"

"That was the feds?"

"No," she mutters, lighting up and opening her window, "that was the outcome of their fine work."

I look at my watch. "If we go to John Wayne Airport, I think I know how we can get a ride back to New York."

"I don't want to go to New York," she says. "I want to go home."

"To Ohio?"

"To Larkensburg," she replies, pulling heavily on the cigarette. "It's east of the Springs."

"Ah, Larkensburg, of course," I say, tearing open the bag of popcorn with my teeth. "What the hell is Larkensburg?"

"Get us to 10 East, will you, Lucas?" she says.

"Wait a minute," I complain.

"Shh, shh! Here it is!" Lucas cries, turning up the radio.

"The Bel Air mansion where actress Lilliana Martin has been living was firebombed this afternoon by unidentified assailants. Witnesses say a traffic helicopter flew over the mansion about two-thirty and a rocketlike projectile flew into the roof of the house, followed moments later by a second, which hit the rear of the mansion. Both projectiles exploded in streaks of fire upon impact."

A woman's voice. "I thought it was a traffic helicopter, you know, just a little one like you always see flying around. And then I thought, gosh, are they landing in the backyard or something? but then this guy was hanging out the side and I thought, oh, my God, that's a gun or something, but it launched like a rocket. It blew up the roof and then he shot a second one into the house, but when it exploded the fire was like liquid, going all over everywhere."

"Two people were severely injured and rushed to the hospital. The whereabouts of Lilliana Martin are not known, nor have police confirmed that she was in the house at the time of the bombing.

"No one has claimed credit for the attack and the FBI is checking for possibilities of terrorism."

"Stop the car!" I yell at Lucas, who was about to drive away from the Mobil Mart.

"We've got to get going," Lilliana says.

"I've got to make a call," I say, jumping out of the car. I race back to the pay phone and call into the DBS newsroom. "This is Sally Harrington. Can't talk but take this down. I was in the Bel Air mansion when the firebombing occurred. I am fine. I will call again as soon as I know when I can go on the air." And I hang up. Then I call back. "Please call my mother and tell her I told you to call and that I am fine." I hang up.

I get back into the car and Lilliana is having a fit. "Who did you call? You called the damned news people, didn't you?"

"Yes, I called DBS News, yes I told them I was in the house and survived the blast. That's it. Not a word about you. Got it? Not a word about you. No one will know if you were in that house or not."

"You reporters are all alike!" she fumes. "You can't keep your damn mouth shut!"

I give her a look that would make most people wither inside. "Gee, Lilliana, and you've been such a joy to know."

We drive on in silence until I cool off and apologize to her. "It's just that if the network is going to have to bail me out of this," I explain, "I've got to give them something. I know NYPD is probably ready to throw me in the slammer for disappearing on them. God only knows what Schyler Preston will have in mind for me."

"Listen," Lucas suddenly says from the front seat, "I've been thinking about this. I don't mind pulling you girls out of the fire and running away from the police and all, but I don't think I really want to know anything more about who all these people are that are after you." He looks in the rearview mirror. "Do you get where I'm coming from?"

"We're already thinking about that, Lucas," I say. "I promise."

Fifteen minutes later an update on the firebombing story says that DBS News has confirmed that their reporter, Sally Harrington, was in the mansion at the time of the bombing and the authorities are looking for her.

"Oh man, oh man, oh man," Lucas says like a mantra.

"Lucas," I say, scooting forward, "could we borrow the car? That way you wouldn't have to be involved anymore. If any of this ever gets back to you, you could just tell the authorities we took it."

He looks in the rearview mirror. "This car's not even one year old. It's my office."

"I work for DBS," I explain, "you know they'll make good on it. And Lilliana—" I gesture. "She's going to win an Oscar, so you know she's going to be good for it."

"Thanks for the vote of confidence," she says coolly. She takes off her plastic sunglasses to look at Lucas in the mirror. She's all charm. "I really wouldn't want your name to get mixed up in this, Lucas."

"Yeah, all right, I guess," he says none too happily.

It is a beautiful car.

"It goes back to 1978," Lilliana sighs, smoking. We're both in the front seat now, me driving. We've left Lucas to his own devices with a little cash and an IOU for the gas he put in the car on his credit card, for I dare not use one or hit an ATM. "It's kind of a long story," she adds.

"We've got time," I say. I glance over. "Can you look in the glove compartment and see if there's a map?"

"I know the way," she assures me, but she opens it, anyway, and lets out a whistle. "Look what Lucas left us."

It is a black handgun. Lilliana takes it out.

"Lilliana!" I protest, swerving across the lane.

She opens the chamber. "Loaded, too."

"Put it away!"

"Safety's on, don't worry," she tells me. She puts it under her seat. "Problem with the nine millimeter, though, is it jams so easily."

I look over at her. "You know guns?" I turn back to the road and say to myself, aloud, "Of course she knows guns. She knows everything. She knows how to get firebombed, win an Oscar and seduce strangers."

She offers a quiet laugh and begins to talk, so that, over the next two hours, I might understand what the heck is going on.

CHAPTER
TWENTY-THREE

"Once upon a time, in 1930," Lilliana begins, and I know right away she must be telling me some kind of legend, for her voice has assumed the slightly awed tone of a child, "a boat docked in Ellis Island. On it was a man named Mario Arlenetta. He settled in Brooklyn and worked for his cousin on the waterfront. He married a girl named Delores and their first child, Joseph, was born in 1932."

Inwardly I groan. I hate long stories told this way. You're supposed to give the relevant news *first,* so you can see the context all this history holds for the present. But hey, she's an actress not a journalist, and so I continue to drive, listening carefully to the facts as she presents them.

Mario and Delores had more children. Mario got a job at the Fulton Fishmarket in Manhattan where he kept track of truck deliveries for the Genovese crime family.

Ah, I think, *now we're getting somewhere. The Genoveses...*

By the time he was fifteen, young Joseph Arlenetta was working for the Family, too. By age nineteen he was running a group of laundromats in Brooklyn and lower Manhattan and by twenty-four, was handling the laundry needs of several restaurants. In perhaps the most important move of his career, in 1953 he married Gina Presario, daughter of

Rocky Presario, a New Jersey boss for the Gambino crime family. Nicky was born 1954, Rose in 1956, Theresa in 1959, Clifford in 1962 and Michael in 1963, by which time Joseph's laundry operations had moved uptown into some of the finest Manhattan hotels.

By the time young Nicky Arlenetta was twelve, he was running numbers in the neighborhood. By thirteen he had a record. Joe packed him off to military school in Pennsylvania. The last thing he wanted was for him to get into the family "business." Nicky ran away and lived with a gang member for two months before Joe could find him. Joe sent Nicky away again and this time he ran away and wasn't found for almost five months, when he was arrested in the Bronx for murder.

Lilliana finally takes a breath and I shift in my seat as I await Nicky's fate.

Nicky got off the murder charge and moved back home to work in the family "business" with papa. As Joe's star rose within the Genovese organization and he was given more and more responsibility to oversee parts of the family's Manhattan hotel and restaurant unions, son Nicky rose with him. Except for another arrest for murder in 1974, for which he was cleared, Nicky was doing well.

Under the leadership of Don Funzi Tieri, the Genovese and Gambino families happily coexisted and Joe's union activities in New York began cross-fertilizing with those New Jersey unions run by his father-in-law, Rocky Presario. In the late 1970s, with legalized gambling moving into Atlantic City, Joe made a bid to control part of the hotel unions there. Rocky might have gone along with it, but his own son, Frankie, wanted the territory for his own, and Joe Arlenetta's attempts were rebuffed.

"This is Cliff's father we're talking about?" I ask. "Joseph Arlenetta?"

"Yes," the actress says, slightly annoyed I've interrupted her dramatic telling of this saga.

"And the brother, Nicky—is he the one who was trying to muscle in on Cliff's union in L.A.?"

"You're going out of order," she informs me.

"I'm sorry, go ahead."

Although his father, Rocky Presario, may have stepped over a few bodies in his day, son Frankie Presario was from the new generation who wanted to use the illegal gains from the previous generations to build legitimate and profitable businesses. Long gone, he maintained, were the freewheeling days of sucking off the unions the way the Arlenettas still did. It was time to build on worker loyalty, strong contracts, good benefits and winning great wages off the boom of legalized gambling in Atlantic City.

"So was Frankie Presario a crook or wasn't he?" I interrupt again.

"He graduated from Georgetown University," she says.

I glance over. "So was he a crook or not?"

Lilliana insists, "He was an ethical guy born into a family of crooks. Making the best of a difficult situation."

"Yeah, right, whatever you say." I smile, driving on.

"Before Georgetown, he went to a seminary, he was going to be a priest."

"All right, I'll take your word for it. So where are we? Frankie's doing his best in a difficult situation...."

"Frankie Presario married a girl from Philadelphia, Celia Bruno—"

"Wait a minute," I interrupt yet again. "This wouldn't be a Bruno as in Angelo Bruno, the don of Philadelphia, would it?"

"Well, yes, it might be," Lilliana admits.

"Ah, no crooks here, not in this family."

Silence.

I glance over and can see Lilliana is ticked off. Too late

do I realize she must know all this information for a reason, all the names, the dates... "I'm sorry, please continue. I *like* Frankie and Celia," I add.

She resumes her story. Frankie and Celia Presario lived in Bergen County, New Jersey. They had two kids, a boy, Taylor, and a girl, Lise. In the fall of 1979, Frank agreed he would pick up Taylor and some of his teammates after school and drive them to an out-of-town soccer match, so he took the station wagon to work. After the kids caught the bus to school, Celia went shopping, but when she started Frankie's Cadillac, she was blown up into a million pieces.

The hit, intended for Frankie, had been carried out by Nicky Arlenetta. He had wanted Frankie out of the way so the Arlenettas could roll into Atlantic City.

Frankie, crazy with rage and grief, promptly sought permission for revenge. It didn't come from New York. He went to Angelo Bruno in Philadelphia, but as enthusiastic as the don was, a few days later he was found in his car with his head blown off. So Frankie Presario went to the feds and turned state's evidence against the Genovese family. Joe Arlenetta went to prison, and even Funzi Tieri was convicted, but died while out on appeal. Young Nicky Arlenetta walked yet again.

"How does this Nicky Arlenetta stay out of prison every time?" I ask.

Lilliana mentions the name of a very famous criminal defense lawyer.

I make a face, looking at her. "Now, why would he ever get mixed up with someone like Nicky Arlenetta?"

"Nicky married his sister when they were seventeen."

"He let that guy marry his sister?"

"She was—" Lilliana drops her voice "—you know. In the family way."

After testifying at the trial, Frankie Presario disappeared. His father-in-law, Rocky Presario, offered amends to Joe

for Frankie's betrayal, and from prison Joe Arlenetta over-
saw the expansion of his territory into Atlantic City. When
Joe died of a stroke in 1986, Nicky "took care" of the op-
position to him within the family and came into power as
his father's successor. In an ongoing overture of peace,
Rocky Presario offered to groom Nicky's younger brother,
Cliff, as his own successor, essentially bequeathing the
whole territory to the Arlenettas. To start, Cliff was to oversee the finances of a very profitable new union Rocky and
Frankie had created, the American Federation of Technology Workers.

Cliff Yarlen's star rose quickly and he brought a kind of
financial sophistication to the union it had been lacking. He
was a high-tech executive, an expert in forensic accounting and combating the troublesome techniques of investi-
gators from the Department of Labor. He was moved from
Jersey to the gold coast of Southern California, more specif-
ically, Hollywood, where he successfully brought Monarch
Studios to the bargaining table with the AFTW.

Greedy and ambitious as ever, Nicky Arlenetta had recently begun pressuring his brother to siphon benefits payments from the union for his own personal use. Cliff told
him to take a hike, it wasn't Nicky's territory. Nick persisted.
Cliff finally told him if he wanted a cut, he had to earn it,
and he should start "protecting" AFTW members from the
other union mobs. Nicky promised to do just that and started
moving his people into place in Southern California."

Lilliana tosses her cigarette out the window and rolls it
back up. "But what Nicky didn't know was, his uncle
Rocky Presario, and his brother, Cliff Yarlen, had been
working with Frankie Presario and the feds for the last five
years to set this up."

I blink, trying to focus on the road.

"They were setting Nicky up for the fall, planning to get
the mob out of the union once and for all."

I can't think. I'm overwhelmed. Finally the full impact of what she has just said hits and I cry, "Are you trying to tell me that Cliff Yarlen was a *good* guy?"

"The best," she says.

I take a deep breath.

"A very brave, honorable man trying to undo some of the wrong his father and brother did," Lilliana continues, unscrewing the cap on her bottle of water.

"Oh, man," I say, trying to snap out of my stupor. I glance over. "And what was your role in all this? As his girlfriend, you were Cliff's confidante? Is that why they're after you? Because of all that you know?"

"No," she answers gravely.

After a moment, I look over again. "Well? So why are they after you?"

Staring straight ahead, she answers, "Because Nicky's figured out I've been a messenger between Cliff and my father."

"And who's your father?"

She takes a swig of her water and swallows. "Frankie Presario."

The light is beginning to dawn.

PART
FOUR

CHAPTER TWENTY-FOUR

"So you weren't romantically involved with Cliff?" I ask Lilliana, as we continue to drive to wherever the heck Larkensburg is in the California desert.

"I should hope not," Lilliana says. "He was my first cousin."

"Wow," I say quietly.

"And I guess Nicky's finally figured that out." She laughs, and the sound is reminiscent of the wise and knowing laughter of the elderly. After what I've just heard, I'm beginning to understand all this woman has seen in her relatively young life.

"There was supposed to be a meeting between Nicky and one of Dad's guys," Lilliana continues, "to see how much he knows, but since Nicky's firebombed the house I guess the meeting didn't go so well." She drinks her water. "I wonder how he could have known I was there."

"So you're Lise?" I ask. I notice that the tremor in my right hand has started again.

"You pronounce it Leeza," she instructs me.

"Leeza. Lise Presario."

"And once they moved me to Ohio, it was Lilliana Martin. Dad picked Lilliana for me." She chuckles. "Martin. Oh, my. That was a stretch."

"What about your brother? You said Frankie and Celia had a son. Taylor." I can't help it. "Kind of a WASPy name, wasn't it? I mean, Taylor Presario?"

She smiles. "It was a generational statement, I think. We're not FOBs anymore."

FOB, Fresh Off the Boat.

"Anyway, they split us up because the Arlenettas were looking for two kids. Taylor went with my father just across the border in Indiana, and I was matched up with the Martins. He had just remarried—"

"So when you told me your mother had died of cancer," I begin.

"That was the cover story. My real mother—Nicky Arlenetta killed her." She rubs her eyes. "I wonder what happened to her portrait in the fire, how badly damaged it is."

"It didn't look like the living room was hit," I say, trying to cheer her up.

"It was stupid to keep it, probably. I guess it doesn't matter, though. It's bound to all come out sooner or later. Actually, I'm glad." She looks down at her hands. "It's a horrible thing to deny the existence of the parents you adored more than life itself."

"I can only imagine," I murmur.

"Anyway," she continues, raising her head, "I was matched up with John Martin—he was a widower moving to Ohio. I was to be the daughter who lost her mother." She cracks the window in preparation of lighting yet another cigarette. "I was part of his cover, I later found out. He was from Omaha or somewhere and his real wife didn't want to go into the program with him. Can you imagine?" She lights up, exhales smoke. "He got a new wife, I got a stepmother. And I saw Dad as much as possible." She laughs to herself. "I don't know how the feds are going to handle this one—John is ex-CIA. And he's pretty old now."

I fumble for a piece of bubble gum. "I'll unwrap that for you," Lilliana says, taking the package from me and pointing, "because we're getting off at this exit.

"After Joe Arlenetta died," she continues, "my father— my real father, Frankie—breathed a lot easier, for the only active mobster around who still had a bone to pick with him was Nicky. Fact was, however, everybody seemed to have a bone to pick with Nicky Arlenetta."

"Why didn't Cliff just get out?" I ask. "Move away and cut himself off from the family?"

"You had to know Cliff. He was very special. He was close to our grandfather, Rocky, and Rocky was the one who taught him that if the family was ever to be truly successful, the family had to run clean businesses. If the Rockefellers could do it, Pop-Pop used to say, so can the Presarios. And that's why my father got into such trouble, because he had tried to steer the Atlantic City union toward a clean slate. And so Nicky tried to kill him and he killed Mom."

From the beginning I thought I identified with Lilliana on some level, and I think this was probably it. Her mother was killed, murdered, and she lives with the knowledge her killer is free to this day.

My admiration for Lilliana, at this point, knows no bounds. This is a hell of a person.

I look at her. "I can't believe your father would drag you into this."

She shrugs, blowing smoke. "He didn't want to, not at first. Then I just went ahead to the feds and put myself in it. They really did need me, someone who could move freely, passing on information as I went."

We are now on the loneliest-looking road into the desert, the kind where you instantly wonder what to do if the car breaks down. I suppose we could call on my cell phone, but I don't feel like being firebombed again or anything.

"Linking Cliff and me romantically I thought was pure genius," Lilliana says, smiling. "It was not an unusual match for Hollywood, and our meetings at different houses, if anyone was watching, could always be construed as us seeking a private romantic getaway or something."

"But you're an actress!" I persist. "You might be getting an Oscar!"

"We don't choose our families." She tosses the cigarette. "Take a right up there."

Now we are bouncing along a dirt road, clouds of dust billowing up behind us like in one of the Mad Max movies. We're heading straight for the mesa.

"Nicky," Lilliana continues, "leaned on Cliff to take on some of his union supervisors from the east. The feds were delighted. This was what they had been hoping for, to watch Nicky set up shop in the union and start stealing. But then Nicky suddenly got suspicious and backed off. Cliff was nervous, something was wrong. He told me he felt sure Nicky suspected him. To help screen Cliff, the feds started rumors of a pending indictment solely against him. Cliff played it up, making the kind of moves that any self-respecting mobster would make toward building a defense. He destroyed records, surrounded himself with a battery of lawyers and consulted with other crime syndicate figures for advice.

"And Nicky took all this to mean that Cliff had been milking the union for himself—the feds wouldn't be indicting him for no reason—and that Cliff had been cutting him out of it. Cliff was damned if he had, damned if he hadn't. In the meantime, everyone wanted to get me out of it now, so I publicly started 'breaking up' with Cliff."

And that's when Spencer and I met her.

"So what *was* that all about?" I ask.

"Oh, God!" Lilliana moans, leaning over and covering her face with her hands. "It was me being drunk and crazy. Oh, God." She sits up, sighing, dropping her hands to look at me. "I don't know what got into me that night. I was just going to make an appearance at the party, but I had a few before I went, and then I got loaded, and I—" She hesitates.

"What?" I ask, glancing over.

"I just felt like having sex." She looks at me, gesturing. "I haven't had sex in about two years! And then when Spencer thought this was a great idea, the three of us getting together, I decided to take you to the Cold Water Canyon house. I knew no one was there, and I certainly wasn't going to bring you home to our house in Bel Air!"

"Our house?" I pick up on this.

"Well, you know, it's kind of where everybody stays at times. Dad, my brother, even Cliff, some of the guys—"

"I don't think you better drink very much anymore," I tell her.

She grunts in agreement. "But the stress had been unreal." She looks at me. "I thought I was entitled to have some fun."

I glance over to meet her eyes briefly.

"I thought you were very attractive," she tells me. She gives a small laugh. "But that was before I got to know you."

I smile.

"So what happened that night?"

"My father got wind of dear cousin Nicky making persistent inquiries into my past. And that night, when I met you, after you left, one of my father's men, Joey—" She shakes her head. "I hope he's going to be all right. It's hard to believe he can be with all that damage."

Joey was the man who had given us orange juice in the basement of her house. "On the radio they keep saying two men were hurt," I offer. "They didn't say anyone was dead."

"I can only hope so." She sighs, looking out her window. After a long moment she continues.

"After you and Spencer left the house in Cold Water Canyon, Joey came tearing in to get me out of there. My father feared a hit. Cliff, in the meantime, was out of contact with everyone on a trip to Silicon Valley. So the next morning when he stopped by the house and found Spencer in the driveway, it was the first he had heard that I had suddenly disappeared, leaving my car behind. I think he thought the worst, especially after he checked the Bel Air house and found nothing. He checked with the feds and they hadn't a clue where I was.

"In the meantime, Nicky Arlenetta's people were watching the Cold Water Canyon address and reported seeing Spencer Hawes waiting around. They also saw Cliff talking to him. I guess they figured Spencer had to be a link to somebody and Nicky said to pick him up, that he might become useful in negotiations. We only figured that out when you told me Spencer had disappeared," Lilliana says. "I called Dad's people and they called somebody and—well, you know the rest. They dumped him." She sighs. "Thank God they didn't kill him."

"So how did I get into all this?" I ask.

"Cliff couldn't figure out where I was. My agent, Richie, told him I had been drinking heavily the night before and had latched on to some pretty girl reporter—"

"But why was he looking for you? He was supposed to stay away from you, I thought."

"Because Richie called the police and told them I was missing. Cliff was supposed to still be in love with me and some jerk at the FBI told him he needed to play the part out and start looking for me. So Richie tells him you were the last person to see me and had just taken off for Connecticut, leaving behind your boyfriend, Spencer, who also can't figure out where I am—and so Cliff just figured I had taken off with you."

I cough a little. "Well, when you think about it, it makes sense. I was a stranger to everyone involved and Castleford's not exactly the center of the universe. If you were looking for a place to hide—"

"Exactly."

We are traveling up a curving road into the mesa. There is a large stucco-and-brick wall up ahead, and a wooden gate, complete with surveillance cameras.

"Whose place is this?"

"I'm not sure exactly," she says. "But this is where Joey brought me last week."

"But if you were in danger," I say, "why did you go back to L.A.?"

She laughs. "Because we found out Cousin Nicky was probing my background because he thought I might be a fed. And if he thought that, I didn't care, because he wouldn't touch me. He wouldn't kill a fed. It was the other that panicked us, if he figured out I was Celia Presario's daughter."

I stop the car at the gate and look at her. "And the fire-bombing today?"

"Well—" she winces "—clearly he's figured it out at long last." She looks thoughtful. "Poor Cliff. I felt so bad because he was so happy when he heard I was okay. I never dreamed Nicky would get him so soon, none of us did." She tosses her head a little. "Okay." She leans across my lap to address the security camera and intercom. "It's me and my friend Sally Harrington."

The gates slowly open and a large man in khakis and a polo shirt walks out to nod to Lilliana. We drive into the compound, because that is all you can call it. This is a walled-in fortress with a cement house built into the mesa. It is one of the most residential bunkers I've ever seen.

* * *

"Dad?" she calls in the front foyer. Her voice echoes over the tile. We continue into the house, which means into the mesa. The walls are plain white stucco, no pictures, no decoration.

"LeeLee?" someone cries. And then a small, stocky man of about sixty comes barreling through a doorway and hugs Lilliana for all she's worth. He lifts her off the ground and then puts her back down, touching her face. "You hurt?"

"No, Dad. We were very lucky. I don't think Joey was, though."

"He's alive," he tells her solemnly, holding her face in his hands. "I wasn't sure at first..." He is visibly upset. "When I heard two women and a man were seen driving away, I thought—LeeLee!" He pinches her cheeks and shakes them. Then he hugs her again.

She's taller than her dad. I can see the resemblance, but I understand at once how she must physically take after her mother. Her father's a bit of a fireplug.

"Dad, this is Sally Harrington," Lilliana says over his shoulder.

He releases her and turns to me. "We have been hearing a good deal about you lately, young lady."

"She got me out of the house, Dad. She helped me get here safely."

"Thank you," he says, holding out his hand, which I shake.

He turns back to Lilliana. "Your brother's here. He was just taking a shower and will be right out. I guess you girls might like to freshen up. You look like hell, LeeLee," he says, rubbing her head to mess up her hair, "you're supposed to be a *boo*tiful actress now." They laugh.

Frankie walks us down the hall when we hear a voice in another room say, "She's here? Lilliana's here? Thank God!" And we turn around to see her brother hurrying out into the hallway, rubbing his wet hair with a towel. "Lil-liana!" he cries happily.

It's Jonathan Small.

CHAPTER TWENTY-FIVE

"Please don't be mad," Jonathan Small says, holding his hand out to me. "I thought Nicky was using you to smell us out."

"Me?"

"I didn't know who the hell you were! It seemed so strange how quickly you guys zeroed in on my sister."

"Me?" I say again.

"It didn't make sense, you didn't check out," he continues. "We knew Nicky was snooping around Lilliana and then when that Spencer guy disappeared—"

"Only because your cousin kidnapped him!"

"Yeah, but we didn't know that. All we knew was that he was pushing his way in with my sister, and then he talked to Cliff, and the next thing we knew, Cliff was dead and Hawes disappeared. What would you have thought?"

I look at the three of them, nearly speechless. Finally I manage to say, "You mean to tell me, you thought Spencer Hawes, the executive editor of Bennett, Fitzallen & Coe, was some kind of hit man for your sleazy cousin Nicky Arlenetta? Are you out of your friggin' mind?"

Jonathan looks to his father.

"Hawes's father is very deeply in debt," Mr. Presario says. "He's about to lose his marina. Your friend Spencer baled him out with a cash infusion three years ago, but it wasn't enough. He's going to lose it."

"But how? They've had the marina forever."

Mr. Presario holds out his hands. "How do you lose the family farm? Times change, a bad season, personal disability, who knows? Hawes was trying to help his father, but kept up the high-flying living. He's got big financial troubles."

Big troubles or no, I am relieved. This, knowing Spencer, makes sense. To infuse cash to keep his parents in the marina, always thinking he'd make up the money somehow, and sinking further and further into debt. Declaring bankruptcy would never occur to him.

"It was the kind of situation," he continues, "that often lends itself to someone like Nicky moving in to take control over their lives." He bows slightly. "We apologize."

"Well at least he's not dead," I mutter. "That's something."

"We understand he's going to be all right," Jonathan pipes up.

This is so weird. Jonathan doesn't even really wear glasses. He doesn't even walk the same. And here his clothes fit; he doesn't look like he's wearing his dad's suit.

"You—" I point at Jonathan "—I'm not even talking to you yet. Not after last night."

"What happened last night, bro?" Lilliana asks him, kneeing the back of one of his legs so he jerks forward.

"I was investigating," he mumbles.

"Yeah, I bet," she says, flicking the back of his ear with her finger.

"Ow!"

"They're basically good kids," Mr. Presario tells me.

And then Lilliana and I are led away to freshen up.

* * *

While we're eating a hastily thrown together meal, the man from the gate comes into the windowless kitchen and whispers into Frankie Presario's ear. Frankie nods. "We'll have visitors in a moment. By helicopter, don't be alarmed. It's our friends from the Justice Department."

"What are they going to want?" I say. "I mean, I'm not sure of my status, what I'm doing here."

"We have to get rid of you," Frankie says matter-of-factly.

From the expression on my face, the three realize how badly chosen those words are.

"I mean we need to send you away," he tries again, "so we can finish this thing."

I nod, and resume picking at my salad. "This is very strange, you know. Sitting with an Oscar-winning actress—"

"My movie's not even released yet," Lilliana laughs.

"A studio boss."

"Ha!" Jonathan says.

"And a—" Whoops. I don't know how to describe the father. Ex-mafioso? I don't dare.

"Microchip maker," Jonathan supplies.

"Really?" I turn to him.

He smiles. "Gotta make a living."

I look at Jonathan. "Did you really go to Harvard?"

"Yep," he declares, taking a bite of bread.

"Who wants some more wine?" Lilliana asks, pushing her chair back to stand. She is in an outfit of loose-fitting white silk slacks and tunic. I am in a pair of Jonathan's khakis and one of Lilliana's blouses, neither of which fit correctly.

Do I hear something?

We're all listening now.

Lilliana tells me to follow her. We go up the staircase we used to go to the bedrooms (that have no windows). We go past that floor, up to a small landing, where there is a couch, easy chair and bookshelves loaded with books. She grabs a handle in the wall and slides up a whole panel of wallpaper, revealing a window looking out the side of the mesa.

A helicopter is gently descending from the night sky, landing in the cement courtyard outside. The blades slow but don't stop. Two figures run inside.

She closes the panel and we hurry back downstairs. There are voices in the front hall. It's Schyler Preston and the other man is introduced to me as Agent Alfonso.

"You've had quite a day," Preston tells me.

"And mine was a cakewalk," Lilliana says, walking over to him. She slaps him across the face, hard. "That's for all the wonderful protection you gave us."

"I can't protect you if I don't know where the hell you are," he says quietly, rubbing his cheek.

"For the love of God, Skye," Frankie bellows, coming into the foyer with his napkin, "what are your people doing?"

"They're investigating the bombing," he says.

"Investigating," Frankie says dully, crossing his arms on his chest. "God help us, next Nicky'll probably drop a neutron bomb and your people will no doubt be investigating vigorously."

"Don't be impatient, Dad," Lilliana says, going to her father and resting the side of her face on his shoulder.

"Sally," Schyler Preston says in a serious tone of voice, "get your things, I want you to go with Agent Alfonso."

"You don't have a problem flying, do you?" Agent Alfonso asks me.

"Not as long as I know where I'm being flown."

"Back to Los Angeles."

"Gee, and we just went through so much trouble to get here safely," I point out.

Lilliana walks over to me. "You'll be okay." She takes my hand and gives it a squeeze. "They won't do anything to you." She lowers her voice and whispers in my ear, "Just do as Attorney Pettuti and Agent Asshole tell you."

I laugh and look at Lilliana. "But I've come this far—"

She shakes her head. "You've got to go. And you've got to keep your word until Skye tells you it's okay. It means our lives."

"Yes, I know, don't worry."

"I know you do," she murmurs, kissing me on the cheek. She smiles and then turns my face to kiss the other side, and then walks down the hall.

It is silent for a minute.

"I better head back," Jonathan says.

"I don't think it's wise for you to ride with us," Agent Alfonso says.

"No, I'm driving." Jonathan rubs his chin and looks at me. "Lilliana's right, you know. And since I'm the only one whose cover is left, my life really is in your hands, Sally. One wrong word and it's all over." He smiles. "Good luck, maybe we'll see you around." He walks back toward the kitchen.

"You're a good girl, I can feel it," Frankie says, pointing at me and winking. "I know you'll do the right thing." He, too, walks away. But then comes back into the hall. "Thank you for saving my daughter." And then he is gone.

I look at Preston. "About that deal of ours. I actually need a little bit more from you so I can hold up my end of the bargain."

He frowns slightly.

"It's somewhat personal in nature, what I need from you," I add, "something I think only a man like you would know how to do." And so I tell him what I want the Department of Justice to do for me. He tells me at once he can't do it, but by the end of our conversation he is swearing up and down he will do it, he will find a way.

"Where the heck is Castleford, Connecticut, anyway?" he asks.

CHAPTER TWENTY-SIX

In the helicopter I beg Agent Alfonso for paper. A pen I've got, and when I finally convince him that unless he rips some pages out of his daybook I will probably cause the pilot to crash, he hands some over.

I frantically write in shorthand names, dates, a schematic of events from—what did Lilliana say? Was it 1930, 1932? Damn it, I'm losing it already. I do the best I can, and as I glance out the window and inquire where we are, I quickly fold up that paper and stick it in my underpants. (Well, I don't have a bra on. That wasn't provided at the bunker house.)

I start writing again, but this time I write what I think meets the requirements of Federal Prosecutor Preston. That I met actress Lilliana Martin last week at a Hollywood party, that we gave her a ride home, that Spencer was mistaken for somebody else—maybe her boyfriend Cliff Yarlen, president of the AFTW union—and was kidnapped. That I tried to find Spencer and crossed paths with Cliff Yarlen shortly before he was killed. That I came to L.A. when Spencer was found, and when I went to the house in Bel Air to see Lilliana to tell her about it, it was firebombed. I escaped unhurt. I have no idea who did it, all I can do is describe firsthand what it had been like. I am cooperating with the FBI to the best of my ability and cannot say more.

I've got a deal with Schyler Preston I wouldn't dream of messing up now.

I look down out of the helicopter and recognize the Valley. "Is that Ventura?"

"Approaching Burbank," the pilot says.

I've never heard of an FBI office in Burbank, but of course I haven't lived here for a while. I work on my story, polishing it.

We zoom over the Warner Brothers lot, sweep past NBC and are heading for a large building I'm not familiar with. The parking lot is in use, but a corner has been cleared and a circle of flashing construction lights indicates where we are to land.

I try to pull myself together as we set down. No doubt it is going to be a long night with the feds. I hope they'll offer coffee because I am running on empty. Agent Alfonso helps me step down from the helicopter, putting a protective hand on my head to duck beneath the blades, and leads me toward the building, my hair flying up all around my face. When we reach a door into the building, I find myself staring at Wendy Mitchell, the head of security at DBS, who is holding it open.

"You've got ten minutes," she tells me, putting a guiding hand on my back and steering me down a cement hallway. A young man appears. "Glen, this is Sally Harrington."

"Finally!" he says, taking my arm.

"Glen? You're not the L.A. news producer, are you?" I dare to ask.

"Not that you'd ever return my calls, lady!" he grunts, hustling me down another hall. "She's here," he yells into an office. "We've got Harrington. Tell Alexandra."

"Where are we?"

"At the affiliate," Wendy says from behind me. "Alexandra's already on the air. They were hoping to slip you in at the end. They'll do a promo right now saying you've been located."

"But—"

I am pushed into a dressing room where a makeup gal looks me over. "You need a bra or something," she says, looking down at the telltale marks my breasts are making against the silk blouse. "What size are you?"

"Thirty-three C," I say.

"Find one," she tells Glen, the producer.

"Okay," she says, rolling up her sleeves, "let's start on this face."

"Don't cover the bruises or that scrape," Wendy says. "Don't make her look too good."

Another guy comes barreling in. The executive producer. He doesn't bother introducing himself, just says, "Dictate questions Alexandra can ask you." To Wendy. "Check it against your list, will you?"

"What list?" I ask.

"Skye gave me a list of buzz words that are a no-no," Wendy says.

"He gave you an actual list?"

She shrugs. "I told you, he knows me. We've worked together before. We're going to honor your agreement and wait for the exclusive."

"Sarah's wearing a 32D," Glen reports, swinging in around the doorway. "She'll take it off in the ladies' room if you want it."

"Close enough, I want it," I say, closing my eyes against the foundation the makeup lady is applying.

Somebody is pushing a cell phone in my hand. I crack an eye. It's Glen. "Alexandra says welcome back, call your mother."

I do. She is very glad to hear from me.

* * *

My surprise appearance on the *DBS News America Tonight* broadcast is in many ways, I know, the highlight of what is to come, because after this I will be barraged and stalked by every other news agency in the country. Which I hope won't happen. But knowing Alexandra, she'll want me to hold some kind of news conference at DBS in New York, as a kind of goodwill gesture, where, no doubt, she'll allow me to tell the competitors everything I already told the world the night before on her newscast.

Maybe, and I am hoping, Alexandra will let me write and produce a two-hour special on the whole affair, which I can work on until such time as it will be safe for the Presarios.

But my mind is racing ahead, partly from fatigue, and as I step onto the interview set while the weather's on, and my microphone is run up through my blouse to my collar, I try to focus on matters at hand. It's tough. I can feel my body starting to fail, the signal being that tremor returning to my hand. I'm not scared, I'm not shaking, it's simply my body warning me it's about to crash.

A production assistant runs up on the set with an open can of Coke. "Alexandra says gulp some of this, quick," she whispers. Smart lady, she knows what's happening to me. I do as she suggests, and allow for a discreet burp. Within moments I feel a little better with the sugar racing through my system.

The weather is finished, they bounce back to Alexandra across the studio and she leads into a break, promising my appearance. On the monitor I see them running a video of the FBI helicopter landing outside the studio.

Alexandra, I kid you not, unplugs her mike, jumps off the set and *skips* across the studio and bounces up on my set. She is beaming. "You are the best!" she declares, giving my hand a quick squeeze before plunking herself down in her chair. They plug in her microphone and for a moment Alexandra ignores us all while she looks at the index cards that have been left for her. She nods to herself. Makes a note in pen—makes another note. Clears her throat, tapping the cards together on the arm of her chair, and crosses her legs in my direction, leaning forward slightly as if she is anxious to hear what I have to say.

She looks at me straight in the eye and smiles. A glance at the floor manager, telling us we're coming back, and then her eyes are back on me and she mouths "You are the best!"

"Three, two, one..."

The red light goes on camera three behind me and Alexandra's expression is deadly serious as she addresses the camera, starting in on the "amazing survival story of one of our own, a young woman who simply went to a party in Los Angeles and found herself caught up in a web of murder and terrorism."

I have to suppress a smile.

CHAPTER TWENTY-SEVEN

DBS arranged for my luggage and things to be retrieved from Century City and allowed me to crash for twenty-four hours at the Four Seasons Hotel before heading east. I slept and I slept. I ate and then I slept again. Saturday evening, now that I feel a little more like myself, I try to return some phone calls. I talk to Mother at length, and to Mack, and am surprised to find out that my brother Rob came home after all. I talk to Buddy, and I talk to Doug, who is, strangely, staying at the Sheraton in Manhattan.

"What are you doing there?" I ask him.

"What do you *think* I'm doing here?"

"I haven't the slightest idea, that's why I asked. Is there like a seminar or something?"

"Harrington, you are *unbelievable.*"

"I'm not firing on all pistons quite yet," I admit.

"I'm in New York because, in case you've forgotten, you disappeared and a lot of people thought you might be dead."

"But I called Mother, and Mother called you."

"And I knew your mother wouldn't know the half of it. 'Hi, Mom, hear about the firebombing in Bel Air? I was in it.' And then—poof—you've disappeared. NYPD says you're missing for days—"

"Oh, Doug—"

"It was not funny, Sal. I didn't know what to do, so I got in the car and went to DBS."

"You went to West End?"

"I figured they'd be first to know where you were, and if you were all right." He laughs a little. "I had no idea the red carpet treatment I'd get. Some guy put me in Alexandra Waring's office! Said *she* said to put me in there. And then they told me they had a room for me here tonight."

"Wow," I say.

"Wow is right." Silence. "Call me crazy, Sally, but I love you. I can't help it. And the idea of something bad happening to you is unbearable."

I inhale sharply, my eyes filling. "I'm afraid I really did it this time."

"No," he says quietly. "What matters is what you do— what we both do—from here on in."

As I listen to the phone ring, I'm not sure how I feel, but when I hear Spencer say "Hello?" I cry, "You're talking!"

"I'm talking!" Spencer confirms, "but don't make me try to...thay...anything with an *eth* in it."

I laugh. "Oh, Spencer, you sound like yourself again." I am determined not to hear his speech impediment, not to make him self-conscious.

"I fweel much better. I don't know where the hell I've been."

"I hear you were at sea!" After grabbing Spencer, Arlenetta's people, I have been told, called in a ticket purchase to Honolulu on his credit card, but no one used it. Instead, they locked him up on an oceanbound garbage barge, another branch of the "family business."

"Oh, God, and I wath tho theathick in the beginning."

"And they just locked you up?"

"Yeah. And then one night I finally got out of there, and

I get up to the deck and I think, oh, God, now what? I can't even thee land, and thith guy comth afther me and so I thtart running—ath ifth I haf anywhere to go—and, lucky me, I fell into the cargo hold. I don't know what wath worth, the pain or the thmell. If you can imagine being a mouthe whoth fallen into an old metal garbage can, that'th eck-thactly what it wath like."

We talk some more about his injuries, his schedule of dental implants, the next surgery on the elbow. He says I looked great on the news Friday night.

He thanks me, too, because he found out I had paid his February rent. And the parking garage. And the phone and light bills. For the sake of his parents, who are staying at his apartment, he is near tears. I tell him not to worry about it, maybe because of what we've got to talk about next.

Spencer does the honors. "Verity told me thee thaw you."

"In Long Beach, at the hospital," I acknowledge. "She said you had been asking for her."

Silence.

"All I want to know is, Spencer, is this something you think you really want? To allow her back in your life?" I sigh. "Because as you may remember, she's not so easily displaced."

Several moments go by. "Thee and Throeder are getting divorthed."

I try hard not to laugh. He sounds so much like Sylvester the Cat. And, too, I've got to admit, I'm relieved. I was right about our relationship. It wasn't working on either side, regardless of what Spencer had said.

"Have you heard about the video surveillance Schroeder was doing on your bedroom?"

A sigh. "I'm tho thorry."

Now I have to laugh. "I'm sorry, Spencer, I don't mean to laugh, but it just doesn't sound like you."

He lightens up, too, relieved, I guess, that I can laugh.

"Buddy came to thee me. He told me about O'Hearn thending it all over town. Your mom..."

"Don't you worry about my mother," I tell him. "She's made of far stronger stuff than you or I." I clear my voice. "Look, I'll come see you when I get in."

"Pleathe."

Pause. "I thought it could work, Spencer."

"We had to try," he says, and I think, he's so right. We had to try. Because both of us needed desperately to make changes in our lives, but couldn't do it on our own. We had to chase after a magic solution first.

Calvin, the burly intern from the DBS newsroom, is waiting for me at the Newark baggage area Sunday afternoon. "Will wants you to stop in at the office," he explains. "And then we'll have you driven out to Connecticut."

"Great, thanks."

We get my stuff and go outside, where Calvin leads me to a black limo. The driver pops the trunk and there is the squeal of car tires farther down the pickup area and then some kind of crash. Within moments Calvin and the driver have shoved me down into the car and slammed the door.

Moments later, as I have succeeded in sitting up, the driver sheepishly climbs into the car. "Sorry," he says.

Calvin, on the other hand, bounces into the front seat and turns around, eyes wide with excitement. "He's a detective, Sally. We thought it might be an attempted drive-by shooting!"

"How wonderful," I say without enthusiasm, craning my neck to look back, but I am unable to see anything.

The detective pulls the car up about ten yards and then over again, putting the car into Park. "Be right back," he says, opening his door and jumping out. We watch as he jogs across the lanes of traffic to the terminal.

"That was so cool the other night," Calvin tells me, turning around from the front seat. "We were all like flipping out at West End. We had another scoop."

I smile. "I'm glad you enjoyed it."

A man is standing outside my window, smiling in at me. He is a businessman, at least he looks like one, with short hair, pin-striped suit and heavily lined trench coat. He's rather good-looking, with large brown eyes, maybe late forties. I smile back. He makes a small circular motion with his hand, and I use the switch to lower my window. "Can I help you with something?"

"You were on TV the other night," he says, smiling. "Congratulations. It was a very good story."

"Thank you. That's very nice of you."

"Not at all." He holds out his hand. "The name's Nick Arlenetta."

My blood freezes. So does my smile. I try very hard to keep my cool. We shake hands. "Hello."

"I believe you knew my brother, Cliff Yarlen."

"Yes," I say, nodding. "I'm terribly sorry about his death. I didn't know him very well, but he seemed like a very nice person."

"A family trait," he assures me. "Okay," he adds, backing away and giving me a vaguely amused salute, "just wanted to say hello. Be well, keep up the good work. We're all watching you!"

"Nick!" someone calls. It's a man standing outside a driver's side door of the Mercedes up ahead of us, waving to him. I sit there watching as the mobster walks to the car. He opens the passenger side door, looks back, waves and gets in the car. And they drive off.

"Who was that guy?" Calvin asks.

Nicky Arlenetta's name is on Schyler Preston's no-no list.

"I don't know," I say, shrugging as the detective comes back to the car, "my first fan, I guess."

* * *

"Trouble wherever she goes!" Will Rafferty announces, coming down the hall of Darenbrook III with his arms wide open. He hugs me. "Thank God you're back in one piece."

He releases me and another set of arms grab me. These I recognize.

"Doug."

"I know," he whispers, holding me.

I open my eyes and over Doug's shoulder see Will smiling at me. I close my eyes again, thinking how different Doug's arms feel now. They feel like the only place on earth where I can live. I open my eyes again. Will's still there. "You wouldn't happen to know how I can get a hold of Wendy, would you?"

"She's waiting for you in there," Will says, gesturing down the hall.

Doug and I part from each other and he holds the side of my face in his hand. "Thank God you're all right."

"Thanks for being here."

"Come on," Will says, "let's go see Wendy."

He points to the door past Alexandra's office, where a conference room is. I let go of Doug's hand and go in. It is now an office. There's a desk, a computer and a printer. Two TV monitors, a tape deck. A ficus tree with a big white bow on it. Some flowers. A couch. It is about a third of the size of Alexandra's and Will's offices, but it's very nice. It has one wall of glass looking out over the little park.

Wendy rises from the couch. "There's something for you on the desk."

I walk over. There is a creamy envelope that reads Sally. I open it. A sheet of expensive notepaper with the initials A.B.W. raised on it reads:

Dear Sally,
Welcome to Alexandra's Merry Little Band.
This is your office.

Your agent has our proposal for you to join us in the capacity of special projects editor. I have not a clue what that is, but we'll figure it out. Before you say anything about not deserving it, remember that my big break in TV news was getting shot on the steps of the Capitol. So yours was getting firebombed in Hollywood—sounds good to me.

A.

"What do you think?" Will asks.

"I think I need to go home and pull myself together," I say, coming back around the desk.

He nods. "Remember, there's a lot of latitude with this job. The one thing I know for sure," he adds, sounding serious, "Alexandra needs a second. She's tired and she's looking for a protégée. At the very least, for someone to take some of the pressure off."

I can't help but smile.

"Down, girl." Doug nudges me with his hip. "He said protégée, not replacement."

I nudge him back. "Why don't you guys go ahead? I need to speak to Wendy for a minute."

After the men leave, I whirl around. "I know," Wendy says, beating me to the punch.

"Nicky Arlenetta was closer to me than you are right now!" I whisper, pointing at her. "What the hell is there to stop this guy from getting to me?"

"Nothing," she says. "But since you're not reporting anything about him, he has no reason to bother with you."

"Oh, great, so when Skye Preston finally says it's okay to run with the story, then I can look forward to having Nicky Arlenetta to contend with?"

"I think that may have been the message he was trying to convey, yes," Wendy says.

"The guy is a murderer."

Wendy smiles sympathetically. "This isn't an easy business, is it?"

I point at her. "You tell Alexandra the story's all hers," I say, edging my way to the door.

"But she doesn't know what it is," Wendy reminds me.

"Then you better make sure I stay alive to tell her when the time comes, hadn't you?"

I nearly run out into the hall. "Please, Doug, let's go home. I'm about to drop."

We say goodbye to Will and head to the garage. In the elevator I look at Doug and say, "I better tell you, a Mafia guy who shall go nameless may want to kill me."

He smiles. "Welcome to the club."

Of course, that's right. Doug's had so many death threats in his career, he thinks nothing of carrying a gun.

"No, I mean really. I could be putting you in danger."

"If our number's up, our number's up," he says. I used to hate when he said this, because he always said it when I was trying to figure out a way to gain control over a situation he maintained was out of our control. But this time, I am very glad to hear it.

If my number's up, my number's up, I think to myself.

So I let Doug drive me home to Castleford.

CHAPTER TWENTY-EIGHT

"I didn't know the Royces wiped out the Tokahna Indian tribe," Mother says as we leave the new Castleford Cultural Center, where some of the History Week exhibits are located. And then she catches herself, as she always does when she finds herself being critical of people. "Of course, it was their ancestors, it has nothing to do with them."

"Except how much money they inherited," I can't help but point out.

"Had," Mother corrects me. "There's not that much anymore."

Up ahead of us is a group of Castleford seniors. We have seen several this morning. Like the others, upon spotting me and Mother, they have begun whispering to one another.

Mother slings her arm through mine and leans into me. This means, *Attack my daughter, you'll have to go through me first.*

"Hello, Belle," one of the women say.

"Hello," Mother says.

Others in their group say hello, and then there is an awkward silence. Mother pulls me forward. "Do you all know my daughter, Sally?"

Murmurs of yes, hello, how are you? although I don't recognize anyone.

"And have you heard our news?" Mother continues brightly.

Yeah, they sure have, I think, wanting to roll my eyes, *I'm a major porno star!*

"Why no," one lady says, playing along.

"Sally's been offered a huge job with DBS News in New York," Mother says.

Oohs and aahs follow and I stand there, smiling, as a little discussion takes place about how everyone in Castleford knew I was destined for great things.

"But you're not going to leave us, are you, Sally?" the woman asks me.

This is a sore point in Castleford, the fact that almost an entire generation has left town never to return. To find a college-educated "Castleford's own" between the ages of twenty-eight and forty-five is a rarity. Everyone's doing well, but it's in places like Atlanta and San Francisco and Phoenix and Boston, leaving their parents graying on their own back here.

"No," I declare, "you're not rid of me yet. I'm keeping a place here."

This gets discussed a bit with Mother, how lucky she is, and finally the group moves on to the cultural center.

As soon as they're gone, Mother slumps a little against me. "Six down, fifty-eight thousand to go."

I smile, putting my arm around her. This is Mother's idea, dragging me around town and pushing me into everyone's face so people know we have nothing to be ashamed of. She says she wants to show people how proud of me she is.

"I think we need some fortification," Mother announces, straightening up and away from me. She points. "On to the Elks tent!" she says the same way she has for the last twenty-one years, and the way Daddy did in the years before that.

"This is so good," I say later, biting into a hot dog. Mother turns toward me, struggling to maintain her lady-like appearance with her own big beef frank with mustard and sauerkraut. They are delicious, as they are every year. Mrs. Stenowski has been serving them up at the Elks tent for forty years. Her secret involves beer with the franks and sugar in the sauerkraut. Whatever, Mother and I never miss her. Next will be a stop at the St. Michael's tent for fried dough, which should be extra special this year because next to it the Lions Club has rebuilt an 1880s industrial steam engine from a Castleford factory. They're having the kids throw wood in the furnace and generate steam, which in turn will somehow generate electricity. Whether or not it actually works, Mother and I really don't care, we're just interested in getting near that furnace since the March air is near freezing.

"You are a wonder and a treasure," my mother tells Mrs. Stenowski.

Over the steaming vat of her hot dogs, the older lady beams. "I might leave you the recipe in my will, Belle Harrington, I'm thinking about it."

"You do that," Mother laughs.

After we finish eating and wiping our hands, we put our

gloves back on and continue walking downtown. There is a huge banner stretching over Main Street advertising History Week, and there is a very large credit thanking the Tokahna Indians. Al honored the agreement, good for him.

Mother says hi to several people, and I'm starting to feel like people are trying to stare through my clothes.

And then I feel Mother seize my arm.

Up ahead is Mrs. O'Hearn. She's selling seedlings at the Ancient Order of Hibernians tent. The question is, what to do? And we are not the only ones wondering about the same thing. Several people around us have noticed the dynamics of our position and are waiting to see how Mother plays it.

Mother throws her shoulders back and dives in. "Those aren't beefsteak tomatoes I see?" Mother asks, pointing to little seedlings under a plastic tentlike covering. Mother pronounces them *tomahtoes.*

Mrs. O'Hearn definitely hesitates. But she swallows, chooses to ignore me, and says, "I can't believe you can tell the difference right off."

And then, without greeting each other, or even really looking at each other, Mother and Mrs. O'Hearn loudly discuss the tragedy of so few beefsteak tomatoes being available anymore, that their tendency to grow in deformed shapes has lessened their commercial appeal and they have been replaced by a host of fruit that simply does not taste as good, nor has such an appealing consistency.

Mother purchases a flat and hands it to me to carry. After money exchanges hands, we move away and laughter breaks out behind us. Mrs. O'Hearn is cackling something to the other workers. Mother starts to turn around but I block her way, muttering under my breath, "Don't, Mother, I'm taking care of it."

Mother looks at me.

"Keep moving," I tell her, "and I'll tell you about it."

And so as Mother and I walk up Main Street, saying hello to people, I explain to her what I've done, the deal I've made with the feds. "But can't they convict Phillip for something?" she asks. "Can't they put him away? Fine him, at least?"

"No. Mother, there's simply not enough evidence. Phillip O'Hearn is in the clear. There's nothing else we can do."

We walk for a long stretch in silence. Finally I hear Mother sigh. I look over. "I suppose it would be some kind of justice," she murmurs. "At least he will be reminded." She looks at me. "How long will they do it for?"

"I will always find someone to do it, Mother," I tell her. "As long as he lives."

We're walking past the local yokel bar, Clancy's Saloon, and I glance in. Then I stop. They've got *CNN Headline News* on in there and I swear I see—

"Sally!" Mother exclaims as I dump the flat in her arms and charge into the bar.

I run inside, squinting against the darkness. Someone calls out hi, but my eyes are on the TV screen. "Oh, my God, no," I say out loud, feeling my stomach turn over. I cover my mouth with both hands and lean on the bar, eyes glued to CNN.

They're showing a covered stretcher being carried out of a building. Police are everywhere. The caption reads "Culver City, California."

"Jonathan Small is the head of production in the motion

picture division of Monarch Entertainment. Details are sketchy, but sources say Small was having a business meeting with Arlenetta when the shooting occurred."

"Sweetheart," Mother says, putting a hand on my shoulder.

"It's about a friend of mine," I say, near tears. I look at the bartender. "What was the story?"

"Some guy died," he says, wiping the bar down.

"But which one?" I nearly yell.

A bleary-eyed guy at the end of the bar, leaning on his elbow, makes a halfhearted attempt to raise his hand. "The studio guy."

"The studio guy died?" I ask, my eyes filling up.

"Naw," he winces, trying to make himself clear, "the studio guy shot some guy in his office."

"He's your friend?" Mother says.

"Ladies, are you buying a drink or are we startin' some kind of garden party here?" the bartender asks, looking at the flat of tomato plants.

What the feds couldn't do, protect his family from Nicky Arlenetta, Jonathan Small, aka Taylor Presario, decided to take care of himself. He called Nicky Arlenetta, saying he recognized him as the new power behind the American Federation of Technology Workers, and invited him to a meeting at Monarch Studios. Shortly after Arlenetta was shown into his office, Jonathan killed him.

"Just like that," I say to Alexandra Waring.

"A witness outside the office says she heard Jonathan Small talking about his mother." Pause. "Do you know what that means?"

"No," I lie.

"Well, do you want to get out there and cover the story?"

"No."

"Sally?"

I regrip the telephone. "Yes?"

"Are you going to tell me what you know about this?"

I take a breath. "Let them make their case, let it go to trial. There's no way I'm interfering."

"He shot Nicholas Arlenetta between the eyes. It was cold-blooded murder."

I say nothing.

"Well, when you're ready," she says. "Get in here. We need you. There's plenty to work on around here besides this."

After I get off the telephone with her, I curl up on my couch, stroking my dog Scotty. He tries to lick my hand.

I would like to send some kind of message to Lilliana, condolences or something, but it obviously would not be appropriate. At least not until I get the go-ahead from Schyler Preston.

I roll on my back, looking up at the ceiling.

Jonathan killed him. And so now I don't have to worry, either.

I'm curious how all this will play out at his trial.

In many ways I envy Jonathan, that he was able to avenge his family's grief. After all, Nicky Arlenetta had killed their mother.

And Phillip O'Hearn killed my father. But I can't get him arrested. I can't get him fined. I can't even get half this town to change their opinion about him.

There is only a small action I can take. I suspect, however, that if I keep it up, it might be enough to punish O'Hearn. If not, to at least make him paranoid and crazy.

CHAPTER TWENTY-NINE

"Say cheese," Mother's neighbor says to us.

"Cheeeese," Mother, Mack, Rob, Doug and I say.

The flash goes off. We break up, blinking, smiling nervously at one another, as Mother profusely thanks the neighbor for coming over. As soon as he is safely ushered out the front door, Mother turns to look at us.

Mother is absolutely gorgeous tonight, dressed in a long blue silk dress and pearls. Mack is in black tie, so is Doug, I am in my black silk dress from Syms again, and my brother is wearing our father's white dinner jacket and black tie from the seventies.

"Last chance, people," Mother says, as if we're a class about to embark on a field trip.

"Let's do it," I vote, looking to Doug.

"Let's do it," Doug says, looking to Rob.

"Let's do it!" Rob declares.

"I bought the tickets, we *better* do it!" Mack says, making us laugh.

We are nervous, though. Scared is more like it. At least I am, for Mother's sake.

Every year the Castleford Country Club has a formal

dinner dance for the benefit of cancer research. As you can well imagine, it is an event particularly important to my mother. Only this year the chairman of the event is Phillip O'Hearn, and until we talked it over, Mother was going to pass.

It was Doug who suggested we all go. We have not yet even broached the subject of where we go from here as a couple, but he is determined to publicly stand by Mother in these difficult days and therefore stand by me. Doug has a golf membership to the club, Mother has a house membership, and Rob and I have junior memberships (at least I did until I turned thirty). "I think it's important your mother takes her town back," he said.

"It was never Mother's town to begin with," I point out.

"You're right. It was your father's."

True. Dodge Harrington was the golden boy in these parts, and just because the man who was once one of his best friends killed him was no reason for Mother to have to stay home. Even if her daughter was having sex on tape all over town.

Mother and Rob and I have our own agenda.

We discuss it in the car on the way over and decide that the ladies are not going to be dropped off at the front door of the club, but that we will all walk in together. The key, you see, will be getting through the front foyer where the club officers will be, and at the end of that line will be Phillip O'Hearn.

We park and huddle against the drizzle as we hurry across the parking lot, Mother saying at this rate she's going to look like Little Orphan Annie. So when we hit that front door, we are laughing.

And so there we are, in our coats and finery, and there is Mr. O'Hearn. The other club officers hurry over to greet

Mother. I have no idea who of these people have or have not seen the video, but they are wonderful. I can only assume they were once friends of Daddy's. Meanwhile, I notice as Doug takes my coat, Mr. O'Hearn's attention seems to be keenly focused on me.

After our coats are checked, Mother leads the way. "Phillip," she says, nodding.

"Wonderful of you to come," he says, having the good sense not to dare offer his hand. "It's wonderful how people turn out for a good cause."

"Yes, isn't it?" Mother says, moving into the ballroom, but not before taking a peek back at me.

Mack nods to O'Hearn and hurries on to take my mother's arm. Rob, on the other hand, practically laughs in O'Hearn's face, saying, "Yeah, *right,*" and walks on. Doug dutifully shakes hands with Mr. O'Hearn, and answers the inquiry as to how his parents are doing in Seattle.

And then there is me. When I offer my hand for Mr. O'Hearn to shake, it is he who hesitates. But he does, finally, firmly, and says in a low voice, "I don't find it funny, Sally, not in the least."

"You're not supposed to, Mr. O'Hearn," I say sweetly.

He glances past me at someone, forces a smile, and then looks back at me. "You leave my family and friends alone. And you sure as hell better stay off my property."

Now I smile for real, because I know how upset he is. And I know it's probably because his girlfriend found a framed picture of Dodge Harrington sitting on her piano in Wallingford.

Or it could have been the picture of Daddy he found taped to the steering wheel of his locked car outside of a restaurant in New Haven.

Or maybe he's already found the picture of Daddy in his locker at the clubhouse at the golf course.

My smile broadens even wider, then, because tonight I know Mr. O'Hearn will find a picture of Daddy waiting for him under his pillow at the O'Hearn mansion on the hill. I dearly hope it freaks him out.

I have a deal, you see, and Schyler Preston has proved to be a most excellent and honorable ally, arranging things for me until such a time as I have learned to arrange them for myself.

As a matter of fact, the pièce de résistance is coming through the front door of the country club right now in the form of Agent Alfonso in a sharp navy blue suit, who shoves his credentials in the manager's face and scans the room. His eyes land on Mr. O'Hearn and he makes his way through the black-tie crowd, booming, "Phillip O'Hearn? Federal Bureau of Investigation." He plants himself in front of him, flashing his credentials. "You're needed at FBI headquarters in New Haven for questioning."

"Phil!" Mrs. O'Hearn gasps as people stare on in disbelief.

"What are you talking about?" O'Hearn asks, face and neck starting to turn red against his black tuxedo.

"You need to accompany me to FBI headquarters," Agent Alfonso says. "Now."

O'Hearn crosses his arms over his chest and squints at Agent Alfonso very hard. "You've got to be kidding."

"We don't kid much in the FBI about the interstate transportation of pornography," Agent Alfonso says in a loud voice.

An audible gasp ripples through the crowd and I have to turn away.

This is too good for Mother to miss.

About the Author

Laura Van Wormer was raised in Darien, Connecticut, and received a B.S. degree in Public Communications from the S.I. Newhouse School of Public Communications at Syracuse University. She joined Doubleday & Company as a secretary and worked her way up to the position of editor. As a freelance writer, she worked with the creators of the prime-time TV shows *Dynasty, Dallas* and *Knots Landing* to write coffee-table books about the shows.

Many of the characters in *The Last Lover* appear in Laura's other novels. Sally Harrington can be seen in *Exposé;* Schyler Preston and Wendy Mitchell in *Just for the Summer;* Alexandra Waring and Will Rafferty in *Riverside Drive, West End, Any Given Moment* and *Talk;* and Kate Weston in *Benedict Canyon.* Laura is also the author of the romantic murder mystery *Jury Duty.*

Laura divides her time between Manhattan and her English-style, stone-and-stucco farmhouse in Meriden, Connecticut, where she is president of the Friends of the Meriden Public Library and sits on the board of directors of the Augusta Curtis Cultural Center.